City of Ghosts

City of Ghosts

A NOVEL

JOHANNA STOBEROCK

W. W. NORTON & COMPANY NEW YORK LONDON

For information about permission to reproduce selections from this book, write to
Permissions, W. W. Norton & Company, Inc., 500 Fifth Avenue, New York, NY 10110

Manufacturing by The Haddon Craftsmen, Inc.
Book design by Chris Welch
Production manager: Andrew Marasia

LIBRARY OF CONGRESS CATALOGING-IN-PUBLICATION DATA

Stoberock, Johanna.
City of ghosts : a novel / by Johanna Stoberock.— 1st ed.
p. cm.
ISBN 0-393-05172-2
1. Triangles (Interpersonal relations)—Fiction. 2. Female friendship—Fiction. 3. Loss
(Psychology)—Fiction. 4. Married women—Fiction. 5. Nepal—Fiction. I. Title.
PS3619.T63 C58 2003
813'.6—dc21

2002015949

W. W. Norton & Company, Inc., 500 Fifth Avenue, New York, N.Y. 10110
www.wwnorton.com

W. W. Norton & Company Ltd., Castle House, 75/76 Wells Street, London W1T 3QT

1 2 3 4 5 6 7 8 9 0

For Christopher

Acknowledgments

I would like to thank Martha and David Ives, Peter and Denise Stoberock, and Jessica Stoberock for their unfailing support. Thanks also to Nina Goss, Kristen Palazzo, Christine Penberthy, Krishna Pradhan, Nick Trautwein, the University of Washington Creative Writing Program, the University of Wisconsin Tibetan Studies Program, the Vermont Studio Center, and the Corporation of Yaddo.

I am grateful to Denise Shannon for her insight and faith, and to Maria Guarnaschelli, whose generosity, creativity, and intelligence have long inspired me. Thanks also to Erik Johnson at Norton who has been vigilant and thoughtful, and to Rachel Wong at ICM. At Norton I also wish to thank Katya Rice, Chris Welch, and Paul Buckley.

Stephen Bezruchka's excellent guide, *Trekking in Nepal: A Traveler's Guide,* helped me map the route toward Kangchenjunga. Kerry Moran's *Nepal Handbook* has also been of great help.

Part One

CHAPTER ONE

A plane crashed in the mountains outside of Kathmandu three weeks before we came. It was a full
flight. Everyone was killed. The first time Danny took me
out of the city, we walked up a slope that was littered with
muddy Thai Airways magazines. The wreckage was gone by
then, the crumpled metal shell of the plane dragged away
from the side of the mountain, and I could not think what
the magazines were doing there, tucked in that rocky crook
between two inclines. I laughed about the magazines. I
shaded my eyes to the sky and pretended to wonder whether
anything more was likely to fall from it. Danny was silent,
and I thought he was as puzzled as I was. It was only when
we got back to the city, aching and exhilarated from the few
days of walking, that he told me about the crash. I got a sick

feeling in my stomach when I heard. It rained that night, the last rain for months. Danny slept with his arms around me and kissed me every time he heard a dog bark or a temple bell ring. I dreamed in his arms. He kissed me all night.

We had gotten married on Cape Cod in early July, and two weeks later had traveled halfway around the world to Nepal. Danny's business was there. He worked as a trekking guide. His apartment, a small block of rented rooms in a falling-down palace, was waiting for us in Kathmandu. We arrived during the last weeks of the monsoon, and the potted plants on the balcony were emerald green. Huge moonflowers looped in vines over the door, opening their white bells at night. Tiny pink tea roses swayed under large drops of water, the water pooling in the creases between their petals where the color concentrated to a deeper red. It was hot and steamy all day, but the rain cooled the air down in the afternoon, and on nights when we had electricity a lazy fan rotated slowly above our bed.

When we came across the first of those magazines, I picked it up in surprise. I remember thumbing through the tattered, dirty pages; I remember the sticky texture of the paper beneath my fingers. I laughed out loud at the fashion and beauty articles. I had forgotten to bring a mirror with me to the mountains and could barely remember what it felt like to have a clean face; fashion seemed to belong to another world entirely. I remember showing the ragged magazine to Danny, remember giggling a strange hysterical giggle that clashed with the glossy pages. I made fun of whoever brought this magazine deep into the Himalayan foothills, wondered how much makeup she had carried with her, whether she had packed high heels to wear at night. Then we kept walking, and the trail of magazines got longer, and finally the magazines spread from the crook between the hills out over the whole steep slope. I put a magazine into my pack—something by which to remember my first step into the mountains. I took it back with me to the city.

I wonder now why it took so long for Danny to tell me about the crash. I wonder if he saw me tuck the magazine away, rolled like a baton, inside my pack. I wonder if he thought then, as I think now, that I brought something back to our home with us, that the panic of that falling plane traveled with me; that sighting its debris marked the moment from which we started to fall. But on that day, before we returned to the city, I shook my head and kept on walking, and when we passed over the crest of the ridge I put the thought of the slope behind me, wiped the tattered magazines clear out of my mind.

I MET DANNY by chance. Anna and I were living together in New York. I was managing an import store, spending my days surrounded by dusty wooden masks from Third World countries, selling embroidered shirts and incense sticks to teenagers. She was taking a sabbatical from her law practice. Matthew had died. Her brother was gone and she needed time and movement to heal, she said. Her mother had given her a ticket to travel round the world. She was almost thirty years old and had never been out of the country. I needed time to heal too, I sometimes thought, the ache of Matthew's absence still sharp inside me. But then I thought that the one thing we can't escape is time, and that it would come to me whether I was unpacking crates from Guatemala in the back room of the store or climbing the side of a mountain behind Anna. Time comes to us no matter where we are. Better to sit tight and wait it out, I thought.

I met Danny because Anna asked me to go along with her when she met him. She wanted information about trekking, and she wanted me to tell her if she could trust this man to lead her safely up and back.

It was January when we went to see him. We met at a café in the West Village. It was raining. There was no snow that year and all I remember of the winter is days and days of gray rain, icy puddles forming in the gullies between sidewalk and street, the constant dampness creeping into my bones. I was wearing my wool winter coat, and when we stepped into the café, Anna just ahead of me, I could smell the water steaming off the wool: warm, animal. That or the sudden heat made me blush.

Danny was sitting by himself at a corner table. He was a tall man; the first thing I noticed was his legs stretched out toward the center of the room, too long to fold under the table. He was wearing hiking boots that looked as though they had actually been used for hiking.

He took Anna's hand.

"Dan Grady," he said.

"Anna Davis," Anna said.

Then his hand enfolded mine, and he had blue eyes, and I couldn't help but return his smile.

"Isabel," I said. "Isabel. Anna's friend."

"Isabel Anna's Friend?" He looked at me with one eyebrow raised.

Did I say that his eyes were blue? They were like a September sky. I blushed again. I could feel my face turn red.

"Isabel Anna's Friend, that's right." Anna put her arm around my waist. "My best friend."

Her best friend. We were meant to be sisters.

Each of us ordered coffee. Danny laid out brochures on the table and unfolded them as if they were maps. The mountains on the covers were jagged and covered in snow. "My shortest trek is three weeks long," he said. "I don't like to work with people who haven't already had extensive experience in the mountains."

I nodded. Anna smiled. She had spent every summer of her childhood in Colorado with her father and her brother. She cared about mountains the way I cared about the sea. I could see her wanting him to ask about her experience.

"We don't do any technical climbing, but I only like to work with people who know what it means to be in mountains, to push their bodies that far up into the sky. I do about four or five treks a year. Three in the fall. Two longer ones in the spring. In the winter and summer there's too much snow or too much rain."

The mountains looked sculpted in the photographs, their lower slopes cut to form terraced fields, rice paddies, trails that rose like stairs. There was a picture of a yak, its sharp horns bound with red ribbons, and a picture of a monk wrapped in maroon robes, holding a staff. A snow-covered peak towered behind him.

"I don't like to do the standard trekking circuits. I'm not interested in those routes. They're too crowded. They feel too much like highways. I take my groups as far away as I can. I take them into the real mountains, the high Himalayas. I take them where we won't be found if we get lost."

I shivered and looked at Anna. She was staring at Danny as if she wasn't sure about whether she could take anything he said seriously. Anna was like that—she couldn't stand it when she thought someone was bragging. "I have plenty of experience," she said. "I'm from the mountains. I'm not afraid of them."

"I am," he said.

She smiled.

"Me too," I whispered.

ANNA AND I lived in an apartment on Lafayette Street, right between Soho and Little Italy, that had belonged to an aunt of my mother's. When she died, my family decided to keep the apartment. An inherited home. The rent was stabilized. We had it for practically nothing. It was an inside apartment with windows that looked out onto the airshaft. A heating pipe ran through my room, and I had to keep a window open always to regulate the heat. Anna slept in the living room, and we shared a closet in the hall. We were nearly the same size, the two of us, and though she had black hair and I had brown, tucked in the apartment together we often felt like twins.

Danny was in the city for six months to supervise a new office the trekking company was opening. He liked Anna very much. She would leave for the first leg of her trip in March and planned to reach Nepal within a year for a trek before returning home. I didn't know what I would do without her. Danny kept her company while she shopped for her trip, telling her what he knew of the countries she would be visiting, what he knew of traveling. "Take as little as possible," he told her. "As little as you can, but make sure everything you do take works. Test it out first. Make sure you love it. Never take anything with you that you don't love."

I met them for dinner a few times after they'd been out shopping, and I could feel the energy between them, the way Anna, laughing, reached across the table to touch Danny's wrist; the way Danny held her coat for her, wanted to carry her bags; the way he was slower and slower about saying good night. Night after night she came into my bedroom, her face flushed with excitement, and flopped down on my bed. "Can you believe this guy?" she said. "Can you believe that this is what is waiting for me almost a year from now? Maybe I should just cancel the rest of my trip and go straight to Nepal. Do you think I should?" She laughed, but she was only partly kidding.

I didn't know what I thought. I loved to watch the two of them together. They looked just right together, and right for New York; I couldn't imagine them anywhere else. Anna always had her hair pulled back, always wore a wine-colored lipstick, had her legs waxed every three weeks. Danny wore his boots everywhere, but the way he carried himself made them look right for the city. He did everything with purpose. When he leaned down to whisper to me—from the beginning I seemed his confidante—I hung on every word.

I heard a conversation once between them. We were on a bus, the three of us, and I sat in the seat behind them. The bus was crowded. It lurched forward and screeched to a stop at the beginning and end of every block. Anna turned her face toward Danny and leaned over to whisper something in his ear.

"What?" I heard him say. "What? It's too noisy, say it louder."

She blushed. A red haze spread out over her creamy cheeks. "Nothing," she said. "It's nothing."

"Tell me what you said."

The bus jumped forward. She swung in her seat to face him. I imagined that she slipped her arm through his. "I feel like I know you," I heard her say in a voice raised just above a whisper.

"You do." He laughed. I liked his laugh.

"No, I feel like I've known you for more than just these weeks."

He lifted his arm up and put it round her shoulders. "Maybe we have known each other longer, sweetheart. Maybe we have."

Anna blushed again. Her cheeks bloomed like roses. He'd called her sweetheart. I saw her smile and settle closer in beside him.

I don't know when it happened. Anna and I had never cared about the same man before. No, that's not true. We had both loved Matthew, but she had loved him as a sister.

One night I came home from work to find Anna and Danny having dinner together. It was raining again, that cold winter rain. Only five customers had come into the store all day. Gina, who owned the store, had dropped by and talked loudly about the slowness of the business, about its being time to let someone go, time to make a change in the focus of the merchandise. "Do what you need to do," I'd snapped.

"I will," she'd said. "Don't worry."

I came home with my hair hanging in my face and my teeth chattering. I heard their voices as soon as I opened the heavy door, and I cursed under my breath. I wanted a bath. I wanted a night alone. Anna laughed, and I could hear Danny's laugh, low, and when I walked from the hall to the kitchen I saw them sitting next to each other instead of across the table from each other as Anna and I sat every morning. The windows to the airshaft were covered with steam. Red roses filled my aunt Mary's porcelain vase.

"Isabel," Anna said. "You're wet! Do you want some dinner?" Tomato sauce stained the corner of her mouth, and she flicked her tongue to lick it off.

"I'm fine," I said. "I just want a bath. Go on and eat."

"Did you see my flowers? Did you see the flowers that Danny brought for me?"

He looked up. His eyes were blue. His wrist, cocked on the surface of the table, was bent at an angle that could be opening or closed. I sucked in my breath and nodded. "Beautiful," I said. "Danny, they're beautiful."

"Like you," he said.

I held my breath again.

"Like me?" Anna said. She laughed. "Like me?" She leaned the distance to his body, turned her head, kissed him on the lips. It was seconds before she moved her face away. His face was red. His mouth was smeared with the wine of Anna's lipstick.

"Like you," he whispered.

"Bed for me," I said. "A bath and bed." I heard Anna laughing again as I left the room. Then I heard nothing, and then I turned on the bathwater and listened to the rushing from the pipes and stepped into the tub and shut my eyes and listened to the water as if it were music, as if it were the rain.

ANNA LEFT FOR the first leg of her trip at the end of March. She was going to New Zealand first, to stay for some months with a family friend. Then she would travel through Australia, Indonesia, Vietnam, and Thailand. She would reach Nepal almost a year later, would go with Danny into the mountains then. They'd had two months in New York together. Two months and then they said good-bye. "Do you think a year is too long to wait?" she asked me. I shrugged. Who knows what a year can mean?

The day she left, the apartment seemed to grow. I stood in the living room, Anna's room, after the door shut behind her, and suddenly I could see the dust in the corners, the paint cracking on the radiator. I had never lived alone before. I stretched my arms out wide and then, self-conscious, drew them quickly back to my sides. "I'm alone," I whispered. I filled a kettle with water and turned on the stove. "I'm alone," I said as I sipped my tea. "I'm alone," I sang when a soft rain ended and the water past my window turned to mist.

Danny was still in the city. He would be there until August, making sure the office was running smoothly before he returned to Nepal. He had been at the apartment the night before Anna left, but was gone before her mother arrived from the Cape in the morning to see her off. "I'd like to meet your mother," I'd heard him say. "Just not now, not when you're leaving."

I didn't see him for over a week. I came home straight from the store every day, walking from the subway station with my winter coat still wrapped around me, my umbrella held up against the thin March wind. The city was gray, but when I climbed the stairwell to my apartment and stepped inside, the first thing I did was light a candle. The walls were warm in the flickering light. The melting wax let off a scent of roses. I would peel my coat off, sink into the couch and shut my eyes. I'd never wanted solitude before. Now I could sit for hours in silence, listening to the creaking of the pipes, watching the candlelight flash on the walls and ceiling. When the phone rang on Friday night, it shook me as if out of a stupor. Danny's voice on the line held the same warmth as the candlelight. I leaned against it as I leaned into the couch.

"Are you missing her yet?" he said.

"Umm, she hasn't been gone very long."

"Enjoying the change?"

"Maybe a little."

"I can understand that."

"You can?"

"I can. Change can be good."

ABOUT ANNA AND me. She was the sister I never had. She was the friend I'd dreamed of before I knew what friendship could be. She was strong, and I would follow a step or two behind her. She walked fast, her legs making strides that I, just as tall but slower, had to take almost two steps to fill. She loved to cook. She loved long skirts and cashmere sweaters. As a child she ran wild with her brother. She grew up in the mountains and then later by the sea. She lived in the city as if she'd lived in it forever. She lived in my heart and I thought she would live in it forever.

I MADE HIM dinner. He told me about Kathmandu. "It's an enormous valley," he said. "It's surrounded by mountains on three sides. At night you can see lights glinting from hills that ring the city—unless there's a blackout, and then you can see exactly which areas of the city don't have light by which hills are glittering and where the patches of light are placed.

"I live in an old palace. In an apartment in a palace. It's close to the center of the city, but you'd never know it once you stepped inside the palace gates. Once the gates are closed, the sounds of passing cars, horns, barking dogs, they fade into a hum. Temple bells chime. The air in March is warm."

He told me about the mountains. "They're not like mountains here," he said. "They're carved with paths, cut with steps. Ridges are steep. The thinness of the air, the clean air, you can't imagine it. You can't imagine how giddy height can make you."

"I've never spent time in mountains," I said.

"You'll love them too," he said.

You'll love them too, I heard. *When will I love them? When will I see them?*

I poured coffee, passed him the cream. He held on to my little finger. "You have to see this place, Isabel. You have to see the mountains."

I MAKE IT sound as though I were a retiring mouse of a girl and Anna were a queen. It wasn't quite that way. I was quiet, and I stood in her shadow often, but on my own I found that heads turned occasionally, that one on one I could make a person laugh. I kept my voice low, but I could raise it when I wanted to. I whispered often, but I thought that, put to the test, I would not be afraid to shout.

The day I received Anna's first postcard was the day I first woke with Danny at my side. He was sleepy in the morning. It took him five minutes to open his eyes. The sun filtered in through the window and lit his body in pale light. I could still feel his hands on my hips. I could still feel his back beneath my hands. I lay there with my eyes wide open—I have always been an early riser—and watched him move from sleep to waking, watched his face, soft from dreaming, harden for the day. When he opened his eyes, I smiled, and pretended I was just then waking up as well. "Sleep well?" I murmured.

"Very well." He leaned a long arm over me. "And you?"

"Very, very well."

It was a Saturday, and mid-April by then. We made coffee, and then, eyes bright, walked forever. We walked in Little Italy, past the old St. Patrick's Cathedral and the fenced-off sculpture garden on Elizabeth Street. We walked down to Canal Street, to Chinatown, and back up into Soho. Then we took a subway north and walked through Central Park. There were flowers everywhere we went, tulips in window boxes, daffodils covering whole slopes in the park. It was almost embarrassing, the perfect sun of the day, the flowers, my arm through Danny's. It was made for a dream, and I almost wince at the perfection as I remember it.

We sat on a bench on a path just off the Great Lawn, watching skaters and cyclists whiz past. I leaned my head over and rested it on Danny's shoulder. He smelled of nutmeg. I didn't want him to see how happy I was, but I didn't know how not to touch him. "Are you a good person, Isabel?" I thought I heard him say. I raised my head, startled. "You are a good person, aren't you," he said now. "Aren't you?" He ran a finger along my cheek.

"I hope so," I said.

"You are. You're better than I deserve."

His voice was soft. He had his arm around me, and from the way he held me I felt as though he were taking great pains to be gentle. He pressed me closer to his chest, warming me.

We were tired when we finally got back to my apartment, and I didn't look through the mail until we were inside. There wasn't much—bills, as usual, a catalogue or two, a copy of *Harper's* magazine, and Anna's postcard. "I feel like I'm upside down," it said, "like I've tunneled through the earth. It's beautiful here. Love you. Give my love to Danny." On the back was a picture of a koala bear. She'd drawn a mustache below its nose.

When I started crying, Danny told me not to. "She would understand," he said. "We are a whole world together. She would recognize it immediately." This after one night. This after a day that felt like years and years of gold.

ॐ

WHEN I CALLED my mother to tell her that Danny and I were getting married, she laughed out loud. "How long have you known him?" she said.

"A few months."

"And you're moving where with him?"

"Nepal."

"You're making a mistake, Isabel. Your home's here. Your job's here. Don't follow him around the world."

"I'm not following. I'm going with him. We're going together."

"You're following."

"I'm not."

"You are."

ॐ

BUT SHE HELPED us plan the wedding. She found the church and arranged the flowers, and both she and my father gave me away.

Danny's parents flew in from California for the ceremony. He wanted his sister, Caroline, at the wedding too, but like him she was a traveler of sorts. She was in Africa, in Kenya; she couldn't fly back on such short notice. His parents were as tall and warm as their son, and seeing Danny with them I could picture him as a child and as a man at once. He must have been a mischievous child, I thought when I saw him put his arm around his mother's waist while he mouthed a sentence to me over her head. He must have been a charmer, I thought when he whispered in his mother's ear and a smile spread across her lips.

His mother took my hands as soon as she stepped through the gate at the airport where we went to meet them. "My daughter," she said. "I finally get to meet my second daughter." I breathed her perfume in, a sweet gardenia scent. I felt her fingers press against my back. Her lips on my cheek were soft as powder. When I looked up from her shoulder, I saw Danny's father smiling down on me. He held his hand out and I took it. "Welcome to the family," he said. "I always thought I'd know my son's bride for a little longer before the wedding, but we have our whole lives afterward, don't we? Welcome."

We have our whole lives afterward. I turned that sentence over in my mind. They had their arms around Danny now; I could see his father's hands across Danny's back, and they looked to me as large and strong and forthright as his son's. *Our whole lives. My whole life with these people.* The thought made me gasp, and then Matthew's face flashed in my mind, his dark hair, his tanned skin and the sharp cheekbones beneath it. His eyes clouded over. His lashes fluttered and then his lids dropped down. I shut my own eyes to that vision and thought again of all the time that lay before me, a whole lifetime, inescapable, present now.

On the night before our wedding, my parents had a dinner at their house. We had lobster and corn on the cob at a picnic table in the backyard. My father steamed clams on the grill. We ate with our fingers, and Danny leaned down to me and said, "You'll be eating with your fingers a lot when we get to

Nepal." I looked up at him, puzzled, but he just laughed. "You'll see. It's how they do it there. I can't wait to show you."

"No lobster in Nepal," Danny's father said. His laugh was as deep as his son's.

"No Himalayas in the States," Danny said.

"No ice in the iced tea there." His father lifted a glass to his lips and drank.

Danny's mother leaned toward me. "They do this every time they see each other—fight over which place is better to live. We want him to come home. Of course we do. We miss our son." I saw her catch my mother's eye. "We miss him, but it's where his home is. And it really is his home. You'll see when you visit them. I've been, you know."

"You've been?" my mother said.

"It's better than you'd think. The city's dirty and noisy and crowded, but it's also beautiful. I couldn't live there, I'd miss home too much. But I saw Danny come alive there, even more alive than here. And I want him to stay if that's where he's happy. I think you'll like it there, Isabel. I think you will."

My mother's hand closed over mine.

"He's really happy there?" she asked.

"He really is," his mother said. "He is, and now that he's in love, I can't think of what more he could want."

DANNY'S SISTER SENT us a telegram on the wedding morning. "I LOVE YOU DANNY STOP I KNOW I WILL LOVE YOU TOO ISABEL STOP CONGRATULATIONS STOP LOVE CAROLINE."

"It's just like her to send a telegram," Danny said.

What did that mean, I wondered. What did all this mean?

The sun shone on us when we were married. The sun shone and the air smelled of salt and gulls shrieked their good wishes from where they soared above the sea.

"Is this right, Danny?" I whispered on the morning of our wedding. The church was by the water. The waves glinted in the late summer light. I wore my mother's wedding dress, a long ivory gown trimmed at the wrists and neck with lace. There were ten people inside the church. The veil blew across my face.

"It's right," he said. "It's right."

The sunlight on the water shimmered. His hand closed over mine. I leaned against him and the wind wrapped my dress around him, wrapped us tight together. I could feel the salt spray from the ocean, sticky and familiar on my skin.

CHAPTER TWO

*D*anny's apartment, our apartment in Kathmandu, was in the top corner of a crumbling palace. I loved to write home about it—*I live in a palace. I live in the princesses' old quarters. There were seventeen of them. Seventeen.* The floor was marble, a black and white checkerboard. Danny had covered much of it with straw mats. The windows were shuttered and reached from floor to ceiling. A fan rotated high above our bed. We took our shoes off at the door.

The air was thick when we first arrived in late July. I could feel it on my skin, could feel it resisting and then parting when I moved my arms out in front of me, when I raised my hand to shield my eyes. Everything was green: the vines covering the palace walls, the waxy leaves of the plants in terra cotta pots on the balcony, the small garden at the edge of the courtyard far below. The light had a hallucinatory effect. It created shapes where there were none, caused tiny pricks of black to dapple my vision. In the afternoon the strange light wavered and turned blue and then purple, and then the rain began.

The rain washed everything away. I have a slow temper, but the sticky heat, the weight of the air, the constant noise, built something inside me that was ready to erupt by afternoon. There was noise, despite what Danny had said about the palace, so much noise even behind the gated walls of the palace compound that I could feel the sound vibrations thrumming through my bones. When the rain came, rushing down in sheets, cooling the air, seeping in under the shuttered windows, it washed my moods away. It washed Danny's moods away as well. I hadn't known he had them. I hadn't imagined two people could circle each other with so much stubborn, uncomfortable frustration. *Don't touch,* I thought in the middle of those moods, and when I reached a hand out to him through the thick, heavy heat, I could see in his recoil that he thought *don't touch* as well. But his moods vanished in the afternoon with mine, the hot air giving way to rain, the heat in our bodies giving way until *don't touch* became *touch, touch,* and then words left my head and all I could feel was his hands, his hair, the salty sweat of his skin as it melted into mine. We lay on gathered sheets afterward, spent, listening to the rain thundering down upon the world outside. Then, in that cool quiet, we pulled in our thoughts to talk about the days to come.

Danny would leave at the beginning of September. The first trek would last three weeks.

"You'll get to know the city on your own terms," he said. "You'll make it your home in a way you couldn't if I was here."

I tried to imagine myself in his apartment, in our apartment, alone.

We had three rooms. A bedroom. A living room. A kitchen. We had a maid who came in daily. She cooked and cleaned and did our laundry. I could not get her name right. "Anjala," Danny kept reminding me. "Anjala, it's almost an English name. She's our angel." I tried to remember the long *a* in the middle, but each time I said her name aloud the *a* flattened into a nasal *e*: Angela. I blushed every time she entered the room. I blush easily. It makes the freckles on my nose stand out. When I was a girl I'd rush to the mirror to see what it looked like when my skin flushed hot. I thought I looked like a rose one moment, like a simple, self-conscious girl the next.

There was another foreign couple who rented an apartment in the palace, but they were away, Danny told me, until the rainy season ended. The bottom floors were held by the Rana family, the family that owned the palace. Ravi Shamsher Rana was old. He dressed always in white, the jacket slightly dirty. His crooked teeth were yellow. His wife was silent whenever we passed. Through our open windows I could hear her yelling at their cook or garden boy—"*Bhai,*" I heard her yell, "*eh, bhai.*" But when I saw her in the courtyard she adjusted her silk sari where it folded across her thick shoulders and looked away.

Once, when we first arrived, Mr. Rana—he preferred the English title—beckoned us into his living room and sent a girl to fetch hot tea. The Persian carpet on the floor was worn thin. A moth-eaten tiger skin covered a couch at the far end of the room, the tiger's mouth open in a weary, frozen snarl. The shades on the lamps were hung with cobwebs. Heavy curtains draped across the windows. The tea arrived, milky and very sweet. It was late afternoon. We'd rushed back to the palace compound just as the rain had started and were reaching for each other's bodies with fevered hands when the door at the foot of the stairs opened and Mr. Rana ushered us in. Now we sipped sweet tea in the dim room, listening to the rain rush down outside.

"I have lived here all my life," Mr. Rana said. "I can remember this room when I was a little boy." His voice rose and fell, slightly singsong, his accent thick. "I remember when my father brought that tiger back. He went hunting often when I was a boy. Large parties, they all went hunting then."

"Thank you for the tea," I said. I heard Danny shift in his seat but didn't look at him for fear I'd burst out laughing at the strangeness of it all.

"I was born here. My father had many children, but I am his only son still living."

There was silence. Mr. Rana looked at each of us. His eyes crossed slightly when he looked at me. Danny cleared his throat.

"Do you have any children?" I asked to fill the silence.

"Yes," he said. "Three sons, one daughter. Two sons in India. In Delhi. One son in England. An engineer. My daughter lives in India as well." He sucked his teeth then, a deep, wet, pulling sound. "My wife is very proud."

The rain outside. It fell like the rushing ocean. It fell like the whispering sea. In the room in the palace, the three of us sipping tea while Mr. Rana talked on about his children, the dust on the tabletops unmoved, it felt as though we'd entered a time outside of time, cradled by the din, by the sheets of rain, the pooling water in the courtyard, the dimness of the light.

"It is quiet here now," he said. "These rooms used to be filled with people. There used to be whole wings of servants. Now the wings are closed. The doors are boarded up. There was a fire. Much of the palace is gone. It is too quiet now. More tea?"

The sugary tea was too sweet; my teeth hurt by the time we left. Outside, I took great gulps of rain-cooled air. I tried to put that musty, crumbling apartment from my mind. The air outside smelled of earth. The rain was gone for the afternoon. Mr. Rana closed his doors behind us and I thought of his rooms as of a dream. *We live above a dream,* I thought. *We live above a past that should already have slipped away.* I tried to picture the palace as it once had been, but the gathered dust and the fraying tiger skin were the only images I could call to mind.

In the evenings we sat on the couch in the living room, our feet twined around each other's, and whispered of our pasts. Danny told me of his sister. "Caroline's been at the embassy in Kenya for three years," he said. "She's only a year younger than me, but she's years ahead of me in her career. She's always had her life together."

"You have your life together."

"I guess I do. But it's not the same as what she has. She's a diplomat, for God's sake. My little sister is a diplomat." He paused. Then, "We've always been close. When we were kids we used to set up a tent outside and sleep out there all summer. I used to tell her that I'd rather have a brother, but I loved her even when I teased her. It used to make her cry. But then after she cried she'd sneak around behind me and pull my hair." He smiled. "You'll like each other, Isabel. I know you will."

"I'd like to meet her."

"You will. Soon enough you will."

The rain fell softly outside. I measured my feet against Danny's. "I would have liked a brother," I said.

"You would?"

"I always wanted one. Matthew was almost as good as a brother for a while. Anna and I used to tease him for hours. We used to hang out in the living room of their house before he went out on dates and pick apart everything he was wearing. He'd chase us around the house. I remember running from him, running in circles and giggling, not being able to stop giggling. That's what I remember most about growing up with Anna. Laughing with her. Everything we did made us laugh."

He shifted his weight, and then I felt his fingers on my toes, his warm hand wrapping around my foot. "She'll be happy for us, Isabel. I know she will. I know she'll understand how much I love you."

I nodded. I smiled. I waited for him to ask me about Matthew. Instead he ran his fingers on my toes and when he spoke it was to say, "I love you, Isabel. I love you."

I NEVER STOPPED, then, to question what it was about him that I loved. I loved the shadows that moved across his face when the sun shone through his tangled hair. I loved the largeness of his hands, and how easily one settled in the small of my back and guided me through crowded streets. I loved the softness with which he talked about his childhood, about his sister and his parents and the discoveries he'd had as a small boy. I loved how hard it was to meet his eyes when he stared straight into mine. I loved the way he seemed to see me. "Isabel," he'd say, and touch my hair. "Isabel," he'd say, and touch a finger to my lips. "The air is sweeter when I breathe it from your skin," he said once, his face buried in my neck. I loved it all. I loved the vibrancy of the world he'd given me, the cleanness of the separation from any other world I'd known. I loved that it was me he said he saw, that he said it was only me.

IN THE MORNINGS Danny took me through the city on his motorcycle, a tiny, sputtering Honda. I sat behind him with my arms around his waist, riding sidesaddle in a long flowered dress, modest and hot, through the streets. He rode slowly for my sake. He told me he liked the feel of my arms squeezed tight around him. "It reminds me that you're here," he said.

We rode to Thamel, that neighborhood crowded with budget hotels and cheap cafés, where the winding, narrow streets were already filled with tourists preparing for the trekking season. We rode to Patan, the valley's second city, across the swollen river, where craftsmen worked with traditional methods still. We rode out on the ring road circling Kathmandu and branched off on the highway toward the valley rim, to Bhaktapur, the third and best preserved of the valley's cities. There, the streets were cobbled and the windows framed with carved wooden shutters, and Danny pointed out to me where thieves had been, where they'd been robbing the valley of its wooden carvings piece by piece. On the highway, heavy trucks barreled past us, belching exhaust from their tailpipes, honking horns wildly. When I turned my head away from Danny's shoulders I saw bright green rice paddies gleaming, and heavy stands of bamboo, thick with light green leaves. I saw women in skirts hiked up to their knees working the fields, the colors of their skirts and blouses glittering like rubies and amethysts against an emerald setting. I saw black water buffalo with pointed horns bathing in pools of mud, and if the wind carried it, I could hear the snuffling sound of their snorts.

WE HAD BEEN in Nepal for three and a half weeks when Danny said he'd like to take me to the mountains. "Not the real mountains," he said. "Just a little trip outside the valley—they're hills, really." Hills. Steeper inclines than I'd ever seen. We went for five days at the end of August. The rain had almost ended, and the paths I followed Danny on were green and bright, crowded with gorgeous, burgeoning growth—huge leaves and brilliant, delicate flowers. My boots were new. I'd bought them just before we left New York. My feet felt heavy, my back hurt from the pack, and I could not stop sweating.

Danny said that the route we traced was not a difficult one. I didn't believe him. By the end of the first day, climbing step after step carved into the mountains, my thighs were burning and my feet were numb. There was no flat land. Every step carried us either up or down. Nothing was level, nothing without a slope. We did not carry much with us. We left our sleeping bags at home. The weather at night was still so hot that sleeping in anything more than a light cloth sack would have kept us up, sweating, all night. We did not carry food; there were guesthouses to eat at along the way. We carried rain ponchos, dry socks, mosquito repellent. We carried water bottles and iodine tablets to clean the water. We carried sandals to slip on when we untied our heavy boots at night. We carried small white candles and lit them in the dark with damp matches. Pools of wax hardened quickly on whatever surface we found to attach the flickering lights to.

It was silent at night in these hills. The only roads through the villages were the footpaths we walked on by day. The humming city, the whole flat valley, hidden behind the green ridges, seemed a dream. Danny joked in Nepali with the villagers as we sat outside guesthouses watching the sun fade beyond the mountains. Even the timbre of his voice was different in this new language. I practiced the phrases I had learned. "*Mero naam Isabel ho,*" I said, and heard back "Eesabel, Eesabel." There were dogs here in the mountains too, and as I leaned my body into Danny's when we finally lay down to sleep, their sharp barking cracked the silence.

"Eesabel, Eesabel," Danny whispered to me, and I breathed in the smell of his body as I drifted off to sleep.

It was on the third day out that we came across the flight magazines. We were walking from one roadhead to the next. On a map it looked like nothing. In the mountains it was forever. Over every ridge I thought we would see the road, see the city, but every ridge seemed to give way to a higher slope. Danny showed me on a map where we were walking. Despite what it showed, I could not help feeling that we were curving deeper and deeper into the mountains. We walked on. Tinny music whined after us on radios propped in village windows. And then, suddenly, we were in a valley, and the earth was littered with paper, and the tattered, red-lipped faces of Thai Airways flight attendants stared up at us from the barren ground. I giggled and joked about my relative frumpiness. Danny, ahead of me, crouched down to look at a magazine. His pack rose into the air as he bent, turtlelike, and for a moment he seemed to disappear. The valley was empty. The wind moaned. Paper rustled. I held my breath, shifted my pack across my shoulders. Danny stood up, turned toward me, his face pale. He took my hand and led me through the valley, and when I asked him what we'd come across he shrugged. "Who knows what you'll find here," he said. "Who knows why the world is the way it is."

I HAVE NOT yet said how beautiful it was, or how happy I felt walking behind Danny, breathing in the early-morning smoky air as we threaded our way along the footpaths from village to village. These villages: they looked like places I had pictured as a little girl when my mother read aloud to me at night of fairies and woodcutters and witches. The roofs of houses were thatched with straw. The walls were made of hardened thick red mud. The children with their large brown eyes and tiny hands smiled and pulled at my skirt, and ran away laughing when Danny said to them, abruptly, "*Jaio,*" and then continued to laugh at us as we kept on walking. The closest road seemed always at least two days' walk away; the city we had come from, another, foreign world; the country I had left was unimaginable entirely. My skin felt clean, even without water to wash in. I could feel my face glow, though I had no mirror, and once Danny looked at me and laughed and wiped a smudge of dirt away from my forehead. At night we were tired, our shoulders and calves and thighs and backs sore. We went to sleep shortly after darkness fell, nestled on straw mats on some shaky guesthouse bed, and rose when the sun rose, when the day was still cool. It was beautiful. Everything was beautiful, the soreness of muscles, the lush greens of the valleys and the hills, the sky above blue and then clouding and then blue again. How could I not have said before that it was beautiful?

At the top of the ridge, on our last day out, in the shadow of a pipal tree wreathed by a wall of stone, Danny and I sat and rested. "The road is two hours away," he said. I could see the trail we had walked on, snaking down to the valley and then up again behind it. Two men walked down the path we had just walked down, large baskets tied to their backs. They looked like ants to me, insects far in the distance, becoming human as they came closer. The back of my neck was sweating. "Two hours, then another hour to get back to the city, and then we'll be home again."

"Home," I said.

"It's not so bad, is it?"

I turned. The path before us led straight down and was cut like steps. The sky was an endless blue. A slight breeze rustled through the leaves of the tree above us. The hills rolled on forever. "It's not bad," I said. "It's wonderful."

The men with their baskets climbed up the slope now. Their necks were bent under the weight on their backs. They disappeared briefly before they reached us, and then rose up suddenly, large, close by. Hills play with timing and perception. A dip in a path can make a person seem to disappear. A rise can make one materialize as if from air. They turned their backs to us, circled the tree to find a clear space on the stone wall, then leaned back and let their baskets settle down behind them. They slipped the ropes back over their foreheads and slid free of their burdens. One lit a cigarette. The other climbed up on the wall and, crouching, spit a stream of saliva to the ground.

"*Namaste,*" Danny said.

They nodded. They looked away.

"*Namaste,*" I whispered.

There were red marks where the straps had worn into their skin. The caps on their heads were covered in dust, the once-bright fabric faded and frayed. One was wearing flip-flops, his brown, cracked ankles bulging thick and knotty. The other wore green canvas sneakers. They both smoked now. The smoke blew toward us, thick and heady. I took a sip of water. Danny asked another question in Nepali. The words rose and fell like music. I couldn't understand a thing. They nodded their heads from side to side, clicked their tongues in a way that sounded like regret. One of them pointed back toward the valley we had come through. Then they both stood, hitched their baskets back up again, and slowly wandered off. I turned to watch them. Soon they disappeared behind a dip, then emerged again, halfway across the valley ahead to the next rising slope.

Do these hills sound like snakes, backs arching and dipping and arching again? They had a sinuous quality, as though they were still alive, still adjusting their rises and indentations. Their green was the color of snakes as well, emerald snakes that in fairy tales turn into beautiful princesses by night. My heart jumped suddenly to realize I was in this country, that it was real as well as part of my dreams.

Danny put his arm around me when they finally disappeared. My pack was off. My body felt small, as though I'd just molted, had just shed a layer of shell. I felt his lips on my neck, and smiled. "Thank you for coming with me, Isabel," he whispered. "Thank you for seeing this world." His skin, even after days of walking, smelled faintly of nutmeg. His four-day-old beard pricked at my cheek. His lips were soft. His hand on my hand was warm.

A FEW HOURS later we stood at the edge of the dusty road and waited for a bus to come. The hills were behind us now, sloping upward. The valley lay before us, cutting down and then leveling out into a great stretching flatness. The city was covered with a muddy cloud of smog. We sipped water. We looked for shade. We watched the sky with squinted eyes, watched for rain. "I think the rainy season's over," Danny said.

"What day is it?" I asked.

"Does it matter?"

And it didn't. That was it—it didn't. In that moment, time seemed irrelevant. For a reason I could not understand, my heart lifted. I could feel my lips open wide to smile. "Maybe it doesn't," I said. "Maybe it doesn't matter at all."

"Except for the treks."

Did I say I smiled? I lost the smile then.

"The first trek's coming up," he said. "Two weeks. Middle of September. The only reason I can think of that what day it is matters."

We stood at the roadside and rubbed our eyes against the dust. It was as though we'd been asleep for years and woken, disoriented, to an altered world. The hills looked torn apart by the road. The road looked a beaten, barren swath of dirt. When a truck finally passed, slowed down, and stopped, I didn't even try to understand what Danny shouted at the driver. They exchanged words. Then Danny picked up both our packs, hoisted them over the wooden sides of the truck, and grabbed my hand. He helped push me up and over and then climbed up himself. Soon we were barreling toward the city, covered with kicked-up dust, sitting on burlap sacks. Traffic purred and then blared around us, music and honking and shouting. I can't remember how we finally got home. All I remember is the city closing in, the noises taking over, my hands covered with dust and soot. We spent that night in our own bed, but try as I might, I can't remember the final steps it took to get there.

CHAPTER THREE

*W*hat would I do when Danny was gone? As days passed, the question pressed on me with greater and greater urgency. Those early days, with their explorations, with discovery round every corner, seemed a break from the rest of life, a discrete time to live without worry, an island in the mountains, I thought. But as much as I tried to live in this splendid isolation, to take in each new sight, each new sound and smell, without imagining how I would look at it, hear it, smell it in the future, the thought of Danny leaving for the mountains was always close at hand.

I had ideas. I had an image of Gina in my mind, of her hard arms around me as—surprising me—she hugged me good-bye in New York on my last day at the shop. "Don't give up your life," she'd said. "Keep your eye out for me.

Keep your eye out for things I can use." At the time I'd shaken my head, heard this as just one more sour thought coming from her mouth. But now I remembered her words, and so I did keep my eye out. I looked at fabric and pictured bolts piled high in her store. I ran my fingers over brass knives lined blade to blade on tables set up on dusty sidewalks and saw their blunt edges glistening through the glass of display cases back home. The incense burned here in monasteries was deeper and richer than the incense Gina carried in her store. I wondered if there would be a market for Tibetan prayer flags, for the gauzy greens and reds and blues block-printed with mysterious script, and how high the markup could be. It seemed sometimes that everything in this city could be sold. But I kept quiet. Though I told myself that what Danny did for a living was a peddling of the country, I was aware, somehow, that he would not see it this way, and thought that he would not approve of my exporting scheme.

One day I rode alone toward Patan. I remembered passing stores along the road when I'd traveled there with Danny, stores with different wares from what the tourist stores in Thamel carried. I remembered the artisan-made copper ladles, the small barrel drums stretched tight with hide. I stopped outside one store that had a sign that read SHANTI above its windows. A bell rang when I opened the door. The light inside was dim. I walked in, and just as the door swung shut behind me a young woman stepped out from behind a curtain.

"May I help you, madam?" she said in English. She wore a suit made of a long, loose embroidered shirt and matching embroidered pants. A turquoise stone pierced her nose. Her hair was tied back in a bun.

"I'm just looking, thank you," I said.

"This is a development project store," she said. "Women from my village make everything we sell."

The store was filled with items made from the same colorful fabric. There were pillows covered with geometrical designs, and kimonos dangling from hangers, and bedspreads and quilt covers and shawls.

"We use fabric that is traditionally woven for *topis,* for men's hats. We also sell some hats." I saw them piled on a shelf, the short, stiff hats that all Nepali men seemed to wear.

There were a few items made from another fabric as well. It was coarse and white and it looked almost like linen.

"We also are finding ways to use a cloth made out of stinging nettles. The women of my village gather it in the hills. They boil it and spin it and find that it is very strong— like flax, I think."

I bought a little purse. When I showed it to Danny, he said he knew the store. "It's a good project," he said. "It makes sense to bring money to the village through the women. When it comes in through the men it tends to go to alcohol rather than to help the families."

I went back to the store a second time, and this time the woman recognized me. "How are you, madam?" she said.

"I'm fine," I said. "And you?"

She smiled. "I'm fine. Today our business is a bit slow. Would you like to see how the fabric is made?"

She showed me photographs of her village. It lay above a small river, and was surrounded by steep hills. The store's looms were set up on a platform close to the water, four looms, each with a woman seated in front of it, each woman with a baby on her lap.

"There's no one to watch the children while they work, so the mothers keep their children with them. I would like to create something like a childcare center, where one woman will watch all the children."

"Do you have any children?"

She blushed and laughed. "I am not yet married. I think it will be some years before I have a child. I hope it will be some years."

I laughed too. Before I left the store that day I thanked her for showing me what she had. "My name is Isabel," I said. "I'm new here. I just moved here. I don't know many people."

"I'm Radika," she said. "Come back again. Come back and spend time with us."

And I did. The third time I went back I told her I'd managed an import store in New York. I told her if she needed help, if she wanted to try to export any of the project's goods, I'd be happy to help. She smiled. She nodded her head. And just like that I found a place for myself. Without Danny's help. In a strange city, on my own, I found a purpose for my days.

ONE AFTERNOON SHORTLY before Danny was to leave, I returned to the palace from the store in Patan, each arm heavy with a bag that carried information about stores in America and Europe we might approach. When I reached the gate to the compound it opened ahead of me as if of its own accord. I looked up, surprised. A woman stood where the gate had been, a woman with hair that glinted copper in the sun. Her skin was pale as milk; her eyes where they stared out below a hand that shaded them—the sun was almost always bright now—were the gray of the sea at dawn.

"Are you Isabel?" she said. Her voice was soft, the timbre low.

"Yes," I said. I tried to reach a hand out to take hers, but the bags, I'd forgotten the bags, and they hung there like limp extensions of my arms. I looked down at them and laughed. "I *am* Isabel. And you?"

"Bethany," she said. "Bethany Andrews. Your neighbor."

My neighbor. The couple that Danny had spoken of. I'd begun to think that they might never return.

"We just got back this morning. I'm still a bit delirious from the flight. Three days. It's too much. I don't know how many more times I can do this." She wiped a damp strand of hair off her cheek. She was small, I saw now, slight, and when she smiled her lips curved wide and her teeth were small and sharp and her smile made me want to smile back in answer. She held her hand out, touched my arm just above the wrist. "I'm so glad to have a new neighbor," she said. "I'm so glad Danny's finally found someone. I've been waiting for him to find someone, you know. I've been waiting for him to bring someone back to that apartment to stay." Her hand on my arm was light, her fingers soft as ferns, soft as breath.

"I'm glad to meet you too," I said. "I'm glad you're back. I'm glad the palace won't feel as empty as before." As soon as I said it I realized it was true. I hadn't thought about the palace before as empty, but now the long, dark halls, the creaking steps, seemed to echo loneliness. The high walls rose behind her. Vines rustled in the breeze. A bird sang. A car's horn blared loud beyond the gate. "I'm glad you're here," I said, her fingers dancing on my wrist, a smile playing on her lips. "I'm glad."

⚭

WHEN DANNY CAME home from running errands later that afternoon, I told him that Bethany had invited us for drinks. "She said to tell you she's got scotch." I sighed deeply when he smiled.

"So they're back, are they? And you've met her? I thought the two of you would like each other. I wasn't sure, but I had a feeling."

"You had a feeling?"

"A feeling." He ran his hand across my back. His hand was warm, the calluses rough. He gathered up my hair, and I felt his lips upon my neck.

"So we'll go over later?"

"So we'll go. But later. Much later."

He led me to the bedroom, and the mosquito net tumbled down around us like long hair falling from a knot.

⚭

"WE LEAVE HERE every year," Bethany said that night. "I can't stand the rain." Her mood was lower now, and her voice, soft already earlier, came out in a whisper. She swirled a clear glass filled with tawny liquid, took a long sip, shook her head. "It's different here now. It's not the same city I first came to."

"I miss the rain a bit, now that it's not here," I said. We

stood out on their balcony. Their balcony that mirrored ours. A dog barked in the street beyond the walls.

"I felt the same way the first year I was here." Bethany stood on her toes and stared down over the balcony rail. It was too dark now to see the ground below. She swept her hand across the stone surface, brushing dust out into the night. "I didn't want to leave, and I loved the quiet that came with the rain, the way the city emptied out. Then we got infested with ants. And mosquitoes. And termites. Now I leave as soon as the first rains start."

Bethany and her husband, Greg, a tall, gangly man, both taught at the American school. They'd lived in Kathmandu for ten years when I met them. Bethany taught English to ninth and tenth graders. Greg taught junior high school math. Their apartment was almost a perfect reflection of ours. Their balcony led out from the far side of the living room. Their kitchen was to the right instead of to the left. Their floor, like ours, was covered with straw matting. Their bed, like ours, was draped with a mosquito net. "Danny brought it back for us from India," Bethany said. "For some reason they're hard to find here. I love sleeping under it. It makes me feel like a princess. A princess in a palace."

"I like sleeping under it too," I said. The men sat inside, and Bethany now took me by the hand and led me through the living room and into the bedroom to show me their bed. I could hear Danny's low voice as we passed. The room seemed to shift and I realized that I must be a little woozy from the scotch. "Danny laughs at how much I like it, but I think he likes it too."

"He likes it," she said. She laughed softly. "He definitely likes it."

I looked up at her quickly, but she had looked away.

Bethany and Greg's bed had a headboard made of wood, dark wood, intricately carved. "It's a window frame," she said when I crossed the room to examine it more closely. "They take them from the old houses and sell them abroad. Antique smuggling. Destroying the city. Greg found this one stacked up against the wall in somebody's house, just sitting there in the damp waiting for termites to get to it. He had it made into a headboard for me, for a wedding present. We've had it for years."

"You were married here?"

"In this palace. We spent our wedding night in this very room."

I looked up at her again. Greg's hiccupy laugh rose through the door. She smiled, and then the lights went off, plunging the room into darkness—a sudden stillness where the whirring of electricity had been.

There was silence, and then Bethany said, "I'd almost forgotten about the blackouts. If it's not this side of the city it's the other. It always seems to happen wherever *I* am. Didn't miss this back in the States this summer."

She lit a candle. The light quivered, and I noticed the vanity across the room, the mirror large, its wavy surface reflecting the candlelight. Long, dark wooden legs disappeared in shadows at the floor. "Greg had that made for me. It's the princess thing. Something about this place makes me want to put on lipstick while Greg brushes out my hair."

In the candlelight, in their bedroom, her words seemed too intimate for comfort. But what was it? A bed? A makeup table? The changed timbre of Bethany's voice trembling in the darkness? Then Greg and Danny called out to us from beyond the door, and we both turned quickly and left the bedroom.

The air in the living room was thick now with smoke and incense. The doors to the balcony were open, but no breeze blew in. Danny's feet were propped up on the coffee table. In the candlelight I couldn't see his eyes. He patted the couch beside him, and I crossed the room quickly and snuggled into his shoulder. I hooked my arm through his arm.

"She's sweet, Danny," Bethany said.

"Isn't she?" he answered.

Hindi music floated up from a battery-powered radio in the rooms below, a woman's needling voice, pitching up and down, the deep, fast, thrumming patter of drums. The walls in the living room were hung with shadows. Candles burned all around, on the coffee table, in sconces on the walls; a kerosene lamp glowed on a table across the room.

"I think she's homesick," Danny said. I looked at him in surprise. He ran his hand over my hair. "I think she needs a friend here." I sat up now, tried to see his face clearly in the shuddering light. "Will you take care of her when I'm gone, Beth?"

"When you're gone?" I said.

"Will you, Beth?"

I couldn't see her face. I could hear her rocking back and forth in her chair; I saw, as if a shadow, saw her draw her legs up to her chest, pull her dress down around her knees.

"When's your first trek, Danny?" she said.

"Next week. September twelfth. Very soon."

"Then Isabel and I have to start spending time together.

We'll spend lots of time together. You don't have to worry about anything."

I heard Greg breathe in suddenly, a loud gasp, the air rushing through his throat. "You'll be fine, Isabel," he said. I couldn't see his face. "You'll be fine. We'll take care of you. We'll make sure this feels like home. We'll make sure you're here when Danny comes back."

"Look at her smile," Bethany said then. I hadn't realized I was smiling. "That's why you love her, Danny, isn't it? Look at the way her face changes, look at the light on her skin."

"She hardly ever smiles," Danny said.

My face turned red. I could feel the blush spreading now.

"But look at her. Look at the way it changes her. I fell in love with that smile."

I looked at him. His eyes shone back at me.

We fell into silence then. Danny's arms were warm around me. I rested my head against his chest and watched the candlelight. The flame quivered and the shadows that it threw onto the wall jerked. *I'm here,* I thought, a catch of excitement in my stomach. *I'm here, I'm here, I'm here.* Bethany leaned forward, took a cigarette between her fingers, and then in a quick flare I saw her face. Pale. Delicate. She inhaled deeply, and passed the cigarette to Greg. He sighed. Danny sighed. The incense was thick; the smoke was sweet. I shut my eyes. *I'm here,* I thought, and then I opened my eyes again and wondered if I'd awakened to a dream.

THE DAYS PASSED quickly before Danny's first trek. Our apartment was filled with gear now. It had appeared one afternoon as if from nowhere. I walked in after crossing the courtyard and nodding to Mr. Rana, after smiling at Anjala and watching her quickly duck her face away. I could hear Danny humming to himself in the living room. I smiled. It was only recently that I had noticed he sang under his breath when he thought no one could hear. I slipped my shoes off, put my bag down on the table, and walked into the living room.

The room was covered with sleeping bags. Dusty tarps were spread out on the floor. Danny had pushed our couch back to the wall, and the low table as well. Two chairs were outside on the balcony. He was crouched on the floor, balanced on his toes. I started to step inside but tripped over a rusty cooking stove. I fell down onto a tarp. I screamed.

"I meant to warn you," I heard Danny say. He was laughing. "It's always like this at the start of a season. Got to check the equipment. Can't trust anyone else with it." His laugh was deep and round. I giggled from where I'd landed. "The house won't be long like this, I promise."

"You promise?"

He held his hand to my cheek. He could hold my whole face in one hand. His fingers reached to my forehead. I rested my chin against his palm.

"I won't be gone for long."

"But then you'll be gone again." I'd stopped giggling, was looking at the floor.

"It's how I make my living, Isabel."

"I know."

"It's how I make our living."

"I know."

The tarps smelled of rain and fire smoke and a sweet, rotting odor that I couldn't place. They stayed draped over the couch and the table, spilled down to cover the floor, until Danny left a week later. A few zippers were broken on the sleeping bags, and once they were fixed, the bags were rolled up and piled by the door. Six of them. One was for Danny. One was for Pemba, who guided the trek. Pemba was a Sherpa from Pangboche in the Everest region, and Danny said he was as much his partner as anyone had ever been. The other four bags were for Danny's clients. When Danny wasn't home I pressed my face against his bag, breathing in the musty odor, wondering where he would be sleeping, what he would be dreaming as it wrapped itself around his body.

ANNA'S NAME CAME up once during that week before Danny left. It rose as the result of a phone call, my mother's voice trailing through the wires late on a hot September night. The ringing woke us up, and I scrambled out of bed to find the phone. It was dark, of course it was dark, it was night, and when I brushed my hand against the light switch in the living room the click was followed only by thick darkness and I cursed the blackouts that seemed to come now once a day.

It was a strange thing, to lift the receiver and hear my mother's voice, delayed by half a second, crackling but present in my ear. I often forgot about my parents. It was hard to think of them when everything was new, when there was so much to think about *here*. Then the phone would ring and my mother's wavering voice, so distant that I could not think what to tell her, would speak into my ear. "It's very early here," she said that night. "What time is it there?"

She knows, I thought. *She knows what time it is, she just wants to hear my voice answering.* "It's late," I said. "It's very late."

"How late?"

"You know what time it is." I wondered why I couldn't answer her, surprised at the coldness of my voice. I stood in the dark, hoping that Danny had fallen back to sleep, that he wasn't listening as I snapped.

"No, I don't. I don't know anything about where you are. I hardly even know your husband. I don't know when I'll see you again. I don't know anything about your life."

"I'm fine, Mom. I'm fine. That's all you need to know."

"I don't know anything. I don't know anything, and I can't even hear your voice clearly. Matthew's the reason that you're there, isn't it? It's Matthew. You can tell me."

There was silence for a moment while she waited for my answer.

"Come home, Isabel," she finally said. "We want you home."

Standing in the dark there, the rough straw of the mat against my feet, I suddenly wanted to tell her that I missed her too, that I missed my home.

"I heard from Anna," I heard her say then. "I got a post-card from New Zealand. She said she's coming to Nepal in March. She said to tell you if I spoke with you that she can't wait to see you then."

Can't wait? I held my breath.

"What?" my mother said. Her voice was thin now, the waves across the wires fading in and out. "What? Don't you want her to come?"

"I don't know," I said. I thought of Anna's hand on Danny's wrist. I thought of her leaning toward him across the kitchen table in our apartment in New York, of her wine-colored lips as they touched his lips, of Danny saying, *She'll be happy for us.* "I just don't know."

"You told me it wasn't serious between them."

"It wasn't."

"Then you should be happy that she's coming. You of all people should be happy that she's going on this trek. It's been over a year now since she lost her brother. You should be happy that she's living again."

"I lost him too, Mom," I said. "I lost Matthew too."

There was silence. I bit my lip and nodded.

"Please come home." Her voice was small now, gray. "Please come home. We miss you."

I shook my head into the dark. "I'm fine here. I'll be home again. Don't worry."

She drew her breath in at the other end of the line. She drew her breath in across the world. "We miss you, Isabel," she said.

"Good-bye, Mom," I said. "Good-bye."

When I climbed back into bed, Danny rolled onto his side. "Your mother worried about you?" His voice was still logy with sleep.

"She thinks I'm going to vanish off the face of the earth. She thinks she'll never see me again." I tried to laugh. He reached his hand up and brushed it across my forehead.

"It's natural that she's worried about you. You're precious, Isabel. I would be worried about you too if you traveled half a world away. You're a treasure. Next time she calls, let me talk to her. I'll tell her how well I take care of you."

"Why am I a treasure, Danny?" It popped out before I could rein it in. "What is it you love about me? What is it exactly?"

"Don't be silly, sweetheart." He cleared his throat. "I love everything. Next time she calls you, tell her I think about you every minute. Next time she calls you, tell her that I keep you safe within my heart."

He gathered me in his arms. His voice had lost the silkiness of sleep. I leaned into him, breathed in the nutmeg scent of his skin, heard the deep, slow rhythm of his lungs. "Danny," I whispered then. "She told me Anna sent a postcard. She told me Anna said to say she'll be here in March. Danny, I'm frightened for when Anna comes. I'm scared to see her. I'm scared of what we've done to her."

He pulled me closer. "There's nothing to be frightened of. We love each other, you and I. We love each other and there's no going back from that. Anna will understand. She must understand already. There's nothing to be frightened of. I love you and I always will."

WHAT WAS IT I loved about him? What was it I loved? I loved the sleepy slowness of his voice. I loved the nutmeg scent of his skin. I loved his lack of worry, and the richness of his laugh. And sometimes, yes, sometimes the thought crept in that I loved him because he had loved Anna first, because he had loved Anna first and still had chosen me.

DANNY LEFT ON a Sunday morning in mid-September. He left early, before it was light out. He had stayed up late the night before. There had been another blackout, and, having gone to bed before him, I woke to find him still sitting at the table in the kitchen, going over a map by the light of a kerosene lamp. His back was bent as he hunched over the table. One hand pushed back blond curls from his face. I stood in the doorway in my nightgown, watching him for what seemed to be forever. The world was silent, and with the loose cloth draped around my body I felt as still as a column, as thin in the air as a ghost. When he looked up I smiled. He smiled back, mouthed, "One more hour," and nodded as I turned around to slip back into bed. When he climbed in beside me, I was drifting off to sleep again. I felt the temperature change with the presence of his body, felt his arm slip over my shoulder, his large hand reach out to cover mine. Then I fell asleep sighing and in the morning woke and through half-closed eyes saw the door easing shut behind his back.

CHAPTER FOUR

should speak about Matthew here before it grows too
late. It was too late by the time I spoke of him to
Danny. I think it was too late. But how to speak about
Matthew without speaking about Anna too? And how to
speak about Anna without first speaking of myself? *We were
meant to be sisters,* I have said, and it is true. We were meant to
be sisters, but before we ever met each other, I was a small
girl by the sea.

I was a good speaker, my mother has told me, a good
speaker until I was four. Great, long words, surprisingly long
words that made new people turn their heads and look at me
hard. And then something changed. My mother said she was
never sure what caused it. One day I babbled, and the next I
sucked words inside myself the way one sucks one's lips after

a taste of lemon. A sour sucking. A puckering up. It was a confusing thing to see in a little girl who had always had a smile. "Overnight a certain melancholy set in," my mother said.

It wasn't until Anna moved next door that I found a friend with whom the words could tumble. I was seven when she arrived from Colorado. I was six and a half months into first grade and had spent the year waiting to meet a girl to become my best friend. It hadn't happened in all those months, and I was getting exhausted. I whispered it to my mother at night with one of the few big words I had left: waiting was making me exhausted.

And then Anna's family arrived. They came in a station wagon behind a yellow truck. Matthew jumped out first. Then Anna's mother, calling after him, "Matthew, Matthew, you get back here." While she jumped out of the car to chase him down, Anna opened another door and slipped out. I watched it all from my bedroom window. I could see the ocean over the tops of the trees. I could see the yellow truck, so far below that it looked as though it belonged to a toy truck set. And I could see Anna, tiny, tiny in the distance, stepping softly from the car, touching her father's arm where it hung over the window ledge up front, then slipping off to the side of the house. She looked in the windows before her mother came back, dragging Matthew by what looked like his ear.

We met formally later that afternoon. I had my mother dress me up in my favorite dress. It was flowered pink, covered with a lacy white apron, and I put on my Mary Janes. I asked my mother to brush my hair back in a ponytail, and to tie a pink ribbon around the elastic. Surprised, she did it, and then we were ready to go. I held her hand as we walked out the front door and down our driveway to Anna's. I held her hand as we climbed Anna's front steps, and held my breath while she rang the bell. I can remember this. I was seven— seven is not always distant in memory. Anna's mother answered the door. You could tell immediately that she was a woman who liked to laugh. You could tell by the way she knelt down to my height and said, "And who is *this*? Is she coming to visit *me*?" And when I blushed she reached her hand out, put it on top of my neatly tied hair, and mussed it. "Anna," she called. "Anna, there's someone here to say hello."

A scramble down the stairs. A rush of feet in the hallway. I realized I was still holding my breath. Anna came round the corner to the front door as if she'd lived there forever. Even at seven she seemed confident; even at seven I saw it in her carriage, in the ease in her shoulders. She seemed tall, though later, when we were friends, we had Matthew measure us back to back and we were exactly the same height—we matched each other inch for inch as we grew up. But at seven and ever after Anna carried herself taller than anyone else, and she seemed almost like a giant to me as I peeked from behind her mother's body.

And then, I can't remember how, I was suddenly upstairs in Anna's room, amid the packing boxes and clothes still folded tight in suitcases. I was sitting on the floor with her. Our legs were crossed. We sat facing each other. Her hair was light brown, though it would turn the rich dark black of walnut as she aged. Her cheeks were flushed the deep pink of pomegranates. "We're leaving my dad behind," she said. "He's driving back to Colorado. I told him I'd miss the mountains and he said he knew I would. I told him we'd come back soon and he said he'd be looking for us."

Her whispered words made me flush with pleasure.

"My mother said we won't be going back, though. My mother said we'd be settling here in the East. My mother said I'd make new friends."

Did she realize we were friends already?

"She said it might take time. Matthew says he doesn't care. He said he's going back to Colorado. He said he's not going to live here with the girls. That's what my dad calls my mother and me, the girls. She's not really a girl, but he calls her one."

I couldn't think of anything to say. She was so pretty, sitting there among the boxes and suitcases, her brown hair against her cheeks. I wanted to reach my hand out and touch the velvety skin of her face. I bit my lip instead, then took a deep breath. "You'll make friends," I said. "I'll be your friend. You can come over to play if you'd like."

Is this too precious? It's exactly the way I remember it. Is it possible that I've invented it, reworked it in my mind? I swear I fell in love with her that first moment I saw her through my bedroom window. I swear I told her she could come over to play. I swear I dreamed for days of reaching out my hand to her, of stroking the soft skin of her cheek.

She came over with her mother and brother for dinner the next night. Their father had driven away in the morning. Matthew was ten, already long and thin. He was silent throughout dinner, playing with a marble he kept on a string around his neck, but then, afterward, when Anna and I ran outside in the early April evening, he chased us until we fell down on the damp ground, laughing. All three of us crept inside finally, our knees caked with mud. We tiptoed to the dining room, leaned our three bodies against the wall. I can remember Matthew breathing loudly close to my ear. I can remember Anna reaching out and taking my hand in hers. "I had to leave him," we heard Anna's mother say. "I had to pack up and leave. The children can't understand now what happens between adults, but they'll understand eventually. I know they'll learn to understand."

And that was that. Anna was tucked into the house next door, and I had found my best friend for life. She and Matthew spent the summers in Colorado with their father. I would wait expectantly at the end of every August for the two of them to return, and was always silent for a moment when they climbed out of the car one behind the other, yammering about who had seen their mother first when they'd gotten off the plane. Would she remember me? I wondered. Would she remember what I meant to her? Matthew would saunter past, pretending he didn't see me, then reaching out just when I thought he was gone to punch me lightly on the arm. I'd turn to look at him, and when I turned back, Anna would have scrambled close, would be right in front of me, her cheeks as flushed as when I met her first, her eyes as bright. *This is my best friend,* I'd think. *This will be my best friend forever.* We'd smile shyly at one another, then Anna would take my hand and lead me, running, to her room. She was home. I couldn't stop smiling all night.

Is this too precious? At night in bed when I was seven, at

the end of that first summer when they left and then returned from Colorado, I'd lie with my eyes open, the late August heat bloating the air around me. I'd kick the sheets down to the foot of the bed and lie there, a vague smile on my face. *I have a best friend,* I would think. *She will be my friend forever. There's nothing I could do that would change that. There's nothing she could do.* The crickets hummed. If I listened hard, I could hear the ocean lapping at the shore. The largeness of the world thrilled me. *My friend is home,* I'd hum. *Anna is home.* And finally I'd fall asleep. Only now can I imagine the world expanding around that sleeping seven-year-old body, can I imagine the swelling of the ocean, the rising of the crickets' throaty noise. Only now can I see my seven-year-old self as just a small part of that expanding world, not the center around which it revolved, as I imagined on those nights before my lids fell shut, as I dreamed before I entered the deeper and clearer dreams brought on by sleep.

AND MATTHEW. WHEN did Matthew become more than just my best friend's teasing older brother? When did he become more than a surrogate brother to me?

One night when I was sixteen I crossed the yard to Anna's house and knocked on the door. I remember I was chewing watermelon bubble gum, and that I cracked a bubble in my mouth while I waited on the stoop. Pink shreds stuck to the corners of my mouth, and Matthew opened the door just as I'd begun to peel them off. He was nineteen and home from college for the weekend. "She's out," he said. I popped another bubble. "You're welcome to wait inside."

"Okay," I said. I crossed in front of him while he held the door.

It was fall then. October. The nights came early, and wind howled through the pine trees that lay between our houses and the sea. We sat down on the couch in the living room together, and the wind shrieking loudly around the corners made me imagine that we were closed in tight in the snug hold of a ship.

"I miss this house," Matthew said. "When we moved here I wanted so badly to stay in Colorado with my father that I never thought I'd want to come back to this place. But now that I'm away, I miss it." He cleared his throat. His hair was cut short, and I thought he looked very much as he'd looked when I first met him, and also very different. His hair was as dark as Anna's. His eyes were the same deep brown.

"I've never lived anywhere else," I said. I wished suddenly that I had some place to get rid of my gum. "I've always wondered what your lives were like in Colorado. Each sum-mer when the two of you left, I always worried that you'd stay away for good."

"You worried about that?"

"You two both talk about the mountains like they're heaven. You talk about your father's house like you'd move there in a second if you could. I used to get stomachaches during the summer when I was little thinking that Anna wouldn't come back." I cracked another bubble, then wadded the gum up in a ball and put it in my hand.

"You worry too much, Isabel." He laughed. His laugh was the same rich laugh that Anna had. His cheeks had the same soft velvet skin, but the bones beneath them were sharp. He leaned over toward me and just as I thought he'd lift a hand to punch my arm as he had done since we were kids, he touched his finger gently to my cheek. Something that reached from my stomach to my toes shifted slightly then. "Anna used to talk about you constantly whenever we went away. She kept a picture of you in her wallet, for God's sake. My father used to tease her that she had a girlfriend."

I laughed too. I tried not to think about his fingers on my cheek. I worked the gum into a ball between my finger and my thumb. He reached out then and touched my hand. "Throw your gum away," he said. "You're acting like a little girl."

Anna and her mother didn't come back for another hour. By then I couldn't take my eyes off Matthew. By then I smiled and blushed whenever he turned his eyes toward me. And that night, just when his mother's car turned in the driveway, the headlights flashing into the living room like lightning, he leaned over and kissed me on the mouth.

Before he left at the end of the weekend to go back to school, he pulled me by my hand along the path that led to the ocean. The autumn wind was furious. The trees that edged the sand creaked and groaned, and the sea crashed against the shore. I found that my hand was warm where it folded inside of his. We craned our heads skyward to see the clouds. When we kissed, I could taste salt on his lips. When my arms circled his back I could feel his jacket damp where the spray from the ocean had blown. "You're like a little girl," he said to me, for the second time that weekend.

"You're leaving," I said.

"I'll be back."

"But I wish you weren't leaving."

"I'll tell you a trick, Isabel." His hair was so short that even with the wind blowing up from the ocean I could see his eyes. "When you worry that someone's going to leave you, figure out how to get away first. Then you're the one who's doing the leaving. Then they're the one who's left."

"But I don't want to go anywhere."

"Make yourself. Make yourself want to leave."

And then I lost sight of him, not from the wind blowing his hair across his face but from the wind blowing my hair across mine. I pressed my hand into a ball inside his hand.

"You're still a little girl," he whispered. "You're just a little girl."

When he kissed me his lips were warm. I could feel the cold glass marble he still wore strung around his neck where it pressed against the hollow of my throat.

AND THERE IT was. At sixteen I fell in love. At sixteen I felt my heart swelling up inside me so large and aching that it almost burst. I remember that year, remember sleeping over at Anna's, lying beside her in her bed, hoping Matthew would call home. I remember picking her for information about him, the memories I had of him from years of growing up next door suddenly not enough. At first Anna laughed about it. Then she grew annoyed. But by the time he came back from college that summer, and in the years that followed, she told me she'd ceased to mind. It was over ten years that he and I were together. Through college. Through occasional breakups. Through occasional lapses in faith.

And then, ten years later, when he was twenty-nine and I was twenty-six, I made him leave. I shut the door behind him. One day I had Anna as a roommate and Matthew as a lover. One day he held my hand in his and told me that he loved me and that he would live with me forever. One day he asked me to love him forever in return. The next day he had vanished to the mountains. The next week he was missing. And then the week after that he was gone.

It took me too long to tell Danny about Matthew, but it was Danny who never asked. He arrived in New York that winter like the sun, smiling, strong, and warm. He arrived, and when he asked me to leave with him, I left. *I'll tell you a trick, Isabel,* Matthew had said. *I'll tell you a trick. When you worry that someone's going to leave you, figure out how to get away first. Then you're the one who's doing the leaving. Then they're the one who's left.* And Anna—she was already in motion, had already flown across the sea. Had I missed my chance? I wondered. Had I missed my chance to leave her? I fell in love with Danny and I fell in love with leaving and I think I even fell in love with the idea that she would eventually come to *me*, that her leaving would, in the end, be nothing but a journey toward me, and somehow with her arrival the pain I felt at Matthew's loss would unknot itself and ease.

CHAPTER FIVE

*B*ethany stopped by the first night after Danny left.
The lights were out. It was a night of no electricity. Anjala was gone already for the day. The living room flickered with the light of a kerosene lamp; words blurred on the
pages of the book I was reading. Every way I turned my body,
my shoulder seemed to cast a shadow across the page. Candle
stubs burned upon the table, their wax shedding as quickly as
streaming water. The flames jumped and danced. I put my
book down and shut my eyes and let my mind drift far.

I think I must have been close to sleep when a quick
knocking jarred the silence. I opened my eyes with a start,
unsure of what the sound had been. The scent of incense
rose from the floors below, sweet and thick and musky.
Another knock came, and now I realized it was a knock

upon the door. "Just a minute," I mumbled, and then I found the door. The coldness of the metal knob beneath my fingers helped rouse me.

Bethany stood in the hallway. She looked tired. She'd shifted her weight onto one hip and was shutting her mouth from a yawn. I thought her stomach poked out slightly. She smiled when she saw me. Her eyes were set deep in shadows.

"I thought I'd stop by to see how you're doing," she said.

I could feel the corners of my mouth turn up. When I said thank you, my voice was scratchy. I cleared my throat.

"Are you all alone here? Of course you're all alone."

I cleared my throat again. "Would you like to come in?"

"I'd love to." She kicked her sandals off at the door, plopped down on the couch, and lifted her feet onto the table. "Aah," she said. "Your couch. I love your couch. I've spent hours on this couch."

Later, after I'd handed her a mug of tea, she said, "I used to spend a lot of time over here. It feels like forever that I've known Danny." She sipped her tea. Her copper hair glistened against the pillow. "You must be going through so much," she said. "I forget sometimes what it was like when I first came here. I can hardly remember being surprised by this place."

"I'm surprised every day. I'm so surprised I hardly remember to breathe sometimes."

"That will change. Soon you'll forget that there's any other world." Even in the dim light I could see steam rising up across her face. Her sharp bones were softened by the hazy vapor.

"When did you first meet Danny, Bethany?"

"Years ago. Maybe ten years ago. I remember I had such a crush on him—you think he's good-looking now? You should have seen him when he was twenty-five." She laughed. She looked up at me. "I think every Western woman in this city has been in love with him at one point or another. I've never been exactly sure what it is. Part of it's his looks. Part of it is his distance. Part of it is something else— that he works as a guide? That his job is keeping people safe? I don't know. What is it that makes us love a person any- way?" She took a sip of tea. "Does he seem distant to you? I've wanted to ask you that. Do you mind if I ask you? He's not easy to be close to. You must have noticed that by now."

Did I mind? Did he seem distant?

I thought of his cheek, his beard sharp after our days together in the mountains, rubbing against my own cheek. I thought of him taking me by the hand, asking me to come here with him, asking me to marry him. I thought of his par- ents at the picnic table behind my parents' house. I thought of his mother pressing my hand inside of hers, calling me her daughter. It was *easy*, everything was easy with him, every- thing moved as if under warm sunlight.

Then I thought of Anna, and then I shook the thought of her out until my mind was clear.

"He doesn't. I've never noticed any distance. I've never felt him keeping anything from me."

"I'm glad," she said. A moment passed. Then, "There are some people who are born to have companions, and some who have to struggle against themselves to have them. Greg's happiest when he's with me. I know he is. I don't know when Danny's happiest."

I looked at her. I wondered what she meant by this, what she had come over that night to tell me.

"He moves constantly," she continued. "From here to the States. From the States back to Nepal. From Kathmandu to the mountains and then back. He can hardly stay seated for more than five minutes. I can't think of him without thinking of motion. When he wrote to me last February to tell me he'd fallen in love, I couldn't wait to meet you. Like I said, I'm sure half the Western women in this city are waiting with their breath held to see what you're like."

The dark room. I wished the lights were on. I wished the shadows on her face were not so deep.

"And you. What were you doing when you fell in love with him?"

"I was managing a store. An import store. If I'd known anything about Nepal we'd probably have been selling things from here." I laughed. She laughed too. Then she stopped, and when she spoke again her voice was pitched to a lower tone.

"Greg has a side business. Has Danny told you?"

I shook my head.

"He exports things. Old things. There's money to be made here if you know what you're doing. More than we get paid as teachers, anyway."

There was a low creak outside. I jumped. Now it was Bethany who shook her head. "I shouldn't be telling you about that." Another creak. "It's the walls," she said. "The walls talk. There's a ghost in this palace, you know." She shut her eyes. "Have you noticed anything strange yet, sleeping here?"

"No."

"Has Danny told you anything about the Rana? About how many wives he had? How many children?"

"Mr. Rana?"

"His grandfather. His grandfather had this palace built. He had seven wives. Seven. And then he had mistresses as well. This whole wing of the palace, as far as I've been able to figure out, was where the mistresses slept. Beds and beds of sleeping women. It was quite the thing for those Ranas—the concubines, the wives, the rows and rows of children. They could do anything. There was a curfew then for everyone but the Ranas. You needed special permission to even enter the city of Kathmandu. Sometimes I walk through the city and try to imagine what it was like before roads were paved and cars were brought in. One of the Ranas had a Rolls-Royce carried in from India by porters. They carried it up the mountains on their backs so he could drive it around his courtyard. And there are other stories. Murder. Rape. They did unspeakable things in these palaces." Her voice dropped suddenly to a whisper. "They say all these palaces are haunted. I've seen her here."

I stared. I could not think of anything to say.

She stared back at me and then she shook her head. "Can I tell you something, Isabel?"

I nodded and raised the mug to my lips.

"I'm pregnant. We've been trying for years, and it's finally happened." She reached out and pressed her hand into my hand. I thought of the scotch she'd been drinking not two weeks ago, of the sweet-smelling cigarette she'd raised up to her lips. "We weren't going to tell anyone until it had been three months, but I had to tell someone. It happened in California. We almost didn't come back. Almost. But this is our home." She smiled. The candlelight caught her smile, caught the hollows in her cheeks, and I held her hand in mine. "We wanted to have the baby in our home."

And then the lights flashed back on. The shadows vanished. The flames of the candles dimmed beneath the electricity. Bethany shook her head again. "I should go," she said. "I should get to bed. We weren't going to tell anyone. I wasn't supposed to say anything." She put her mug down on the table and stood up. At the door she turned to me. "You be careful not to vanish here in this apartment, Isabel," she said. "You make sure to go outside. It's not healthy to spend too much time alone. It's time for you to make this place your home. Please come visit often. Please come by anytime you feel even a tiny bit lonely. Our doors will always be open for you."

She stood in the doorway. I reached out suddenly and touched her arm. "Do I know Danny, Bethany?" I whispered. "Do I know him if I don't know his past? If I don't know his history?"

She hesitated a moment, then lifted her hand and touched my hair. She stroked my cheek. "You know him, Isabel. You know you love him. You know he loves you. His life before you doesn't matter. His life before you came was already over when you met him. He loves you, Isabel. I told you he wrote me all about you from New York. He loves you."

I leaned my head against her shoulder. I nodded and felt the sharp bone beneath her shirt, felt it against my cheek. "Thank you," I whispered.

When she left, I stood in the doorway and watched her

walk back down the narrow hallway. From behind, her hips were thin, her body slight. The hall was dark. Her skirt reached to her calves. *His life before I came is over,* I thought. I nodded. I saw her grow faint, and then with one more step she vanished. *His life before I came is gone.*

Afterward I put our mugs in the sink and looked around. It was true that this was Danny's home. The pictures on the walls were framed photographs of mountains he had climbed and people he had met. The furniture was pieces that he had chosen, that he had ordered bundled up and carted over here without ever thinking of me, without having met me. How could he have created this place without me? How could he have been the same person before we met? I blew out the candles, flicked off the light switch, went into the bedroom, and climbed into bed. It was only when I put my head down on the pillow that I let myself remember what she'd said. *When he wrote to me last February to tell me he'd fallen in love, when he wrote to me in February.*

I screwed my eyes tight in the dark. *When he wrote to her in February,* I thought, *when he wrote to her in February, Anna hadn't left yet. When he wrote to her in February I was just his lover's friend. I was just her friend.*

ANJALA CAME THE next morning, slipping quietly through the door as she always did so that not having heard her come, I'd turn around to find her in the kitchen boiling water. Anjala was small, but muscles bulged in her arms as she worked. She wore her long black hair knotted in a bun at the nape of her neck. A small clear stone sparkled from her left nostril. Her blouse, made of patterned cloth, tied at her neck and at the side below her left breast and again at the bottom at her waist. Her skirt was faded and covered in pink flowers, and she pulled it up just enough to let her crouch on her heels on the floor. Her skin was a soft brown, like cinnamon, and her chin was pointed. I watched her sometimes as she balanced, crouched on her heels, on the balcony, and thought that she looked like a bird, delicate, ready to take flight.

But she wasn't delicate at all. She scrubbed our laundry in cold water with a square of soap and a stone. She hefted large kettles of boiled water over her shoulder and poured them into the filter tank and never spilled a drop. She bent low to sweep the floors, her broom without a handle, and when she was resting she crouched down again on the balcony on her heels and lifted a cigarette to her lips. She saw me watching once and quickly put it out, but later I saw her cup it in her hand again, lift a match, and light it when she thought I'd looked away. I don't know why she thought I'd care. I don't know why I was afraid to ask.

I tried to help. I think I tried to help. I smiled at her whenever we made eye contact. I tried out the words I had learned. "*Namaste,*" I would say when she arrived in the morning. "*Namaste.*"

"*Namaste,*" she would answer, and then break into a fit of giggles. "*Namaste didi.*"

I wondered how old she was. I wondered if she was married. I wondered how long she had worked for Danny, and what she thought of me, and whether there had been anyone here before me. She giggled and stepped into the kitchen. We paused awkwardly throughout the day whenever our paths crossed; I always tried to smile and then thought that she must think I was either crazy or without a heart, smiling while she cooked for me, while she scrubbed my marble floors and swept the straw mats and hung my laundry out to dry.

That day I watched her work and wondered what it was she knew about my husband that I did not yet know. Did she look at me and think that I was just another woman in a long line of women he'd taken to his home? Would it surprise her to know that he'd moved from my best friend to me in less than one week's time? I watched her working and I wondered if she watched me too, if she kept her eyes on me in the same secret way that I kept my eyes on her. I wondered if she knew the history of the palace ghost and whether she was ever frightened as she roamed the dusty, creaking halls.

I RODE OUT to the store in Patan during those weeks that Danny was gone. The more I showed up, the more the women talked to me. I wrote letters to stores throughout Europe and the States, and while I waited to hear replies the women talked about their lives. Radika came from a small village in eastern Nepal. Her father owned an inn. The family was prosperous. She'd gone to high school in Kathmandu, to a girls' boarding school where all classes were taught in English. She would be married soon. Her father was deciding now upon a suitable husband. She lived with an aunt and uncle in Patan.

"I would like to stay here in the city," Radika said one afternoon. "I would like to stay with my aunt and uncle and help them with their children and continue to run the store. I would like to be a businesswoman. I would like to travel throughout the world. I would prefer not to be a village wife."

"Can't you stay?" I asked. "Can't you tell your parents you would rather stay?"

"It is not so simple," she said. "This store does not make money yet. The women in the villages donate their time, donate hours at their looms to make this fabric so that someday they might bring money to their families. My father would rather that I get married than spend my life in this endeavor. Perhaps if you find us a place to sell our wares. Perhaps if you can help us make a profit. Or maybe he will find me a husband who will let me keep working here." She smiled. She continued with her sewing.

"Do you want a husband?"

She laughed. She ducked her head down.

"Will you teach me how to make a blanket?" I asked her then. "Will you teach me how to sew a quilt?"

"Teach you how to sew?"

"I'd like to make a present for my neighbor. She'll have a baby in April. She just told me that she's pregnant."

"And you don't know how to sew?"

I nodded. Sometimes in this new world the skills I lacked made me wonder how I'd made it this far through life.

Radika helped me gather scraps of cloth together. Then she helped me lay them out in a square. I wrote letters and I sent them out, and then I spent the days with her learning to sew, helping to keep her store, learning her system for keeping books. As I pulled the needle in and out through the rough, brightly colored scraps of cloth, my heart thrilled to what I was learning, and my mind told me to block out worry about what I did not yet know.

CHAPTER SIX

*W*hen Danny returned three weeks later I was already deeply immersed in the world of the store. He came in the early evening, just as the sun was falling beyond the mountain peaks, when a purple light twined through the streets of the dusty city. I was inside, just home from work, exhausted and stretched out on the bed. I lay half in and out of sleep. He burst through in a loud, clamoring way, called my name even as the door was opening, and when I raised my head he threw himself down on top of me and kissed my neck over and over. "Isabel," he said, his voice thick through the dusky light. "My sleepy bride. Wake up, it's me."

"Is it you?" I whispered. "Are you really home?"

He pulled me from the bed. He pulled me to the living

room, where I sat cross-legged on the couch and listened to him talk about the trek. "They were crazy, Isabel," he said. "I missed you so much. I missed you every day." I stared at him, at his shaggy blond hair, his skin still covered with dust from the hills. *He moved from my best friend to me,* I thought, and then I shook my head. "I thought the people would make me lose it, but the mountains—the mountains are always beautiful."

He stopped talking and looked at me. The purple light from the setting sun was nearly gone, and the air was dark between us. I could see the whites of his eyes. I could see the last light of the day caught in his blond hair. I ran my finger over his lip, wondered what he could see of me. His voice was soft now, murmuring like a lullaby, and then he took my hand and held it to his face, then took his hand and held it to my neck. His hands were bigger than I remembered. I could smell the dust still on his skin. His fingers moved across my throat and down, his lips on my breasts, my lips on his hair. It was as though he'd brought the mountains back with him, the smoky campfires, the days and days of walking. We fell asleep that night twined about each other, and I dreamed of frozen ground and endless skies and my lover calling to me from a dark cave. His sighing was the wind; his heart, the earth beating deep below.

WE SPENT THE next morning at home together. The crispness of the autumn air through the open windows felt almost like the crispness of the autumn air at home, and as I helped Danny pull clothes from his pack I laughed and imagined we were in New England, just back from hiking

through the changing trees. I imagined picking apples, imagined drinking cider and getting ready to light a fire at night.
I haven't even known him a year, I thought. *I haven't known him
through the change of seasons. I don't even know if he likes the fall.*
"Do you like the fall, Danny?" I asked.

"Love it," he said. I knew he would.

"Is it your favorite season?"

"I think so. I think so." He laughed.

"Do you miss the trees here? The changing trees?"

"You know, I don't think about it much. I kind of forget
that there's a world where seasons happen differently. I find I
forget a lot of things, and when I go back to the States I'm surprised by them even when, if I think about it, I know I've
known them since I was a kid. I like that it's a different world."

I giggled. "They're walking around there upside down for
all we know." I pulled a fleece shirt out of Danny's bag. I
pressed it to my face. It smelled of smoke and dirt. "Did you
camp when you were a boy?" I asked.

"All the time. I used to set up a tent in our backyard and
sleep out there all summer. The whole thing drove my
mother crazy. I couldn't sleep once it was light out, so I used
to wake up outside and come in and wake everyone in the
house, no matter how early it was. She didn't mind that I was
sleeping outside. She just minded that I was making everyone else stick to my new schedule. 'It's natural,' I used to say.
'We should be getting up with the sun.' Eventually she
started locking their bedroom door."

"I would have been too scared to sleep alone outside."

"Poor Isabel," he said. "My scaredy-cat. Poor scared
Isabel."

I blushed. I could feel it in my face, the blood rushing upward. I pulled another shirt from his bag, pressed it to my cheek, then tossed it away. "Anjala will have to wash these," I said. I picked up another shirt and hid my face in its musty folds.

HE WAS BACK for two weeks and in those two weeks the world blossomed. I watched—we all watched, Danny, Anjala, and I—as Bethany's stomach began to swell. It seemed to happen overnight, in opposition to the seasons. As the nights grew colder and mist draped itself across the city for longer and longer in the mornings, a dazzling sun seemed to ray out from beneath Bethany's skin. One morning I watched her from above as she walked across the courtyard hand in hand with Greg like two small schoolchildren from a children's book. Her stomach was slightly rounded. She wore a white dress. Her copper hair was tied back with a blue ribbon. That afternoon I watched the two of them return and her belly seemed to have swelled in the few hours that she had been away. She walked now with one hand in Greg's and one hand covering her stomach. Cradling it, I thought. Seeing if the baby was really there.

At night Danny and I would thread our way down the halls to their apartment, and we would all sit with our feet on their coffee table and speculate about what the baby's name should be. "It's a boy," Bethany said. "I know it's a boy."

"Yesterday she thought it was a girl," Greg said to Danny and me.

"I did not."

"You did."

Even at night, when they were together the two of them reminded me of children. Greg was so tall and loose-limbed and gawky, his legs folding this way and that as he crossed and recrossed them, that he seemed stuck physically in permanent adolescence. Bethany, now with her loose dresses and hair growing longer, looked like a little girl. And as the weeks wore on and her belly grew, she seemed to laugh with the joy of a child, her peals of laughter echoing from one corner of the palace to another.

Watching them, I wondered when Danny and I would have children. "Do you want one?" I asked him one night after we'd come back to the apartment. "Do you want a baby?"

"Not for a long time," he said. "My parents would love a grandchild. I'm trying to get Caroline to work on it, but from what she writes it sounds like she moves on to a new boyfriend every month."

"I'd like to meet her."

"You will. You'll love each other. She'll think you're perfect." He paused, then looked at me. "And you? Do you want a child?"

Did I want a child? I'd never liked babies all that much. I'd always been afraid to hold them, with their heavy heads and soft bones, their twisting back and forth in my arms. I'd never been able to hold one still. But I looked at Danny and it was hard not to keep my heart from swelling right then, the thought of his son in my arms, the thought of his daughter inside me. "I'd like one," I said. "I'd like your child."

He smiled. It had been the right thing to say. "I'd like for you to have my child," he whispered, leaning close to me. Then he moved back. "But not now. Please not right now."

When we moved toward each other in bed that night the thought of a baby flashed into my mind. Afterward I lay with a hand draped across my hollow stomach and smiled and thought, *Not now, but someday. Someday there will be a baby for us.*

BETHANY LIKED TO gnaw on the sour inside rind of melons. I had lunch with her one afternoon at an outdoor café where classical music blew across the garden courtyard, where water in a fountain trembled at the slightest breeze. She wore a large hat, and her face was dappled with light, and she held the green flesh of a melon to her lips and smiled when green juice dribbled down the side of her chin.

"I was at the doctor's yesterday," she said. "He said that everything is fine."

I nodded.

"He said I'm gaining weight exactly as I should. He said he could hear the baby's heartbeat."

"Can you feel it? Can you feel it like another person that's inside you?"

She smiled. "It's hard to describe what it feels like. The best I've been able to come up with is that I feel more whole than I did before. And I'm starting to think of it as a real baby, where before it was a much more abstract idea. But it's hard to imagine it ever outside of my body. I really do think it will be a boy."

"Will you raise him in Nepal?"

She smiled. "Our home's here. He'll be born here. This is where I want us to live forever."

It was afternoon and the sun was warm, though the air now, the air that even in this tropical world smelled to me of fall, was cool. A waiter, a thin young man, stopped by and poured us each more tea. Bethany smiled a thank-you, and he nodded his head. There was a stillness there in that garden, the music falling like rain. Bethany raised the melon to her lips again. She gnawed past the fleshy green and into the sour white.

"We'll live here forever," she said. "Me and my baby. We'll be here until the end of time."

I'D NEVER HAD a friend who was pregnant before. Danny sometimes looked at me when I chattered on about my days with Bethany. "The baby this," he said. "The baby that. Are you sure you're not getting ready to have one of your own?"

I blushed. "Of course not. But it's just so amazing. Every day she looks different. I swear she does. Every day. Don't you think it's exciting? Don't you think it's incredible?"

He laughed. He lifted my face in his hand. We stood out on the balcony together drinking beer, watching the sun drop below the mountains. The plants in the clay pots were dying, the cold autumn nights turning their leaves a dull brown. "You'll be a beautiful mother," he said softly. "You'll bear a beautiful child."

I thought, then, I thought he meant that I would bear his child. I thought then that he was imagining our lives together, our children, our lives spent caring for our children. And I could see them—I could *see* our baby, Danny's baby, my baby, a little boy with curly golden hair, a child toddling back and forth between our outstretched pairs of arms. I stared up into his eyes. "I will," I said. "Our child will be beautiful."

"Someday," he said. "Someday."

ONLY ONE THING happened in those first months of Bethany's pregnancy that threw me out of that beatific state. I came home from the store in Patan on a Thursday afternoon, humming to myself, swinging plastic bags filled with cloth scraps for the baby's quilt so that they hit each other and bounced back in the opposite direction. I felt like a girl. The weather was perfect. The afternoon sun was warm, the air clean; the promise of a cool night lay ahead. Danny had a meeting with Pemba, it was Anjala's day off, and as I pushed the gates open I smiled to think of settling into the empty apartment by myself, to think of beginning my project. At first when I stepped through the gates, the courtyard seemed as still and sheltered as it was in my dreams. But then, when I let the gate clang shut behind me, two figures stepped down from off the wide stone terrace.

Two men. One Nepali, one with pale, Western skin.

I nodded at them, wondered who they were, but kept on walking.

"Excuse me, madam," the Nepali man said. He was tall and broad and his fingers were thick. "Excuse me. We're looking for Greg Andrews. Can you tell us how to find him?"

"He should be at school," I said. Did I say that the sun

shone, and that a cool breeze blew? It seemed, then, that the breeze vanished and the air closed in, tight and still.

"At school?" The Western man had a British accent. He was tall, even taller than his companion, but thin. A blond mustache fell low across his upper lip. He pushed his hair back from his face.

"The American school. Where he teaches."

"Right. Right. When will he be back?"

"I don't know."

"You don't know?"

"How should I?" They both were staring at me, and now the bags I carried were heavy at my sides and the empty apartment upstairs seemed less a blessing. I wished that someone were home—Danny or Anjala, it didn't matter—and would step out onto the balcony and call to me to come up. "I've got to get home," I said, and took a step to move past them.

"We have a message for him."

"I'm sorry I can't help you."

"Tell him Ram and Anthony were here. Tell him we have business to discuss."

"I'm not his message service."

"Just tell him."

A door opened behind them. Mr. Rana stepped out onto the terrace. With the two men towering above me, Mr. Rana, in his white suit, with his black cane in his left hand, seemed thin and pale, a remnant from a world now gone. And then he cleared his throat, and the sound broke the strange hold of the two men, and he said, "Isabel, please come inside for tea."

I nodded. The two men looked at me. I pushed my way

around them, pushed my way through air that now seemed thick. When I got to the terrace I knew my face was burning, my hands were trembling, and sweat had begun to trickle down the nape of my neck.

"Tell him," I heard behind me. "Tell him," and then Mr. Rana linked his arm through mine and we walked inside together. I spent the afternoon with him instead of by myself, and he told me stories about the palace until night began to fall.

He didn't mention the two men until I rose to leave. He walked me to the door and opened it, and now we both stood looking at the courtyard, the sun sinking low toward the mountains to the west. "There are bad men in this city, Isabel," he said. He tapped his cane once upon the floor. "There are men to watch out for. Please be careful who you talk to. Please be careful when you are coming home alone."

LATER, WHEN I told Danny what had happened, he shook his head. "I've told Greg over and over not to deal with those two."

"Who are they? What did they want?"

"They're just businessmen. Greg does some exporting through them. They're a little sleazy, but I wouldn't worry. They were just trying to intimidate you, just because they could. Don't worry about them, Isabel. I'll talk to Greg about it."

"It felt like they were going to hurt me. It felt like they weren't going to let me by."

"They weren't going to hurt you. They were just trying to

scare you. Probably because you look like you get scared so easily."

"They did scare me. Mr. Rana saved me."

"He didn't save you. He just invited you in for tea."

"He saved me."

"You just like the idea of being saved."

I laughed. But even though I laughed, I still felt uneasy about those men, and when Danny left to talk to Greg I made sure to lock the door behind him, and I made sure to draw the locks shut on the doors that led to the balcony. I sat on the couch and pulled my knees up to my chest.

WHEN I ASKED Bethany about Greg's business, she shook her head. "I knew I shouldn't have ever brought it up with you that night. It's just a sideline that he has. Exports. Clothes. Those little brass figures you see on tables in Thamel. Kitschy stuff. You know, to make extra money. Everybody's thought of it."

I blushed: it was true. I *had* thought of what those brass knives would bring.

"It's no big deal. Ram and Anthony act like thugs, but they're harmless. They help him get his shipments together. Teaching doesn't pay very much. It is good work, but it's barely enough to cover expenses. Most expats in this city have other business on the side. We're actually friends with Anthony when he's not acting like a bully. You'll see—he's fine." She pressed her hand to her stomach, and I felt bad, then, to bring up any ugliness around her when what she was carrying inside seemed so pure.

I spent hours piecing together the bits of fabric from the store before I started the actual sewing. The scraps were brilliantly colored, reds and greens and blues, and the patterns were geometric, but because I had only a bag of scraps the patterns that the pieces formed seemed a wild geometry, promising logic but none that I could easily understand. I went to the fabric stores close to Indra Chowk, the oldest part of the city, where bolts and bolts were piled up in small stores, and sipped tea with a shop owner and then picked out two meters of red velvet to act as a base for the quilt. Birds chirped from cages as I wound my way through the crowded streets toward home. Buildings leaned in toward the street, bicycle bells chimed, dark alleys led to small stone shrines.

Later, I sat on the floor in the apartment and laid out the scraps on the velvet. Anjala paused her humming and squatted on the floor beside me and helped me rearrange the pieces. "For the baby," I said, and she pressed my hand and smiled. I imagined Bethany swaddling her child in the blanket, wrapping the baby up in my brightly colored quilt, and the baby dreaming of dazzling sunsets on the slopes of white mountains. *We'll have a baby here,* I thought, and though I was surprised at the excitement that rose within me, I moved through the surprise quickly and let myself bask in the excitement as if basking in the sun. *A baby, a baby, a baby,* and slowly the blanket began to take shape, and slowly Bethany's stomach began to grow.

"I'd like a baby," I whispered to Danny one night when we lay side by side in bed. "I'd like your baby. I'd like a part of you to gather in my arms."

"It's just because you're so excited about Bethany," he said.

"You don't really want a baby. Not now. You've barely started building your life here. You've barely started working."

"I know. But think of it—your child. Think of holding your own child."

"I don't want a child to hold. I have you. I just want to hold you." He stretched his arm around me. I felt his hand upon my stomach. I felt his breath upon my neck.

"But Danny, don't you want to see us grow? Don't you want to be a father? Will you ever want to be father?"

I felt his lips upon my shoulder. I felt his hand upon my thigh. "Someday," he whispered, and his voice, his voice at my ear, I felt his voice vibrate through my body. "Someday, but now I just want to hold you. Now you're the only one I want to care for."

I sighed. How could I not sigh in his arms? But later, in the lazy moment between waking and sleep, I thought I felt a child in my arms. I thought I felt a small weight upon my chest, a baby nodding to sleep against me, and I thought I heard a soft murmuring, mewing noise, a baby sighing in its dreams. *Someday,* I thought, and smiled. *Someday I'll hold your child in my arms.*

BETHANY CALLED ON a Friday three days before Danny was leaving for his second trek. "I was too tired to walk over," she said. "I wanted to invite you two to a party Anthony's having for the full moon."

"Anthony?" I asked.

"Anthony Parnell. The bully? You met him with Ram, remember? Danny will know who he is."

"You're going to a party at his house?"

She laughed. "You met him on a bad day. I told you, we're friends. He and Greg have patched things up."

I swallowed hard. I held the receiver to my chest and, whispering, asked Danny if he'd like to go to a party. "Where?" he said, and when I answered, he shook his head forcefully no.

I put the receiver back up to my ear. "You have to come," Bethany said. "You can't say no."

"Tell her no," Danny said again when I looked at him. "We only have three more days together. No." I nodded in relief.

"We can't," I said into the phone.

"Can't? What else do you have planned? You're coming."

"Really, we can't," I said, giggling. Danny looked at me strangely. "We can't."

"Put him on the phone. Let me talk him into it."

"It's not a question of talking him into it," I said. "He's leaving on Monday. We only have a little time left together." I looked to Danny for help, but he'd turned away now, was looking for something through a pile of papers on the table.

"Put him on."

"Okay. Okay, I'll get him."

Danny was in a mood. There was a propane shortage and our tank was empty. We'd had no way to boil water for days and had begun to drop iodine tablets in water from the tap. He glared at me when I handed him the phone and he looked ready to throw it on the ground. "What?" he said, both to me and into the receiver. "What do you want, Bethany?" He cradled the phone in the crook of his neck and continued to leaf through papers. "We can't come." Anjala was in the kitchen, and as Danny's voice rose, I saw her slip through the living room and out the door. "Stop talking for a second and listen to me. We cannot come to the party. We cannot come."

And then something changed. Danny's face softened. The red beneath his skin faded, and he gasped, laughing suddenly. "No," he said. "No, really," and laughed again. When he put down the phone it was settled. We were to go to Anthony's house for a full-moon party on Saturday. He was still laughing as he told me. "What?" he said when he saw me looking at him. "What? I can change my mind, can't I?"

I nodded yes. At least he was not leaving until Monday. At least we would have Sunday night alone together.

THE MOON ROSE the next night as large as a lake. It hung over the rice fields to the east and bathed the earth in silver light. Horns sounded from the Tibetan monasteries surrounding the Boudha stupa, the Buddhist reliquary mound that rose like a large white dome capped with azure eyes that stared out in all directions across the valley. The sounds of the horns were loud and deep.

Bethany met us at the door of Anthony's apartment, her long skirt trailing on the floor behind her. She held out her arms to us. She kissed me on the cheek. Her hair brushed against my skin. She smelled of roses. I took a deep breath. Danny crooked his arm through mine. The moon shone on our backs as we climbed behind her all the way up to the rooftop. Horns echoed after horns, and as the night turned black, the stupa began to glimmer with the light of butter lamps.

"We'll go to the stupa," Bethany said when we reached the roof. "Not yet, but soon."

It was dark on the roof. Lanterns stood on tables, the glass orbs and flutes glowing gold. Sticks of incense sent streams of perfumed smoke skyward. I felt as though I were floating on a raft above the earth. Danny and I nestled down on two cushions. I pulled my shawl tight around my shoulders. A few people stood beside a table where bottles of beer were set out. Danny ran his fingers through my hair. "This is like magic," I whispered to him.

"It is," he said. "I'd forgotten how beautiful it is up here."

Bethany pulled a chair over close to us and sat down. I could see Greg across the roof. "It's been forever since I lived in Boudha," she said. "I lived here before I moved into the palace, before Greg and I were married. I still sometimes feel like it's my home. I went to teachings at the monasteries as often as I could. I don't know why I stopped. When I lived here I didn't think I could stand to live anywhere else. It does me good to see the stupa. It does me good to hear the sounds from the monasteries."

"It does me good too." Danny tightened his arm around my shoulders and breathed deeply.

"It's getting crowded out here now. Anthony says they're building another house in front of this one. Tibetan refugees keep coming. Villagers keep coming from the hills. More and more students of the lamas come to live here. The valley is filling up."

I wondered where Anthony was. I thought of his eyes and the coldness of his voice, and wondered how it was that he had chosen this beautiful place as home.

Bethany poured a glass of beer from a bottle and handed it to me. She poured another for Danny, and a glass of water for herself. "Cheers," she said. I raised my hand, breathed her perfume briefly as we leaned toward each other to touch our glasses. Her fingers grazed my fingers. Another horn sounded across the fields. "We should go soon," Bethany said.

I smiled. She pressed her hand down on my knee.

"I love that smile, Danny," she said. "I love to make her smile. You'll come find me, Isabel? You'll visit when Danny's gone again?" And then she swept away, carrying the bottle of beer with her, and walked to where Greg stood with a group of people across the roof. When she set the bottle on a table, the candlelight glowed a rich amber through the brown glass.

The air was cool. I could see my breath when I sighed. There was no wind even high up on the roof, and the night had a sense of stillness, a floating outside of time and motion. *We'll stay here forever,* I thought. *If we don't move, the night will never change.*

A man walked toward us, his hair pulled back in a ponytail, a lock escaping and hanging down over his left eye. Danny ran his finger over my cheek, not yet seeing the man. *Don't let it ever change,* I thought, and then the man kneeled down on the cement floor beside us and Danny looked up.

"It's been a long time," the man said. Shadows hollowed out his cheeks and a mustache draped over his top lip. I realized it was Anthony. My hands knotted up in fists as I looked up to meet his eyes.

"It has," Danny said.

They looked at each other. They shook hands.

"Who's this?" the man said. "Who are you hiding there?"

He looked at me, and I thought he looked right through me, looked through and behind to someone else. I pressed back, silent. The cushions were so thick I couldn't feel the wall.

"Isabel," Danny said. "Isabel. My wife. We were married in the States."

"We've met," I said.

"I'd heard you'd gotten married."

"Yes," Danny said.

"You always find the pretty girls."

I blushed. I waited for Danny to say something, but all that he responded with was a tight-lipped "Yes."

And then the man turned to me again, and it seemed his eyes were darker than the sky. He held out his hand and said, "Isabel, I'm Anthony Parnell. It's good to meet you again. Good to meet you under better circumstances, on the night of a full moon. Welcome to my home." His hand around mine was warm. His voice was low. Something more than the cold made me shiver, and when everyone got ready to leave for the stupa, I nodded and held Danny's hand like a little girl. This place, these people, felt old to me, and I felt very young. I followed quietly behind the group as we made our way down the stairs and across the hardened furrows that ran between the rice fields. The moon shone so bright that there were no stars in the sky. The blaring of horns grew louder as we approached the stupa. I wondered if I would wake up and find myself in bed in the early morning in New York.

A deep chanting came from behind the gates of the monastery closest to the stupa. Each level of the stupa overflowed with circling pilgrims whispering mantras. Each prayer on a full-moon night was magnified ten thousand times,

Danny told me; each time I let my hand drift across the prayer wheels embedded in the stupa's side, the spinning prayers extended ten thousand times across the valley. Tiny butter lamps shimmered at each level's edge, and the smoke from the butter lamps rose black into the night sky. Monks circled, their maroon robes blending into the smoky darkness, and Danny held his arm across my lower back and we circled together, silent, breathless in the cold night, the golden flickering light.

We circled until I was dizzy. At the street level, along the cobblestone courtyard, I held out my right hand and ran my fingers along the wooden prongs of prayer wheels, spinning them faster than we spun ourselves. We climbed up a small staircase, onto the first rounded level, and then up again, and up again, until we stood at the top. I saw Bethany circling below us, her stomach large, her elbow linked through Anthony's, whispering to him, her face lit from below by the light. She glanced up, nodded her head, and looked at Anthony again. The air was cool. A monk brushed past. The chanting grew louder, a horn sounded, high, then dropping low. I breathed deeply, breathed in incense and cold air and the starless sky.

"Let's go home," Danny whispered, and I nodded. "Let's go home now."

We circled until we found Bethany, circled until we said good night. She took us both into her arms. It was cold now and her arms were warm, and I could feel her stomach when she pressed me close. When we climbed into a taxi, I leaned toward Danny and put my head down upon his shoulder. The sonorous horns faded. The car pulled away, and then we were gliding through empty roads, the meter ticking evenly, and finally we were home.

Part Two

CHAPTER SEVEN

I grew up by the ocean, along the sandy beaches of Cape Cod. I spent my summers under the sun, body-surfing in the cold water. I spent the winters walking through thin snow until I reached the sand. I had no sisters or brothers. When I was small I prayed for a sister, a sister whose hair I would tie with ribbons, who would trail after me on a small red bike, whom I would dress up as a doll and wheel around the neighborhood in a carriage. My mother always shook her head when I asked her for a sister. "No, Isabel," she said. "You're enough for us. We love you so much we don't have anything left over."

I didn't spend much time with my father. He left early in the morning for work and came home late. My mother would feed me dinner at the kitchen table and sit with me while I ate, but she waited to eat her own dinner with my father. I was supposed to be asleep in bed when his car pulled into the driveway. Sometimes I only pretended to sleep, and would slide out from between the covers when I heard his car whirring to a stop. I would steal down the hall, down the stairs, and peek around the corner to watch my parents together. They ate sometimes by candlelight. My mother leaned forward in her seat, staring at my father's face. My father would cut into the meat, then pause, look up, see my mother, meet her gaze, and smile. I loved to see the two of them together without their knowing that I was looking on. *This is a family,* I thought, even as a very little girl. *This is what love is like.*

During the summer my mother and I hunted on the beach for shells. We made tall pitchers of sticky lemonade from a mix and drank glasses of the yellow liquid all day. I ate spaghetti in the early evening while she sat and watched. Before I went to bed my mother gave me a bath. She'd scrub the day's sand out of my hair, then lift me from the tub, dry me off with a rough towel, and sprinkle my skin with talcum powder. I remember lying in bed during those years, the fresh smell of talc on my skin, a breeze through the scrubby pines outside, my mother's voice, low, murmuring on the phone.

He was home all day on weekends, my father. I looked forward to those days, but I also hated them. He would let me jump into his arms when he climbed out of the car late on Friday afternoon, still in his suit from the office. Then he would look down at the sandy tracks on his dark pants and sleeves and step warily back. "Let Daddy get changed," he'd say and look up at my mother. "Let me just get changed, then I'll be back down." Sometimes my mother followed him upstairs to the bedroom. Sometimes she came right back down. Sometimes they stayed up there until dinner.

One Friday night in late July, when my parents were together in their bedroom and the crickets were humming and the waves, farther away, were crashing against the shore, I slipped outside. There was a path behind the house that led from the back door directly to the beach. The first part of it was narrow, closed in by pines. I remember walking past the outstretched branches, breathing in the scent of pine needles mixed with a salty smell from the sea. The second part of the path was bordered by wild roses, thin, flat flowers with bulging orange hips. I could hear the ocean. The sky was black, the stars not yet out; the moon was a thin sliver far away above the sea. I could only guess at where the water licked the sand. I was wearing sneakers, and the sand gave way beneath my feet, but I did not know how far ahead of me the water lay, and I caught my breath suddenly and realized I was not certain where the path I had stepped away from was, where I could find the path that led back to my home.

My mother tells the story of walking downstairs, finding me gone, the screen door rattling behind me. She called out for me, called, "Isabel," at the top of her voice, and when there was no answer, she ran down the path to the ocean in her bare feet. She stumbled over sand-covered roots and stubbed her toes. Pine branches scratched against her legs. She stopped where the path opened up to the loose beach, the sky opening above, the ocean, endless, slipping back and forth beyond her in the darkness. The water surged and fell, surged and fell, the sky as dark as the water, the water black as night. When she found me, finally, I was sitting on the sand, my knees pulled to my chest. She wasn't sure whether I had been crying, whether I was huddled against the cold or against the largeness of the sky. She threw her arms around me and picked me up, despite my size. She carried me back up the path to the house, and the only time I have ever heard her yell at my father was when we stumbled through the door and found him sitting on the sofa in the living room, reading the paper, his glasses sliding far down the slope of his nose.

My mother never asked me what I'd been thinking of there on the beach. I'm not sure I even know. I've revisited that night in my mind: her arms around me, the sharpness of her voice calling my name into the night. I think I remember the wind around me. I think I remember nestling into the sand. I think I remember knowing I would never find my way home, and pausing there to think about it before I reacted to that knowledge. I've always been one to pause after action. I've always been one to act and then wait, frozen, for my mind and heart to catch up with me. I was wrong, at any rate. I got home. I slept snug in my bed that night. When Anna and Matthew moved in next door in the spring of the following year, I never thought to run to the beach alone again. Instead I held on to Anna's hand and followed behind her away from the sea.

THINGS WERE DIFFERENT after Danny left that second time. I no longer felt lost. There was a world of my own to go to, a world that knew me without Danny, that knew me alone. *Isn't this what I was longing for?* I sometimes thought as I rode across the city on a bicycle in the mornings on my way to work. *A life of my own? A life created without Anna?* I thought of my childhood then, of the emptiness I'd felt before Anna appeared and the fullness I'd felt after she came. *I feel full on my own now,* I thought. *I feel complete without her.* I tucked my skirt between my legs, pulled sunglasses down across my eyes and a scarf across my mouth, and wove in and out of crowds in the cold morning light. I liked that ride in the morning, when my limbs were still stiff from slumber, when each pump of the pedals sent a rush of hot life through my muscles. I'd chain my bike to a post in front of the store, then unlock the heavy metal door. I was almost always the first one there.

With the exception of Radika, the women I worked with were shy with me. A few of them spoke English, enough to practice wishing me good morning, anyway. Enough to ask me how I felt. They laughed sometimes, and taught me Nepali phrases: How are you, they taught, *Kasto chha?* And *Thik chha,* I'm fine. They told me how many children they had, or blushed and said they were not yet married. They asked me when I would have a child and I blushed and said, "Someday." These were light, feathery kinds of friends, friends I knew by presence alone and not by intimacy of thought, but friends. These women knew me outside the home. They knew me on my own as I knew them—not well, not with a great deal of understanding, but as they were, alone. *These women know me only as Isabel,* I thought. *These women know me only according to what they see.*

Radika was in charge of the project in her village. She was young, and she hummed to herself all day. She dressed in a sari except on days when she boarded a bus for the long ride back to her village in the east. On those days she wore a two-piece *salwar kameez.* "I would like to stay in the city," she told me several times. "Or go to India. Or Hong Kong. But I will marry soon. I know that I will marry soon."

The fabric that we sold was of two kinds—there was brightly colored cloth woven from cotton on small looms, patterned in abstract geometrical designs. Traditionally it was used to make men's caps, *topis,* but in our store we sold it refashioned into jackets and skirts and pillows and bags. The second type of fabric was rougher and bleached a yellowing white, made from fibers spun from stinging nettles. It was strong fabric, and when woven it resembled linen. Radika told me stories of blisters that formed on women's hands and arms as they harvested the bitter nettles from the steep sides of hills.

In early November I heard from Gina. "I'll give it a shot," she wrote. "I'll see if there's a market for it." *There will be,* I thought as we sorted through our wares, trying to decide what to include in that first shipment. I waited with my fingers crossed to hear from her again.

I WALKED THE halls to Bethany and Greg's after work on the day I received Gina's letter. "It's going to happen," I told them. Even to my ears my voice rose high—the excitement of a child, I thought, and then decided I didn't care what I sounded like. "It's going to happen. Gina's going to take care of everything in New York. We're going to ship her the fabric. We'll ship some purses and pillows too, and I know they'll sell."

Bethany smiled. Her stomach had swelled larger, and when she leaned forward from her seat upon the couch to hug me in congratulations, she had to pause to push herself up with both her hands.

"That's fantastic, Isabel," she said. "Greg, don't you think that's great?"

"It is," he said. "It sounds like a great project that you're working for."

Bethany's arms around me were heavier than they had been when I first met her, just weeks—no, now months—before. She seemed still in a way that she had not been that first day, when the sun had gleamed gold through her hair.

"I might be able to help you on the export end," Greg said. "I do some exporting myself."

Bethany turned her face away from me, turned away toward him. I looked up over her shoulder.

He shrugged and cleared his throat. "If you want. Only if you want some help. We'll include your box in my next shipment out." He coughed, breathed in. Bethany sat back down. I saw her shake her head from side to side. Greg put an arm down on her shoulder. "It's fine, Beth," he said. "Ram will do a good job. He always does a good job. There's nothing to worry about."

"Ram?"

"You've met him once. With Anthony. I think he scared

you." Greg laughed, but I thought his laugh was thin. "He takes care of all the shipping for me. He'll help you out."

I nodded. I remembered Ram's thick fingers, his loud voice. I remembered Anthony's sallow face, and Mr. Rana opening the door behind them and ushering me in, and then I remembered the lanterns glowing on Anthony's rooftop, the lanterns and the horns from monasteries and later the prayer wheels at the stupa turning beneath my hand.

"Do you think he's really okay to work with?"

"Trust me," Greg said. "I think he's fine."

When I got home there was a fax waiting from Gina, telling me to rush. And crumpled in my palm was a scrap of paper with Ram's phone number written on it in bright blue ink. I read the fax. I looked at the scrap of paper. I thought of the half-answers I'd received since I'd come here— Bethany who changed the subject, who misdirected inquiries, Greg with his strange laugh. Even Danny. A hard frustration fell on me, a heat that the evening breeze did nothing to cool. I picked up the phone and dialed Ram's number.

In a city where blackouts fell almost every night, where phone lines could usually not be trusted, the connection worked. "I'd be happy to take care of it," I heard at the end of the line. "I'd be happy to ship the boxes for you. I take cash. Just bring them over and I'll get them ready to send out."

Late the next morning, I walked into the bedroom, where, in the back corner of a dresser drawer, a roll of money nestled between my underwear and socks. I peeled off bills. *I'll get the money back,* I told myself. Then I walked over to Greg and Bethany's apartment and had Greg help me find a taxi. The taxi waited outside the store while Radika helped me pack the boxes. We carried them to the taxi together. Then I brought them, taped shut, to Ram.

CHAPTER EIGHT

*D*ays passed. A week passed. The shipment went out and I forgot my wariness and gave myself over to life. I almost burst with excitement then: my job; the women I had met; the new Nepali words they'd taught me; the first shipment on its way to Gina. There was so much to tell Danny and I counted the days until his return. And then one day I came home from work and saw his boots, heavy and caked with mud, in the hallway outside the door. It was a day early—he'd returned a day early! My stomach jumped, and I bit my lip to keep myself from crying out loud. I shut my eyes while the door swung out. I opened them to the smell of a campfire, to my husband—*my husband*—at home in the afternoon. But I opened them to something else: to his hunched back; to a strange silence.

His hair was long and needed washing—I could see that right away. His hands, his hands were larger than I'd remembered. They cupped his cheek, and as he sat on the couch with his head cradled in them, I could only think that they had grown, that these were not the hands he'd had when he had left.

I startled him. When I shut the door his head jerked in his hands, and he looked up in surprise. "Isabel," he said. His voice sounded a thousand miles away. "I'm back early."

I hardly recognized his voice. The sun shone in such a way on his hands and shoulders that they looked as though they were made of wax. His jaw worked back and forth. I stood just inside the doorway, the door closed behind me, the room ahead suddenly enormous. "Why are you back early, Danny?" These were my first words to my husband. "Why are you back now?"

"I'm just so tired," he said. And then his shoulders began to shake, and he began to cry. I rushed toward him, but he moved away.

"We were almost home, Isabel. We were almost all the way to Pokhara." His shoulders shook again. I'd never seen him cry. *You haven't been with him long enough to see him cry,* I heard a voice whisper inside my head. I took a deep breath. I wrapped my arms around him even though he flinched. "A terrible thing happened. A terrible thing."

"Did someone get hurt?"

"Yes," he said. He nodded his head.

"Did someone get badly hurt?"

His body trembled. He leaned against me. I held his head to my chest, felt his tears through the cotton fabric of my shirt. His hair was knotted and rough. It smelled of fire, it smelled still of the mountains.

"Did someone get badly hurt?" I said again, and the salt water of his tears seeped through the fabric to my skin.

It wasn't as bad as I had thought at first. No one had *died*. Death is the first thing that jumps to my mind at any sign of real trouble; there have been many times when I've been sure that death is what is being discussed when in fact the topic is a disaster of a lesser order. So it wasn't death that Danny had encountered, that had reduced my husband to tears. It was a broken ankle, and his reaction to that break. When I think about it now, I think he must have been crying at his own panic. But then, then it seemed as though the world had ended.

They were almost back to Pokhara, that mountain city built around a lake, when one of the women he was leading slipped. Patricia, he called her, Patricia, and with his shaking voice and his hunched-up back, she became the world of the trek for me. Patricia was walking in the back. She'd "had it," she said over and over. Too many days in the mountains for her. Too many days watching her husband speed on ahead, watching him crouch at the top of ridges with the porters, smoking Yak cigarettes with their thick, oily odor. She hated sleeping in a tent, she'd found, though it wasn't her first time—"Just somehow different this time, somehow different here." She hated walking. Walking everywhere, every day, with no choice but to keep walking up and up and then steeply down. Once she claimed she couldn't take another step. She sat down on the stone wall built round a pipal tree, pulled on her windbreaker, and said, "That's it." Danny left

Pemba behind with her. Furious at being relegated to the role of baby-sitter, Pemba didn't speak to Danny for what seemed like days.

At night, when, sometimes, on some trips, the group would sit around a fire, their tents in a ring around their smaller, human ring, and tell stories about how they'd ended up here, at night this group would retire to their tents and complain about the day. They didn't like the food. It made them panic to realize that there really were no roads close by. They picked up trails of children when walking through villages, children screaming "Hello, sexy" and "Ink pen" after them for miles. Tent walls don't keep sounds out. Everyone could hear everything that was said by everyone else. "I was with them for only two and a half weeks," Danny said. "I've never seen so much bickering in such a short time. Never."

Then, two days before they were to reach the roadhead, Patricia slipped. Danny was up ahead. He didn't see what happened. He remembered hearing her voice behind him, calling out, calling, "Danny, come look at this," and then the voice trailing downward, as if in a cartoon, the high notes sinking low, "Danny, come looooooooook," and then silence. Danny stopped in his tracks. It seemed that a hush had fallen over the entire mountain. He froze for a second, then wheeled around and raced back. Pemba was already there. A crowd of children in dusty school uniforms, appearing as if from nowhere, were there as well. Patricia lay in a gully just off the path. The sky above her stretched bright blue. The snow-capped mountains in the distance watched in silence. She lay frozen on the ground, her skirt tossed up around her knees. Danny couldn't see her face. It wasn't far that she had fallen, but far enough so that he held his breath. And then a whimpering rose up from the gully, a low whimpering, and he still couldn't see her face, but he began to see her shoulders shake.

They had been moving quickly, were two days away from the roadhead if they kept up their pace, a day ahead of schedule. Danny climbed down off the path, into the gully, and checked for broken bones. When Danny touched her body, she reached up and clutched his arm, and wouldn't move her hand off it to let him finish his investigation. I pictured her holding on to him as he tried to lift her up, her fingers working into his arm, her body pressing close to his, a whimper still escaping from her throat. If they had been farther out, they would have radioed for a helicopter. As it was, they decided that Danny would walk ahead with Patricia and one of the porters. They took turns carrying her. My husband carried her on his back up and down mountains to reach a road. My husband.

The rest of the group would be arriving in two days. Patricia's ankle had been set. The doctor said she would be walking without crutches in two months. Danny had left her sleeping at the clinic. "You should have heard the sounds she made while I carried her," he said. In my imagination, she was transformed into an animal. "I was certain that something else had been hurt, something inside her, that she would die on the way back and it would be my fault."

"It was just a broken ankle," I said. "It wasn't your fault at all."

"What if it had been high up in the mountains? What if we'd had trouble getting a helicopter to come get her? I've never had to helicopter anyone out. I've never had anyone get hurt before. Who would hire me if something happened? How could I live with it if someone I was guiding didn't come back?"

It seemed so small to me now that I'd heard the story. A slip, a twisted ankle, the bone broken, but now set, now the woman—Patricia—now Patricia sleeping soundly at the clinic. So small compared to everything else imagined that had seemed so large. Danny's hair fell down over his face. His cheeks were rough with his bristling beard. He sat on the couch, his knees pulled to his chest. This was not the man I had imagined. I gathered my arms around him and rocked him against my chest. He began to cry, his tears hot on my neck. I rocked him and thought of him as a child, and he cried and he cried until he stopped and I realized he was asleep.

WE WENT THE next morning to see the woman. When I told Danny that I wanted to come along, his first answer was simply no. But he was still so shaken and I was suddenly so firm that at last he hung his head between his hands and said in a low, tired voice, "Fine. Come with me if you want."

He drove us on his motorcycle through the foggy streets. The roads were crowded with children on their way to school, men and women on their way to work. Danny nudged the motorcycle between cars and bicycles and puttering three-wheeled motor rickshaws, and eventually we wound our way up a tree-lined avenue and pulled into the driveway at the clinic. Patricia was still in bed when we arrived, awake, a small, blond woman with long hair brushed back from her face, red lipstick spread across her lips, a pale face beneath tanned skin.

"Danny!" she called as we reached the door. "Danny! You came." As if it was a surprise that he would come. She seemed not to have seen me yet.

"You look much better," he said.

"I am much better. I'm so much less frightened. I'm so glad that you're here." She reached her hand up and touched his face. I swear, though I could not see clearly from where I stood, that she tapped her finger lightly on the corner of his mouth.

"How are you?" I said. She looked toward me for the first time. It took a moment for her eyes to clear. "I'm Isabel," I said. "Danny's wife. Isabel Grady."

"Oh," she said. She looked puzzled for a moment. "Oh. His wife. Isabel. I didn't know that you were married, Danny. Isabel, thank you for coming." She held out her hand to me. It was small in mine, a very small hand. "I don't know what I would have done without your husband."

I didn't know that you were married.

It's true that when I think of her I still get a tight feeling in my jaw. I hated her lipstick suddenly. I hated her voice. I hated the way she reached her hand out to my husband's hand, I hated that after only one night in the clinic she'd somehow managed to have her fingernails painted. I hated that she'd never heard of me. How could he never have spoken of me?

A nurse came in, a large woman who seemed caught moment by moment between scolding and holding her breath. "Now don't tire her out," she said.

Patricia smiled, a weak, small smile. "It helps so much to have visitors. It's frightening to be hurt in such a very foreign country. I was scared, Danny."

"I was scared too." He cleared his throat. The nurse checked the scratches and bruises on Patricia's arms, purple and yellow where she'd fallen. The morning was cold. I shivered slightly, and seeing me, I swear it was from seeing me, Patricia began to shiver too. The nurse shook her head and brought over another blanket.

"You'll be fine," she said. "You'll be ready for the trip home in no time. Soon enough you'll forget you were ever here." She sucked in her breath and turned away.

"Soon enough?" Patricia said. "Soon enough? How will I travel like this?" Her voice rose high. My head began to hurt.

"Danny, I think I'm going to go," I said. The nurse and I met each other's eyes. She shifted her weight from foot to foot, and shook her head slightly. I could see through the window that the fog was nearly gone, that the sun was shining bright, drying up the dampness of the morning. "I'll walk," I said. "You stay here. The exercise will do me good."

Patricia sighed a whistling sigh from her bed. "Walk while you can," she said. "You never know when something's going to come along to stop you. You never know what lies ahead."

The nurse gasped, a quick intake of breath that sounded like a laugh. When I looked at her, she had turned her back and was walking toward the door.

I left the two of them there in the cold clinic and walked out into the November air. Vines still flowered along the stone walls, their last delicate blossoms before the deeper cold of winter. The sound of the city rushed over me like water. When I turned back I thought I saw through the wavy panes of the window that Patricia had raised both hands to Danny's face, that she cradled his face between them and that his head was bowed. I thought again that he might be crying. I stood frozen, noise from the city washing over from ahead, worry overwhelming from behind. *Did she touch his face? I saw her through the window. Did he let her touch his skin?* A horn blared just outside the gate. *Who is he when he's away from me? Who is he when he's away?* I turned again to look, but now the windows were misty and the light inside was dim. *Who have I married?* I thought. *Who is he?*

Cars careened by as I walked at the edge of the street toward home. A high, vine-covered wall jutted up beside me. The sun was strong. The traffic made me dizzy, and I ran my fingers against the wall to steady myself. The stones were coarse. I shut the door behind me when I got home. I filled a glass with clean water and sat down on the floor and drank it in large gulps. My fingers were rough where they'd pressed against the wall. My throat was dry. When I shut my eyes I could still see cars swerving past.

WHEN DANNY CAME back that afternoon, it was as though we'd both agreed that we would talk no more about Patricia. He held my hand and told me of the trek, and I murmured my fascination with the places he had seen. I told him of my job, I told him about the store and Radika and Gina and the boxes that had been shipped out, and he smiled and squeezed my hand. *We live in the present,* I thought. *This morning doesn't matter. What matters is now. The only thing that matters is right now.*

It was cold when we went to sleep that night. Our windows were shuttered closed, but the damp night air crept in through gaps between the slats. I lay awake in the dark and thought of the empty palace, the creaking stairs and the walls hung thick with cobwebs. My eyes were heavy. Danny's breathing eased beside me, his back turned toward my back. I let my lids drift down. *Good night,* I whispered in my mind to the empty palace, the empty halls stretching wide around us, the years of lives lived there echoing through the dusty passageways. *Good night,* I whispered, and then my lids dropped down, and I drifted into sleep. Danny's breathing turned into the ebb and rise of the ocean. I saw waves move forward and away in my dreams.

When I woke it was to another cold morning, light the color of lemons breaking its way through the slats across the windows. I woke still thinking I was at the ocean, and all day I kept turning my head, certain I could hear the shrieking caw of gulls.

CHAPTER NINE

I wonder now if there was a time when my mother was pregnant with a second child. There was one summer when Anna and I were twelve and Matthew was fifteen, when we were all still mostly children, that Anna and Matthew stayed on Cape Cod for the summer. It was hard for my mother and me to drag ourselves home from their house at night during those hot months. My father seemed to work later and later. Even in the long days of summer he still seemed to arrive home well after dark had settled. My mother had become good friends with Anna's mother, and on those summer nights we'd often have dinner on the patio behind their house.

Anna and I would rush upstairs to her room while my mother and her mother talked. We lay on her floor on our stomachs, the pink carpet spread out around us like a field of candy, the whirring hum of crickets throbbing at a steady pulse. I loved to watch her even then. Maybe even more so than when we got older—yes, certainly more so than when we became adults. She blew her bangs off her forehead by sticking out her lower lip. She wore her hair pulled back in a ponytail every day. Her hands were so tanned that they were almost brown, and only in the creases between the fingers could I see the original paler white.

"He's getting married," I heard my mother say to my father one night long after I should have been asleep. "He didn't want the kids this summer. Can you believe that? He didn't want the kids."

I wanted to ask Anna about that, then. Every night while we lay on our stomachs on her carpet I wanted to ask her if she knew. *Do you know he doesn't want you?* popped into my mind so quickly that a few times I caught it only when it had reached my tongue: "Do you know—"

"What?"

"Nothing."

"What? What do you want to know?"

"Nothing."

"What?"

"Do you know . . . do you know what time it is?" I acted still with the clumsy guile of a child despite the fact that by twelve my body was already stretching long.

We had many things to discuss, Anna and I. We always did. She was trying to learn to surf. She said that if she couldn't go to Colorado—she never mentioned why—then she could at least learn to do something at the ocean. We discussed what kind of outfit she should wear when balanced on a board. We discussed how to get the deepest tan. We discussed whether she should ask Matthew to teach her how to keep her balance, or whether it was just too geeky to have a brother get involved.

"Ask him," I said.

"I can't."

"Why not?"

"I just can't."

I loved the scratchy feel of her carpet on my stomach. I loved the feel of my skin still holding the heat of the summer day, and the crinkly sensation I got when I touched my nose. My hair smelled salty like the sea. There was a white line between my big toe and my second toe on each foot where the thong of my flip-flop rested. Anna talked on and on about how she'd be able to ride a board by the end of summer and I nodded and pressed my finger on the arch of my nose and told her I'd be on shore to cheer her on.

It was a good summer for me. I think it was a good summer for Anna as well. I know it was a good summer for Anna.

AND MY MOTHER? She and Anna's mother talked with each other late into the nights. Sometimes Anna and I paused in our recap of the day's greatest pleasures and crawled, instead, still on our stomachs, to the window by her bed. "I don't know if I'm ready for another," we heard my mother say once, her voice carrying up to us on the salty wind that blew inland from the ocean. "I don't know if Nick's ready. It's not something we ever planned on."

"Even if you're not ready now, you'll be ready by the time it happens." There was something about Mrs. Davis's voice that reminded me of music. It was low, lower than most women's voices, and rich. Sometimes I thought it seemed to vibrate. "I always wanted two, but Matthew was still practically a baby when Anna was born. It was a lot to handle. But you rise to it. You have no choice."

"I know," my mother said. "I know. It's really not a matter of choice."

Anna and I stared at each other. We scuttled back across the floor and broke into fits of giggles. I can't say now exactly what it was we laughed at. I can't say now that we knew for sure they were talking about another baby. But we laughed and we stared at each other and then looked away, and as soon as we'd caught our breath and calmed down, we caught each other's eyes once more and broke out in another peal.

"Okay, girls," my mother said five or ten minutes later. "Okay, girls, it's time for bed. Isabel, we're going home."

"Do we have to?" I said, my sides aching, the laughs turning into hiccups as I tried and failed to catch my breath.

"Yes, we have to. It's almost ten. It's way past your bedtime."

"Anna, time for bed," her mother said. "Anna. Say good night to Isabel."

And then we were home and I was in bed and as my mother bent down to kiss me good night I whispered, "Where's Daddy? Why is he out so late?"

I could tell then, in a slight difference in the weight of her hands, in a shaking that filled the edges of her voice, that I'd ruined the night. I'd ruined it. A perfect summer night, now gone.

"He's at work," she said. "He'll be home soon."

"Okay," I said. And then I tried—it can't be said that I didn't try. "Give him a good night kiss for me."

She tapped me on my nose. She ran her hand through my tangled hair. "I'll give him a kiss. I'll tell him you said good night."

When she left I rolled over on my side and stared out the window, across the night to Anna's house. I watched the lights turn off from room to room, and even with my eyes open I could picture her mother walking softly through the house. The light went off in Matthew's room, and then went briefly on again. *Their lives are set,* I remember thinking as I stared out into that summer night. *The changes have already happened to them. They've already made it through.* Above their house I could see the stars. Above the stars I could see the moon. *A change is happening here now. A change still lies ahead for us.*

I NOTICED MATTHEW in a new way for the first time that summer. He had his own friends on the beach, older boys, older boys with legs and shoulders and arms tanned to a golden brown. It was hard for me to walk past those groups of boys. My towel always seemed to trail behind me and tangle in my legs. I felt too skinny in my suit. The slapping of my flip-flops got louder whenever I approached them. Most of those older boys would turn away when Anna and I came near. But Matthew, Matthew always smiled. Matthew always had a teasing word. "Isabel," he said once. "Isabel, your skirt's falling off," and I looked down and there was my towel, curled up like a snake behind me on the beach. "Isabel," he called out another time, "Isabel, don't keep your sunglasses on or you'll get eyes like a raccoon." My face turned red, and I pushed my glasses up to rest upon my hair. When I reached Anna where we'd set up on the beach and told her that Matthew had called out to me, she shrugged.

"He just wants attention," she said. "He can't stand it when he thinks no one's noticing him. Don't let him bother you."

Anna never managed to stand up on the board, but she tried every day and got the attention of the lifeguard. He was in high school, and he called out to her when she crawled, dripping, from the surf. "Hey, kid," he called. "Hey, kid. You've got a lot of courage out there, kid. You'll make it up one day. Don't give up. You'll get the hang of it." Anna ignored him, as we both knew was the right thing to do, but when she got back her face was flushed and she raised one eyebrow and said, "What can I say? Is there anything more sexy than being a surfer chick?" and we both collapsed in giggles and lay with our faces down on our towels, peeking up occasionally to see if he was looking.

And then a few times—a few times, I can almost count them now, they were so few—Matthew came and sat with us. I loved to watch the two of them together. He hit her shoulder softly with his fist. She said, "Ow! Stop it," and he smiled. She said, "You're such a jerk," and turned away. He hit her softly on her shoulder one more time and then they leaned back in silence and lay side by side, the sun soaking deep into their skin, their faces, eyes shut, slight smiles on their mouths, looking suddenly very much alike, as if the same deep satisfaction passed between them and settled upon both their lips.

I watched them then. I watched the two of them together. A brother and a sister. The same soft skin. The comfort in each other's breathing. A world that existed only between the two of them.

One night when my mother sat outside talking with Mrs. Davis, and Anna and I lay on our bellies on her carpeted floor, a soft knock sounded on the bedroom door. "Who is it?" Anna said, her legs kicking in the air. "Anyone but Matthew's allowed to come inside." The knock came again, a gentle tap. "Oh, okay. Even Matthew can come inside, but he has to promise to leave his cooties in the hall." I laughed. Anna looked at me and grinned. She nodded her head, motioned me to speak.

"If it's Matthew, he can come inside, but only if he doesn't smell," I said. She laughed. I loved to make her laugh.

"And only if he promises to introduce us to his friends at the beach tomorrow."

I looked at her in surprise. I thought I was the only one who had noticed them. "And if he promises not to talk too much."

The door opened. Matthew stepped inside. "You want to meet my friends?" he said. "You two are crazy. You're only twelve years old. They're not interested in you."

"Whatever," Anna said. "You want to stay or not?"

"Whatever," I said in echo.

Matthew lay down on his stomach next to us. He pulled

at the marble that hung by a leather strap around his neck and put it in his mouth. We were cutting pictures out of a magazine and pasting them on a large sheet of construction paper to make a collage. I had collages taped up on all the walls of my bedroom. I was teaching Anna how to make shapes from other pictures. How to reposition them to suit her own perspective. He began sorting through the images and found one I'd cut—large lips covered in gooey pink lip gloss. He held it up to his mouth. "Gross," I said. "Put that down."

"Gross," he said. "Ooh—boys are sooooo gross."

Anna shrugged. I shrugged. We continued with our cutting.

There was silence then, except for the slicing of scissors, except for the rustle of pages as Matthew flipped through a magazine, except for the pulsing of crickets and the faraway murmur of the sea. And then, as we lay there in silence, my mother's voice rose from the patio outside.

"Nick wants me to give it up."

"What do you want? What do you want to do?"

"I don't know. I just don't know. I loved holding Isabel when she was a baby. I loved being able to cradle her whole body in my arms. But it just seems like such a huge thing to start over with. And if Nick doesn't want it—it makes me feel alone."

"You won't be alone. He'll come around."

"I know. At least I think I know." My mother's voice caught, then, and where before we'd listened in transfixed silence, now I felt Matthew jog my foot.

"Is she pregnant?" he whispered.

I looked at him with an open mouth. Anna and I had never voiced the question. Anna and I had only listened. Now she hit him on the shoulder.

"What?" he said.

"Just listen," she hissed.

"I always wanted another baby," Anna's mother said. "I wanted a whole houseful of kids. But Jack was overwhelmed. And I guess by the time we would have started planning for the third one, things had started getting strained between us. Now I can't imagine another kid." There was silence, and then, "I can't believe Jack's getting married. If he has a baby with that woman, I don't know what I'll do."

Now I raised my head and looked at Matthew and Anna, but as if by some silent agreement, the two continued to stare out through the screen at the dark night. Neither turned to meet my eye. Only Anna's feet moved where they swatted at the air.

"I know it must be hard," my mother said.

"You have no idea," Mrs. Davis said. "You have no idea."

THAT NIGHT AS my mother was tucking me in, I held my arms around her neck and pulled her down. She lay next to me, her body so long that she stretched the whole length of my bed. "I want another baby," I whispered. "Can we have another baby?"

She stroked my hair. She ran her hand across my back.

"I don't know, sweetheart." She didn't quite speak in a whisper, but her voice was low. "We'll have to ask Daddy about that. We'll have to see what Daddy thinks."

"Why does he get to decide?"

She was silent for a moment. I opened my eyes, but the room was dark and I couldn't see her face. "It's complicated, honey," she finally said. "It's too complicated to explain right now. We'll see what we can do."

That summer passed by in a series of cool nights and hot days, in a series of sunburns that faded into deep tans, in a series of shoulders getting sore from punches and legs aching at night as they grew in length. The three of us, Matthew and Anna and I—that summer we grew into one unit, Matthew peeling away from us by day at the beach, but joining us again on the floor of Anna's bedroom; I peeling away at night, but joining the two of them in the morning as we walked down the path to the beach. I watched the two of them together all that summer and felt a hollow above my stomach each time my mother told me to say good night, each time I followed her out the door and across the lawn to our house.

During the days Anna and I rotated from our stomachs to our backs on the hot sand and it was only the sound of loud voices that woke us from our stupor one hazy afternoon. "You can't," I heard one voice call. "I can," I heard another say. Anna kept her eyes shut. She sighed and stretched and burrowed her feet in the sand. "Just watch me," I heard. I pushed myself up on my elbows and scrunched my eyes. A group of boys stood at the edge of the sand. The lifeguard looked asleep. Two boys were paddling into the water, stretched on their stomachs on surfboards.

"Anna," I whispered. "Matthew's in some kind of race."

"Whatever," she said.

"I can't tell what they're doing. They're just paddling and paddling. I can hardly see them."

They were dropping farther and farther out of sight, the crashing waves sending spray up that covered them from shore's view. I knew that Matthew was on the left. I couldn't tell exactly what it was they were racing for. There was no mark to reach out there in the waves. The two shapes grew smaller and smaller and I was still certain that it was Matthew on the left, and then the boy on the right stopped and seemed to bob up and down and then I thought he must be turning around. And he did, he did begin to grow bigger, he must have been paddling back to shore. But Matthew, Matthew continued to grow smaller.

"Anna." Now I shook her until she opened her eyes. "Anna, Matthew's paddling out into the ocean."

She sat up. She stared. It took a moment until she found him. She stood up and ran over to the group of boys that stood and watched. "What is he doing?"

"We had a bet to see who'd go farthest without chickening out."

"Why isn't he turning back?"

"Who knows. It's Matthew. Probably forgot he was even allowed to turn around."

He was so small, and now other families on the beach were standing up and staring, and finally a woman shouted at the lifeguard, who roused himself with a large shrug. "There's a boy getting lost in the ocean," she shouted, but to me it did not look as though he were getting lost. It looked as though he knew where he was going, that his intended destination was the middle of the sea.

And then a whistle blew, and the lifeguard dove into the water. I watched. Anna watched. I glanced over at her once. One hand held her long hair off her face. The other shaded her eyes from the sun. "What's he doing?" she whispered.

"I don't know," I said.

Matthew was pretty much banned from the beach by the time the lifeguard got him back. He didn't look tired and he didn't look scared. He high-fived his friends, but he didn't seem to be paying them very much attention. I wondered what it had felt like, so far away from shore. I wanted to ask him, but Anna pressed close before I could and yelled at him. She yelled and yelled and then she started laughing and the two of them left the beach together and I grabbed our towels and followed.

No baby came. In the end, Anna's father and his new wife had no children. By the end of the summer my father came home again at normal times. By the end of the summer I stopped finding my mother in the kitchen crying when I came up from the beach for lemonade when the sun hung high in the sky. By the end of the summer it seemed odd to have ever entertained the thought of a sibling, to have imagined a world as intimate as the one I saw hovering between Anna and Matthew every day.

CHAPTER TEN

*W*eeks passed. Months passed. The trekking season
ended. I didn't ask Danny often about money.
We had no bank account in Nepal, and I never was able to
quite follow when Danny explained how he financed our
life. There was the trekking, and that paid well by Nepali
standards, but was it, I wondered, enough to even buy plane
tickets home? Enough to keep us alive during the seasons
when commercial trekking came to a standstill? There was
the money I kept rolled up in a sock at the back of my
drawer, two thousand dollars in one-hundred-dollar bills, the
money I'd drawn on to pay Ram to ship the boxes. The bills
had been crisp when I'd first put them there, but now, after
the monsoon and the winter dampness, they sagged and softened whenever I checked to make sure they were still intact.

I checked often. I liked to count the bills. Their size and bulk and color felt clumsy after months of smaller rupee notes, but the weight and size was what I wanted, their overgrown clumsiness somehow reassuring. The job at the store paid almost nothing. They weren't making any money yet, and I waited, still, for a phone call from Gina telling me that the boxes had arrived safely. The women at the store could barely cover their own salaries, and I found myself telling them to wait to pay me until their merchandise began to sell in the United States. They needed the money more than I did, I thought, but the truth was, it wasn't easy even as a foreigner to live without an income.

I peeled bills reluctantly off from that wad in the drawer month by month and changed them into rupee notes in a carpet shop in Thamel, but still, how was it we managed to live? What was Anjala's salary? What was our rent? Danny knew about my money, but he never asked to use it. He never wanted any contribution toward the rent. When I asked him about these things, he shrugged his shoulders and made up something to make me laugh. When I pressed him about it, he said, "Isabel, I asked you to come here. I asked you to leave your life behind. I'm not going to ask you to pay the rent, too. Keep your money for yourself. I'll take care of the bills."

But once when I came home from the store and slipped quietly through the gate, I heard Danny's voice raised loud. I propped my bicycle against the wall and walked toward the entranceway. Danny was arguing with Mr. Rana. I could hear the old man's voice rising in response to Danny's, but I couldn't yet make out the words. I swallowed. My hands were wrapped in thick wool mittens, and the wool scratched against my face when I reached up to wipe away a bead of sweat. I could not tell if I was hot or cold then. The heavy dampness made me sweat despite the chill.

Mr. Rana's voice kept jumping pitch. It moved from high to low like a swooping bird, high to low and back up again, with the sentences blending together. "It has been three months," I heard him say. "Three months that you have been back."

"I know," Danny said. "I know."

"I do not give you the apartment for free. I do not let it out for my pleasure. There are many people who would like this apartment."

"I'm sorry," Danny said. To me he didn't sound sorry. He sounded slightly annoyed but as if trying hard to be patient, the way he sounded when my mother called at three in the morning. "I'll have it for you tomorrow. I will come down tomorrow and give it to you personally." I heard Danny's feet upon the stairs. They fell heavily, and even from the outside the walls seemed to shake.

"It is three months' rent. What do you expect, that I let you stay for free?" Mr. Rana's voice rose even higher as he called after Danny. Then it dropped to a low grumbling. I opened the door. Mr. Rana stood in the hall. He turned his face toward me and the light through the doorway caught on his glasses and glared back. I couldn't see his eyes. "Your husband is very late with the rent," he said.

I looked at him for a moment, and then I realized my mouth was open. "I'm sorry," I blurted. My hands were hot inside the mittens. "I'm sure he didn't mean to be."

"Sorry." He shook his head. "You tell him it does not help to be sorry. You tell him to hurry up. You cannot come to this country and expect to live for free. He is very, very late." He turned around and shut the door behind him. I stood in the hallway alone for a moment, not wanting to follow Danny up the stairs quite yet.

It was dark there, in that hallway at the foot of the stairs. The floor was checked with large square marble tiles. A crystal chandelier wreathed with cobwebs dangled from the ceiling. I could hear a *sweep-sweep* from behind the Ranas' door, and pictured their servant girl bent over, brushing a broom softly back and forth across the floor, knocking the dust off the surface of the rug. It got dark early then. It was almost dusk, despite the hour. I pictured the darkness closing in outside, the dark hallway at the foot of the stairs encased in greater darkness from without. *Sweep-sweep,* I heard, and footsteps creaked across the ceiling above. *Sweep-sweep, creak-creak,* and then I shook my head, shook my head to myself, pulled off the mittens from my sweaty hands, and walked softly up the stairs.

Danny paced across the living room and ran his fingers through his hair. I opened the door quietly, as quietly as I could. It was a moment before he realized I was there. When he did, he paused in mid-stride, his hands clutching two fist-fuls of sandy curls, and for a moment he looked as though he'd torn it out.

"Are you okay?" I whispered.

He stood there staring at me.

"Are you okay? Is everything okay?"

"Everything's fine," he said finally. "I just had a run-in with Mr. Rana. Everything is just fine."

"I have money." I realized as soon as I had said it, from the way his face flushed, from the way his lips grew thin, that I should have pretended I had no idea what had happened.

"I don't need it."

I nodded. Could he hear the thumping of my heart?

"You shouldn't have listened to our conversation."

"What was I supposed to do? I didn't try to hear it." I realized again, too late, that I shouldn't have said anything.

"You shouldn't have listened."

"I know," I said. It was as if I were walking backward, stumbling down a hill. "I know, I didn't mean to listen, and I didn't want to listen, but I heard what I heard. I have money. Do we need it?"

He shook his head, picked up his bag, and walked past me. The air changed, he passed that close to me. The air changed, and I thought, just for a moment, that he wouldn't keep moving past, that he would put his arms around me, that he would laugh suddenly, smile, and the smile would be in his eyes as well as on his lips, and he would take me in his arms and everything would be all right. He moved past me. The air changed. The door slammed behind him. That was the last we talked about that.

I LEARNED WHAT not to bring up, what to simply do on my own. I twirled for him in dresses I'd had made, but I never told him what I'd paid for them or where I'd bought the fabric. I brought home pastries from the German bakery in Ghairidarha, but I never told him what they'd cost. Sometimes I'd bring home a bottle of bourbon, and we'd add it to cups of black tea and laugh deeply and long, and I would never tell him that the roll of bills at the back of my drawer was dwindling. I'd never tell him that sometimes I lay awake at night feeling as though I were deliberately stranding myself on an island.

I still liked to watch him while he slept. I still liked to watch his soft breath move in and out, his large hands reach up and scratch his face. His face softened while he slept. His breathing, like everyone's, evened out. Once, I sat up reading by candlelight after he'd fallen asleep. He whimpered softly, then rolled over on his stomach and sighed. The candlelight made his skin glow. I reached out and stroked his neck. The skin was hot and firm. I pulled the blanket away from his back, traced my fingers across his shoulder blades. His back was strong, the muscles etched clearly through the skin. I leaned forward and laid my cheek against it. I brushed it lightly with my lips. The hot skin, the slight taste of salt, a lingering smell of nutmeg—I wanted to press my face against his back forever. It was cold, and he reached his hand sleepily behind him, tugging at the quilt. I pulled the quilt up, blew the candle out. When I leaned my head against his shoulder his skin was smooth as polished stone and soon I fell asleep too, snug and warm, my husband's strong arms reaching out to encircle me.

IT WAS COLD now, really cold, winter cold, a damp that stayed in the bones all day, that turned to ice in the joints at night. I wrapped myself in one layer after another: a shell-colored silk undershirt, a worn cotton T-shirt, a soft flannel button-up, a gray wool sweater, a green pile vest. The layers worked to mute the cold but not to silence it altogether. It still pricked at my skin, still left me achy and stiff for a good few hours in the morning. That kind of creeping cold is unfriendly. It makes everything knotty, makes you clumsy so you bang into corners, sway into walls, and always the part of your body least protected—a hip, a knee, a wrist where the shirt pulls back—is what finds the point of impact.

We had a space heater, and we had the balcony to sun on. Nothing ever froze. The cold made me think I'd wake one morning to a soft white covering of snow, but all I woke to was the eternal creeping mist that wound throughout the courtyard and wound around the outside corners of the palace, covering the stems of dried-up plants with tiny droplets of water. The space heater softened the air in the bedroom slightly, but, like a campfire when huddled round, it only warmed our front sides; our backs stayed damp and cold.

"Let's go south," Danny said one night in early December. "Let's go to India for Christmas." We'd been to a movie at the American club, *Key Largo*, and we both were dreaming of the ocean. "Let's go to Goa, or Kerala, somewhere where there's a beach." He had a smile on his face like a little boy's. His tongue stuck out just at the corner of his mouth. I wanted to kiss him right then.

"Let's," I said. "I want to be somewhere warm right now, right this minute."

"We'll ride the motorcycle down. We'll ride the motorcycle all the length of India."

I sucked in my breath. This was an adventure I had never

dreamed of. This was an adventure that Anna had never mentioned when she talked about traveling the world. "Yes," I said. "Yes, that's exactly what we should do."

We looked at each other, and I'm sure my eyes were shining exactly as brightly as his were. We held each other's hands, the excitement prickling back and forth between us. A vacation! Long walks on the beach. My pale skin, unwrapped from all its woolly layers, exposed to the sun. Flowers tucked in my hair. Fresh fish, fresh fruit, a gentle breeze rolling off the waves.

But the next morning we realized that the rent was late, and neither of us brought up the trip again.

TWO THINGS BROKE up that cold month for us. Two things? No, it was really three. The first was a phone call Danny received late one night. I sat on the couch in the living room and watched a smile spread out over Danny's face as he held the receiver to his ear. "Yes," he said. "Yes, please come. Of course you can come. I can't wait to see you." I looked at him with one eyebrow raised, but he shook his head and held his left thumb up. "And you'll get to meet Isabel. We'll count the days until you're here."

It was Caroline, his sister, who would come to visit in February. "She's coming for two weeks," he said. "I've been trying to get her here for years. I can't wait for the two of you to meet. You'll love each other, Isabel, I know you will. I know you will."

The second event came in the form of another phone call. This time when Danny answered the phone his brow creased and then eased back into place. "The Terai?" he said. "For two weeks? What kind of pay?"

It was a jungle trip that he signed up for. He would go as the guide, but all the traveling was done by jeep, and the group would stay in platformed tents at a camp in the Terai, the lush southern swath of Nepal. "Basically they just need someone to be a liaison between the tour group and the camp. I'm just being paid to look official and be nice. But the money's good, Isabel. I'm going to do it. I would be crazy not to do it."

Two days later he was gone.

And the third event? The third event came late at night, the very night that followed the day on which he left.

CHAPTER ELEVEN

*B*ethany was five months pregnant by December. She was five months pregnant when she got sick. That afternoon, just hours after Danny left, I heard a motorcycle ride into the courtyard. I peeked out the window into the winter sunlight and saw a man climb off the bike and rush into the palace. He carried a large leather bag, and it wasn't until he'd rushed across the courtyard that I realized it was a doctor's bag. It was late in the afternoon when he came. Anjala had brought in the wash from the line she'd strung across the courtyard and had begun preparations for dinner. The apartment smelled of spices, turmeric and cardamom. The man ran up the stairs and vanished down the hall, and then I heard voices, faint, through the palace's thick halls, and then a door shutting, and I sat in my living room wondering how ill Bethany might be.

I thought of them all night, as the shadows filled my bedroom, as I tossed on the wide bed and tried to picture Danny asleep in a tent. The sight of the doctor taking the stairs two at a time kept creeping back to me. The air was cold, colder even than it usually was, and I tossed and shivered and huddled beneath the blankets. When I woke in the morning, I pulled a skirt on, brushed my hair quickly, and walked down the echoing halls to their apartment. Cobwebs swirled as I passed below them. The curtains that hung at the few windows looked ready to crumble into dust at the merest touch. Thinking their black formation was a long crack on the tiled floor, I nearly stepped on a line of ants. The halls between our homes seemed to stretch longer than they ever had.

Finally I turned the corner to their door. The stairway that ran parallel to ours, a twin staircase, stretched down to the left. I turned and stood still, and then I knocked. I don't think I realized quite how early it was until Greg answered the door, still in his pajamas, his hair pressed down against his forehead, black circles under his eyes.

"Who was that man last night?" I asked.

"Our doctor." His voice was low and thick. I wanted him to reach up and push the hair away from his brow. "Bethany's had a fever."

Her fever was so high that the doctor had told them it would hurt the baby. In her fever she had screamed; in her fever she wouldn't let anything touch her. She shook and cried from the cold, but the minute a blanket touched her skin she screamed in pain. "It's so easy to get sick here," Greg whispered. "It's so easy, we shouldn't have come back. But I haven't seen her get sick like this in a long time. I've never heard her crying from a fever. I should have made us leave."

She was asleep now, he said. He took hold of my elbow and pulled me inside. His hand on my arm was weak, and I thought he was shaking too. I reached out and touched his forehead. I held on to his hand. A gasp came from the bedroom. Greg stood up again, I swear he swayed, and then he disappeared through the bedroom door. I thought I heard him crooning. I pictured him with his hand on her cheek, singing softly in her sleeping ear. I wanted Danny badly then. I wanted him there next to me. I wanted to feel the warmth and weight of his hand on my skin. *He's awake now,* I thought. *He's awake now and the tents are packed up and they've had their tea and are off, riding on the backs of elephants until late in the day. Riding and riding until the sun begins to set and darkness falls upon the jungle.* I looked up. Greg stood in the bedroom doorway, and when he met my eye his shoulders jumped and he began to sob.

The doctor came again late that morning when a mist still hung across the city. Greg was in with Bethany. When the doctor knocked, it was me who opened the door. He shifted his weight in the doorway, black leather bag in hand. I tried to speak, but he had already brushed past me, and I bit my lip and shook my head when, turning, he asked me whether anything had changed.

I heard Bethany's voice as the bedroom door opened to let him slip inside, but then the door shut again and I was alone in their living room once more.

I've never been very good with sickness. I've never found

the right touch for a fevered brow. Once, a year before we met Danny, just after Matthew had died, Anna had a fever that came on suddenly and lasted for two days. I sat beside her and made her tea and called the consulting nurse at her doctor's office, but even when she whimpered from cold and even when her hand was small and damp inside of mine, all I could think was that I hated being there, hated the thin sweat on her skin, the heat from her hand, the cries that racked her body as the fever slipped away. Now I looked for a way to leave, a reason to walk back through that dusty hallway to my home, for something pressing that awaited me. Nothing. I could think of nothing. Another knock on the door, and when I opened it Anjala stood there, a thermos of milky tea in her hands. "Thank you," I whispered. She nodded. She handed it to me and then she disappeared.

The sun was out now; morning was gone. Their apartment mirrored ours, and when I opened the door to their balcony and stepped through, it was as familiar as stepping out onto my own. In the courtyard, Mr. Rana's gardener had the hood of the Bentley open. He revved the engine, tightening and loosening its purr. A dog ran across the knobby grass. The smoke from the rubbish heap billowed, and I saw Anjala walk toward it, a plastic bag in her hands. The air was cold on my skin. I could see the edge of my own balcony just peeking from behind a corner of the palace, far away. The sky was bright, bright blue. A voice called from inside. I wrapped my shawl around my shoulders and stared out past the high walls of the palace compound. The voice called once more. I turned and stepped back inside.

The doctor stood in the living room. His face was covered

with a thin sheen of sweat. "They're going to go to Thailand," he said. "They'll leave on the next flight out. The hospitals are better there. I don't want Bethany to risk staying."

He spoke to me as if I were her mother. He spoke to me as if I needed to be convinced, as if it were my permission that the journey rested on.

"I'll call ahead from the clinic. Greg shouldn't have a problem getting them on the plane."

He paused, and when he met my eyes I felt again as if he were waiting for me to tell him this was the right decision, to give him permission to take my child away. I nodded.

"The fever's not unusually high for the valley," he said. "It's just that she's pregnant. It's just that the fever hasn't come down. I can't hear the baby's heartbeat. I think she's lost the baby."

His eyes lifted quickly and then returned to my face. I turned around. Anjala stood in the door, her head cocked to the side.

"Will you take care of things here?" he said. "Can I tell Greg to just take her to the airport and go?"

I nodded, but when he kept looking at me it seemed there was more expected. I cleared my throat. "Of course," I said. "Of course. Anjala and I, we'll make sure everything is right here. We'll clean up. We'll call their friends."

He stepped back into the bedroom and shut the door behind him. Through the heavy wooden door his voice was low, and Greg's voice was low in return. I wanted to hold my ear to that wood, but Anjala still stood in the doorway, still stood and looked at me.

"Anjala," I said. "Anjala, they're leaving." She looked at

me, her eyes wide, and I wondered if she understood what I had said. "They're leaving on the next plane to Thailand. She's too sick to stay. The baby," I said, "she's lost the baby."

Anjala nodded her head, and it seemed to me that she was going to respond, but then a high-pitched wailing rose from the bedroom and the two of us pressed our lips together and listened to the cries in silence.

THEY WERE GONE within two hours. Anjala rode with them, to take care of Bethany while Greg arranged for their tickets. Greg wrapped Bethany in a large blanket and carried her downstairs to a waiting taxi. The doors stayed open behind them, and when the taxi had pulled through the compound gates and the gates had swung slowly shut behind it, I stood in the empty apartment and chewed on a fingernail. It was quiet. The air was still. The bedroom door lay open, the room inside was dark, the windows shuttered close. I took a breath and stepped inside the room.

The sheets were crumpled and kicked to the floor. The smell—the air smelled of damp skin, of stale water, of candles burned to stubs. My eyes adjusted quickly to the dim light. I circled the bed, ran my hands over the carved chest that huddled at its foot. The wood was smooth and worn even as it caved in and out in patterns. The door to the closet was ajar, and Bethany's sandals peeped out. I pushed the door open wider and slipped my right foot into her shoe. Her feet were smaller than mine. My heel barely fit inside. *They're at the airport now*, I thought. *He's paying the driver, he's pushing her through the airport doors, his arms still wrapped around her. I* tapped my sandaled foot on the floor, three quick taps. The sound was sharp in the dark room. I slipped my foot out and shut the closet door. *They're walking through customs. They're walking toward the plane.* It all seemed so fast. The cries at night, the long morning, Bethany carried down the stairs—it all seemed gone in a rush. I breathed again. I sighed and breathed again.

It took no time to straighten up their bedroom. I stripped the sheets off the bed and left them in a pile for Anjala to wash. I found another set in a closet by the bathroom—the same closet where I stored my sheets, folded neatly on the same shelf where my sheets were folded. I opened the shutters to let the cool December air pour in through open windows. The morning fog had burned off, but away from the sunlight the apartment was still cold. I picked up the clothes that lay scattered on the floor. Her blouse smelled of roses. Her skirt had the shimmering lightness of silk. I put her clothes in the pile with the sheets. *They're full of fever,* I thought as I dropped them softly on the pile. *Everything should be washed.* I pushed the sheets and the clothes together to a corner of the room.

When I returned to my apartment, I could see dust whirling in the beams of sunlight that shone in through the windows. The air smelled of boiled milk and sugary tea. The rooms were silent, and stayed silent as I sat down on the couch and tucked my feet up under me. The silence had a weight to it and covered me with the thickness of a blanket. I shut my eyes, tried to hear Bethany's crying, but found instead a pleasure at the soft weight of the air around me, the couch beneath me, the silence folding me in. I fell asleep on the couch in my silent apartment in the middle of the day and slept until it was night.

WHEN I WOKE again the rooms were dark, and when I reached to turn on a lamp nothing happened: another black-out throughout the city. I woke suddenly, my eyes wide before I'd completely left sleep behind. I thought there were shapes moving around me. I rubbed my eyes, and after I'd opened them again and let them grow used to the darkness, I saw that the curtains swayed softly where wind blew through the open window. I fumbled about until I found a box of matches. I struck one. It hissed into a flame. The shadows grew longer in the light. I touched the match to a candle, then to the wick of a kerosene lantern. The shadows flut-tered now against the walls.

It took moments to remember what I knew of the day. The doctor running up the stairs, black leather bag in hand. The dusty passageway. Bethany's cries from behind the doors. The taxi pulling out of the compound, gates clanging shut behind. Bethany's clothes in a pile on the bedroom floor. Bethany and Greg were gone. I looked at the clock. They were probably already at the hospital in Thailand. The second floor of the palace was empty but for me and what-ever echo of their baby it was that had been left behind.

I heard a board creak. I heard a soft brushing sound over the kitchen floor. I heard a bang, and then a shutter flapping in the wind against the outside wall, which sounded hollow at each knock. I pulled myself up on the couch. The curtains at the window moved again, a soft, quick shiver of white fabric. I heard a moan in the bedroom. A moan? A sighing, a low sighing. I know I heard it, I swear that I heard it. I bit my lip, a prickling running like moths' wings up my spine. Another bang of the shutter on the wall outside. *I fell asleep without shutting the windows,* I told myself. *I fell asleep without putting anything away.* That moan again, low, and I sat frozen, not sure whether to shut my eyes and will away the noises, or to rush for the bedroom door, to find out what was inside. *It's empty, the room's empty,* I thought, I nearly whispered, just to hear my voice. But an empty room, I could not bear to enter it. Another bang. The couch seemed a raft and I was frozen to move from it.

And then something changed. I smelled flowers suddenly, honeysuckle, jasmine, and the smoky scent of sage. I bit my lower lip, still trembling, but now I breathed deeply, inhaled the smell of vine-covered walls, of temples vibrating with chants and pouring streams of incense out like water. I know I smelled this, I know that my trembling slowed and that the air must have grown warm, because soon I was lying down again, soon I was shutting my eyes while the lamp burned on, and soon I kicked the blanket away and let my feet dangle, uncovered, in the night air. I know that I shut my eyes, and when I shut them I imagined running my fingers through lush twining flowers, imagined their perfume rising in a strong gust as the bruised petals brushed against my fingertips.

When I woke again it was morning and the early sun poured in through the unshuttered windows, and Bethany and Greg were gone and the world healed so seamlessly that it was as if they'd never been there at all.

CHAPTER TWELVE

*J*ust two times, twice in the first four months that I
was there, were there letters for me from Anna. I recognized her handwriting on the envelopes immediately, the
long, looping letters, the way she underscored my name. The
postage was unlike anything I'd ever seen before—the first colored with Australian stamps, the second with Indonesian. I put
them away without reading them. I couldn't. I couldn't open
them. I couldn't bear to see what it was that she would say.

I WENT SOME days in that first week that they were gone
to Bethany and Greg's apartment. *Just to check on things,* I
said. *Just to make sure everything's okay.* What was there to
check on? *Lives,* I thought when I was there alone. *There are*

lives lived here to be checked. There were photographs of the two of them that were gathering dust. There were clothes in the closets that began to smell musty. The carved wooden headboard at the back of the bed became coated with a milky film that grew slicker day by day. The apartment was still, but sometimes when a board creaked or a bird sang by the window, I thought it echoed with the memory of its former life. *Who lived here before Bethany and Greg?* I wondered. *Who lived here when this palace really was a palace?* Sometimes I walked down the steps to the courtyard and up the flight that led to the east wing. Sometimes I walked through the cobwebbed passage that twisted from our apartment to theirs. Doors along the way were locked. There were small windows high up along the passage's south wall that let in watery traces of light. *Who walked in these halls?* I wondered, almost aloud. *Who lived here before us?*

I thought of Bethany's stomach, of its rising life now gone. I held my hand over my own stomach, thin now, thinner than I'd ever been: thin from sickness that mere drops of the city's water brought. I thought of the lack of winter rain, of plants shriveling for want of water despite the creeping dampness that lodged inside my bones. *Please let life return,* I whispered. *Please make the world whole again.* But I was alone as I whispered, alone in the echoing palace, alone.

DANNY RETURNED. HIS face folded when I told him.

"They're gone," I said. "The baby's gone."

I loved him then, for his voice that shook, for the paleness of his face below his tan. "Will Bethany be okay?"

"They'll stay in Thailand for the winter. Greg said they'd wait until it got warmer to come back. The school gave them leave. He said he thought the time away would help them heal."

"I wish I'd been here. I should have been here."

"What could you have done?"

He swallowed. "There's always something that you can do, Isabel. There's always something."

"That's not true. Sometimes you can't do anything. Bethany got sick. She lost her baby. Your being here wouldn't have helped at all."

He nodded. He buried his face in his hands. When he looked up his skin was no longer pale. When he looked up his eyes had cleared. "It's just you and me alone here then," he said. "It's just you and me alone."

ALL JANUARY THE air grew colder. It was odd that the warmest place was outside, but during the day Anjala would take her work out onto the balcony or down into the courtyard below, and I would follow her, wrapping myself in a shawl and sitting in the sun. Anjala crouched low to the ground, her skirt hiked up to her knees, sorting through grains of rice and lentils in a large, flat basket laid on the floor in front of her. I watched her hands as they moved quickly through the grains, plucking out pebbles like frogs snapping at flies. Her hair was braided down her back. She wore small, buckled shoes. She wrapped her shawl in such a way that it hung tight against her body but left her arms to stretch out free. Sometimes she turned her head to look at me, and then I looked away, my own face flushed.

IT WAS COLD when Caroline arrived in early February. Bethany and Greg had still not returned, and the palace felt empty. Day by day a tight, churning knot in my stomach grew as I realized that Gina had still not received the package. It was three months now, three months since I'd given the box to Anthony and Ram to ship. Three months since Greg had promised I could trust them. But where was Greg now? And in this land where people vanished, what did it mean to trust?

I was surprised that nobody I met in Kathmandu spoke to me of the plane crash. One hundred thirteen people dead. The remnants of the crumpled wreck lay just miles beyond the city. How could all those people have vanished without mention? Was it that their names were hushed when I drew close? Was it that the grieving occurred in private? Or was it something else, a voluntary forgetting, a shutting away of grief? As the nights stayed long and the air grew colder and the mist in the morning hovered for longer and longer into the day, I began to think of that plane again, of the downward movement through the clouds that ended in a rocky mountain wall.

In that cold weather, Kathmandu seemed a city made for vanishings. Buildings shifted in and out of sight through mist. Walls were so covered with creeping vines that they disappeared behind the twisting stems. Crumbling roofs hid behind the walls, made visible only by a sharp angle of the neck. And the vanishings of people—Bethany gone so suddenly from the palace, Greg disappearing with her; it seemed within days of their absence that they had been gone forever, that they would never return. Almost, I thought, that they had never been. *There are ghosts everywhere in this city,* I thought. Figures twined in and out of mist. Sounds were hollowed, muffled in the dampness. I wondered at the ghosts who had no one to remember them.

JUST BEFORE DANNY and I were to leave to pick up Caroline from the airport, the phone rang. I heard Radika's voice on the other end. "Please," I heard her say. "Please, Isabel*ji*, can you come to the store now? Can you come here? It's about the package. It's news about the box."

"Of course."

How could I not have said "of course"? It was my work. It was, I realized then, my life. It had come to be my life.

"I'll be back in a few hours," I told Danny. "I'll meet Caroline then. It will be good for you two to have time alone together."

Danny nodded. I reached up to kiss his cheek, and thought he turned his face slightly to the side.

I RODE MY bike. Radika stood waiting for me outside the store. A wool shawl was wrapped around her, around her shoulders, across her mouth, covering her head. "What is it?" I said as soon as I caught my breath. "Did Gina send a fax?"

"They arrived empty," she said.

They arrived empty.

"They had both been opened."

They had been opened.

"It was just two boxes," I said, and then I looked into her eyes and she stared back at me and I said, "Everything was gone?"

"Everything."

"Let me see the fax."

Everything. The shirts that we had folded so carefully. The bolts of cloth woven from nettles that had swollen the women's hands as they picked them. The bags, the bags that I'd watch them stitch together. *It was just two boxes,* I whispered to myself over and over, but the two boxes were gone. The boxes that I had sent were gone.

"What will we do?" Radika whispered.

I shook my head.

"What will we do?" she said again, and her eyes welled with tears and my hands shook as I reached out to touch her hands.

"ISABEL! FINALLY!" CAROLINE'S voice carried loud across the room and then her arms were around me. When she pulled away at last it almost seemed that I was staring at Danny, at the same blond curls, the same rangy height, the same smile that opened up her face like the sun. "My sister," she said. "I finally get to meet my sister."

They sat in the living room, the two of them. They settled back down on the couch next to each other, Caroline's legs tucked up beneath her, her short hair curling around her face. She reached out and patted Danny's foot from time to time—absentmindedly; absentmindedly she cradled his heel in her hand.

"It's all so new here," Caroline said. "I don't know how many years it's been since I visited Danny. It's so much more crowded. And dirty. If I hadn't seen them before, I wouldn't believe that mountains ring this city."

I pulled my chair over close to the couch and poured myself a glass of beer and watched the two of them together, brother and sister, and all the while my stomach ached with worry.

"Coming from one Third World place and traveling to another, I just somehow assume that the new place will be familiar. But the smells, the sounds—they wash over you here like the ocean."

Like the ocean. I smiled then. It was good to hear someone else speak of feeling pulled under by waves.

"It's true," I said. "It's true. Even though there are mountains everywhere, this city feels just like the sea."

"Isabel misses the ocean," Danny said.

Caroline lifted her hand from Danny's foot and placed it on my knee. "I love the way this city takes you over. You get washed under by sounds. You want to follow your eyes down alleys. In the taxi on the way back from the airport, I saw a woman walking with a round flat tray in her hands. Her forehead was coated with red powder, rice and red powder. Her sari was pulled up above her ankles so that it didn't drag on the road, and I wanted to follow her. I wanted to follow her and find out exactly what she was doing, exactly what the noises sounded like to her—the temple bells chiming, the dogs barking, the blaring of the taxi's horn."

I liked her. I liked this woman, my husband's sister, my sister. She smiled at me. I smiled back. Her hand was heavy on my knee, a good weight, a weight to let me know that she was there. I put my hand down on her hand and we smiled at each other and later that night as I lay beside Danny I thought of the ocean and that it could be made of a substance other than water and affect me with the same strange beauty, the same enveloping strength.

Danny and Caroline seemed to read each other's minds. Danny said, "Do you remember—" and Caroline jumped in and said, "—how we used to build forts in the woods behind the house?" and they both stopped short and stared at each other and then broke down in large, whooping laughs. Caroline's pinkie finger curled in the same way Danny's did. She hummed under her breath when she was reading, and it was the same as the way he hummed under his breath when he sat by the window during the late-summer months, waiting for the rain to end. When she stretched, her body seemed a female mirror of his. When she laughed, it was his laugh raised an octave.

She was here for two weeks. I wished she could stay forever. "Tell me more about Danny," I said to her. "Tell me about him as a boy. Tell me everything I don't know."

She smiled. "He was the same then as he is now. We were always at each other's throats. We're both stubborn. We both like to get our way."

"Did he have friends? Was he popular? What was he like?"

"He always had friends. He was always at the center of a group. If he said I could tag along, his friends went out of their way to be nice to me. People always wanted to follow him."

"And girlfriends? What were his girlfriends like?"

She laughed. "He hasn't told you much, has he? He's always been one for privacy. I remember he didn't tell my mother about his first real girlfriend for months. He was in high school and I knew they were dating, but for some reason he lied and lied about it to my mother. She thought he was on drugs, all the sneaking around he was doing. I teased him about it, and I've never seen him get so mad. 'It's none of your business,' I remember him yelling at me, and I remember his face turning red, and all I could say was 'What? What?' My mother figured it out eventually, and then all she wanted was to meet the girl—she wanted her to come for dinner. She was *excited* about it, for God's sake. Danny wouldn't even introduce his girlfriend to my mother."

"Maybe he was shy?"

"Maybe. I guess that's what it was. Me, I've never been shy. I've always been pretty open about what I want."

They fell asleep leaning against each other, once. Caroline's head was on Danny's shoulder and Danny's head rested on top of hers. They fell asleep on the couch, and it was late at night, and empty beer bottles covered the table. Their breathing matched each other's. They both sighed at the same time. Danny's hair fell across Caroline's cheek, and could have been her hair. Caroline's hand rested on Danny's arm, and it was only the grace of the long fingers that made me certain the hand belonged to her and not to him. Caroline opened her mouth and then shut it again. Danny shifted against the pillows. *They are sister and brother,* I thought. *They have each other as surely as they breathe.* I watched them sleep. My heart grew large with love.

৩ঠ

AND THE BOXES? The boxes were gone. Our hopes were gone. *It was stupid anyway,* I told myself. But when I looked at Radika and she looked at me, it was not stupid at all. The boxes were gone. It was not just the merchandise that was gone. It was the hope of what it held.

"What will we do?" Radika said.

"We'll figure something out."

"What can we figure out? The items in the box were stolen. The shipping fee. The export fee. We have no money for this. Do you have money for this?"

I thought of that roll of hundred-dollar bills, already thinner with the fallow months. "I'll find money," I said. "Don't worry. I'll find a way."

That afternoon I left the store early. I rode straight to Thamel, to the carpet shop where I'd brought Ram the boxes. The light was dim inside. A woman sat on a stool in the front room of the store. "Change money?" she said when I walked in. Tibetan carpets hung from the ceiling, the traditional rich colors washed out here into modern beiges and pinks and blues.

"Is Ram here? Or Anthony?"

She shook her head. She turned away. She took a long sip of tea.

"I need to see them."

She shrugged her shoulders. And then I heard a voice, loud, from behind a door that led deeper into the building, loud and speaking Nepali. It was Ram. I was certain it was Ram.

"Excuse me," I said, and walked past her through the doorway.

Ram sat behind a wooden desk. He held a phone to his ear. His face was thick and his words were loud and the woman spoke in a stream of words so fast that I could pick nothing familiar out of them. He put the phone down. He looked hard at me. "Isabel."

"Everything in my box was stolen."

"And what do I have to do with it?"

"You shipped it. You guaranteed it."

"I think you are mistaken."

"You told me it would get there safely. You told me everything would arrive in New York safely."

"How could I guarantee the way it would arrive?"

"You said it would be fine."

"It is just two boxes, Isabel. Why are you so upset?"

"I want money for what we shipped."

"Not possible."

"I want a refund of everything I paid you."

"Talk to Greg. I am not the one you have your trouble with."

"What does Greg have to do with this?"

"I am very busy, Isabel. Please come back another time."

"Where's Anthony?"

"Come back another time. I cannot help you."

He stood up. He crossed the room, moved close to me. His body was large. The room was small. He reached out his hand. Before he could touch me, before he could put his hand down on my shoulder to turn me, I reeled around and left. I rushed out the door, and when I bumped into Anthony outside the store and shouted at him that he owed me money, he laughed and kept on walking through the door, and I shouted after him and then left them both and pedaled home, anger surging up around my ears.

⁊⊚

THE APARTMENT WAS empty when I got home. Danny and Caroline had ridden to the valley rim. They wouldn't be back until evening. I sat on the bed, held the roll of money in my hand. Seven hundred dollars left. Seven large, soft bills.

It was frustrating; I cannot say that I didn't want to cry out in frustration. Greg had said that I could trust them. Greg had said they'd get my package safely to the States. He'd said they'd send it with his shipment. But what of his shipment? What was he sending, and did it arrive safely as well?

I walked the back passages then. I walked across the creaking boards, through dusty walls of cobwebs. *What was he sending? What was he sending away from here?* The door moaned when I pushed it open. The shuttered windows rattled softly—like teeth chattering, like a disembodied cracking of knuckles—and a dim light spilled between their slats. I coughed in that dim room, and thought vaguely that Anjala should air it out, that I should ask Anjala to clean it. *Tell her to clean it,* a voice inside me whispered. *You should* tell *her to clean it.* I slipped my sandals off and walked barefoot across the cold tile floor.

Their bedroom. Their bed. The carved wooden window frame looked in the thick low light as though it framed a window from which one could peer into another world. *He made it for me,* I heard Bethany say. *He had it made for me. A present for our wedding night.* The vanity stood across the room. I looked up and the face I saw in that mirror at first resembled no face I knew. It was long and pale, and the haze that spread across the glass looked, momentarily, like a veil. *I sit there and he brushes my hair.* I moved. The face moved. My face. Of course it was my face. *He loves to brush my hair.* I shut my eyes. I opened them again. The face stared back. I stared back into myself.

There was only one closet in that room, just as there was only one closet in the bedroom that Danny and I shared. Our closet was deep, but the back was filled with tents and stoves and packs—it emptied and filled as the season passed. I opened Bethany's closet now. I could smell a soft rose scent that grew stronger when I ran my hand across the hanging fabric. The fabric then, in the dark of the closet, felt like gauze. Like the soft cocoon of a worm before it opens to a moth. I thought to wrap myself in that fabric, to wrap myself and wait, but then my thinking cleared—Have I said how hazy it had become? Have I said how sleepy that dark air had made me? *What was he shipping? What was he sending away from here?* came back. I pushed past the shoes. I pushed passed the hanging dresses, the starched shirts, the small suitcases strewn upon the floor. And there, behind them, beyond them in the dark, I stumbled on something hard.

It may seem that I moved as though in a trance, and in part it is true that I did. During those dark winter days in the dusty palace it was easy to give myself over to the crumbling, soporific aura of that place. When I think back on that year, I think sometimes I gave myself too easily to those walls, those corridors, even to the hypnotizing streets of that city. I think now that perhaps it was less that I was transported than that I volunteered myself for absence. *Take me,* I'd thought since I climbed off the plane into the sweat of monsoon. *Take me,* I'd thought since I met Danny on that cold winter day across the world in New York. A place cannot take you, a person cannot take you unless you give yourself. I gave myself, I think now. I gave myself. I was not taken.

What did I find in that back corner of the closet? I found treasure. Carved wooden statues. Carved wooden window frames. Masks with rolling painted eyes. Cornices from temples. Goddesses with six raying arms and breasts as round as apples. *What does he do with this?* I thought. But I knew. I knew already. *He smuggles it. He smuggles windows. He smuggles temple carvings from the country. He transports the city piece by piece.* Extra money. An apartment in a palace. *This is our home,* I heard him say. *We wanted to have our baby in our home.*

And the baby? The baby was gone. Bethany and Greg were gone. Discarded treasure gathered dust in the back corner of their closet. Gods and goddesses spread out their many arms into the dark. *This is what I helped him do. This is how he sold away the store's goods, those women's money.* I sat down. *He needed a cover to ship these things home.* I leaned my head against a window frame. *I'll find a way out of this,* I thought. *I'll find a way.*

When Caroline left, two weeks after she came, I thought that part of my heart would leave with her. She stood up to wrap her arms around Danny. In each other's arms they were like two sunflowers. They were like two rangy lions.

"You're my sister," she breathed into my ear when she held her arms around me to say good-bye. "You're my sister," she said, and then she left.

Danny and I held hands for hours that night, and just before I fell asleep he whispered to me, "I miss her already. And I miss you."

CHAPTER THIRTEEN

*I*n mid–February, at the height of the festival of Shiv-
aratri, we walked to Pashupatinath, the great temple
complex to the north of the city where pilgrims traveled to
worship Shiva. It lay half an hour away on foot through
crowded streets. The crowds grew denser as we drew near
the temple complex. "We won't want our bikes there,"
Danny had said. "You'll see. We won't want to watch out
for anything." The road down to the temple—I remembered it from earlier excursions as a wide avenue, a hill
dropping down to a gate that led to a wall above the Bag-
mati River. But now, now it was so filled with people, with
young men walking hand in hand with other men, with
women herding their children in front of them, with whole
families, with men in orange robes who had dreadlocked

hair and red, wild eyes, that now it seemed another place entirely.

"Don't lose me," I called to Danny. He was pushing ahead of me, finding a route for us amongst the people. "Don't forget I'm behind you."

"I won't," he said. "Follow me." But he was walking faster than I could follow. Every time he took a step, it seemed that someone would jump in front of me, use the space he created to move forward with him. I watched his plaid shirt, kept it as my compass, but always another head popped in front, a surprised face turned toward me when I tried to push past.

"Hold your horses, madam," a young man said, and I realized I was pushing on his shoulder. "We're all crowded here, take your time." I couldn't see Danny anymore, and suddenly, in a great press, I was through the gate and into the temple complex, and down below, across the river, in between the smaller temples, the stone lingams, the shrines, were thousands of people, and a great cloud of incense rose up, and the sound of drums beating pulsed throughout the complex, and whole walls were covered with marigolds where vendors selling garlands had set up their stands, and bins and bins of different-colored tikka powder, pink and red and yellow, lay spread out across the ground. I thought I saw Danny far away, and rushed toward him, but when he turned his head I realized it wasn't Danny at all, just another Westerner in a plaid shirt. The sweet, thick smell of hashish hung in the air. The noise was so great that it seemed to mute itself, sounds piling on top of sounds until they became one thick blanket that covered everything. I took a deep breath, dizzy, and the noise and smells and colors came in, surged in, and Danny was nowhere I could see, and all I could do was move with the press of the crowd, move on.

The sadhu, the wandering ascetics who renounced their lives to worship Shiva, the sadhu with their gray skin, their bodies covered in dust and mud, their piercing eyes, were everywhere. Their robes were tattered and faded to a brownish red. Their hair, long and thick and gray, was piled high upon their heads like baskets full of woolen snakes, sticks and leaves thrown in, birds' nests, snakes' nests twining in and out. Some had eyes rimmed in red. Some had shriveled limbs: arms held high for years in worship, the skin and muscles withering away; sticklike calves bound to thighs so that once-thick legs became thin stumps and looked as though they'd been severed at the knee. Some carried tridents. Some cupped their hands over chillums, straight clay hashish pipes. They breathed in deeply and then exhaled streams and streams of cloudy smoke. Their fiery eyes turned glassy.

The crowd pressed me forward, and then I found that I had crossed a narrow bridge and that sadhu sat in circles on slopes to the left and to the right. The slopes were covered with a few sparse trees, which up above thickened into densely wooded groves. To my left a group of sadhu sat cross-legged around an open fire. Their skin was gray with ash, and on their foreheads were smudges of white powder surrounding a smudge of gold. One beat a drum slowly, rotating it in his hand, two strings with weights thrumming against one side and then the other. Another's right arm rested in the crook of a forked branch driven deep into the ground. He cupped a halved skull in his left hand, lifted it to his lips, then passed it to the left. They moved slowly, as if

underwater, and the drum beat slowly, and even the shuddering flames of the fire seemed to reach slowly toward the sky.

I stopped to stare. How could I not? They seemed crea-
tures more of my imagination than of the earth. The one
with his arm propped in the branch looked up and caught
my eye. His face was pointy like a cat's. His eyes were red. I
could not guess an age for him; any wrinkles on his face were
smoothed out by mud or ash. He opened his mouth, bared
his teeth, and hissed. I jumped back. The crowd pushed me
forward. He hissed again, then shook his head and lifted a
chillum to his lips. *Where's Danny?* I thought, and the crowd
kept pushing. *Where's Danny?* And then we'd moved on, away
from the circle, up toward the woods.

It was quieter there in those dark groves. Pilgrims wandered wordlessly round broken stone statues, around lingams
rising straight up from the earth. Here was the shrieking
laughter of a child, the rising voice of a parent calling; here
were sounds I could make out. The drumming and chanting
from below became like an ocean in the background, crashing waves, crashing voices, so constant it could be forgotten. I
leaned against a wall and heard in that din the ocean of my
youth, the sea beating against the shore. Then I opened my
eyes and watched as an old woman clothed in white walked
past. I breathed the scent of cedar and burning sage, and realized, suddenly, that my arms were wrapped around my body,
that I was squeezing my ribs in a sudden surge of joy.

When Danny finally found me, I'd lost track of when the
day had started. I felt his hands first on my waist, and when I
turned my head and saw him he said, "Isabel, where are you?
I've been calling your name forever." I couldn't tell him

exactly where I was. The wintry air was warm for just a moment, the sky a deep, deep shade of blue. In the distance I could see the river thick with bathers, standing calf deep in the icy, holy water. Out of the corner of my eye I thought I saw a flash of the sea, a flash of my home.

We wandered the temple complex together, then, holding hands, my hand small inside of Danny's. The air was thick with sweet smoke, and when I breathed in deeply it seemed to be an intoxicating breath. I wondered if my eyes were glassy, and looking into Danny's I thought his were, and we smiled at each other and continued moving through the crowds. We didn't get home until late that night, and when we did and finally tumbled, tired, into bed, I'm sure we dreamed the same dream: a sadhu's wrist twisting to the beat of a drum, blue sky above, white walls draped with orange cloth and wreaths of marigolds, and shouting, laughing, wild noise.

AND THE BOXES? I peeled off money from the roll and packed a new box tight. Danny and I took it to a friend of his who was traveling back to the States and who, for a large fee, agreed to carry it with him. He left us with the keys to his house, and asked us to check it for vandalism while he was away. With his keys in my hand as we dropped him at the airport, I didn't doubt that we could trust him. In a week we received a fax from Gina. In three weeks she told us to prepare another box, that she could sell the weavings as fast as they came in. "Money is on the way," she wrote.

"Money is on the way," Radika and I shrieked, holding

each other's arms and jumping up and down. I didn't tell her that the money I'd spent to send the box back safely was almost as much as the merchandise would bring.

AT THE END of February there was Losar, Tibetan New Year. We went to a party at Pemba's home. We got to his house early in the afternoon. A woman with high cheekbones greeted us at the door in a gray *chuba,* a long, straight pinafore with a deep red blouse beneath. Her black hair was piled high upon her head. "Come in," she said, "*tashi delek,*" and, laughing, bowed to us with hands cupped in front of her chest. "There are *momos* and beer."

She turned, and we followed her up the stairs. Danny leaned down to whisper, "She's his sister."

The apartment was crowded with people eating dumplings. All those we said hello to nodded. Beer or tea in hand, they pointed to their mouths: *too full to talk,* the gesture meant, *too full and fat and happy.* Danny brought us plates of dumplings and glasses of beer. "Look at the stupa," he said, and pointed through the window out across the field. It was garlanded with prayer flags like a girl with ribbons in her hair. The yellow arcs, newly painted, shone a saffron yellow; the eyes stared out, bright, unblinking, across the valley. I bit into a dumpling. The pastry burst in my mouth, a spicy ball of meat. A finger tapped my shoulder. I turned around, my mouth full, and Danny linked his arm through mine. "Good?" he asked. I nodded. We heard horns sound across the barren rice fields and in a minute Pemba's sister began to run back and forth telling us to gather up our things, it was time to get to the stupa.

I went to find my coat. We'd piled them on Pemba's bed downstairs. I could still taste the spicy dumpling on my tongue, garlicky, peppery, and hot. It was quiet in that room, though I could still hear laughter from above. I sat down for a moment, ran my fingers across the green silk bedspread. A shadow crossed the floor. When I looked up, Pemba stood in the doorway, sunglasses propped upon his head. "Isabel," he said. His voice was warm. "Happy New Year."

I smiled. His eyes were warm and the horns sounded loud and spring was on the way.

"Have you been well?" he said.

I nodded. He, too, wore a chuba, a man's version, a dark tunic belted at his waist, one arm threaded through a sleeve, the other bare, the sleeve hanging loose in a traditional manner. I'd seen him before only when he was preparing for a trek, in jeans and a pile jacket. He stepped into the room.

"I've been telling Danny to bring you along on a trek."

"I don't know if I could make it."

"I'm sure you could. You should see some of the people we take."

"You think so?"

He laughed. He held my jacket while I pushed my arms into the sleeves. We heard footsteps rushing down the stairs. I pulled the zipper of my jacket up.

"Go find your husband and start the new year side by side," he said and smiled. "Tell him that he should take you with us. There's no reason to leave you behind month after month."

He pushed me out the door and I could feel him follow close behind, and then I found Danny again, coming inside to look for me, smiling, then looking past me, his smile broadening when his eyes met Pemba's. "I was looking for my coat," I said. He nodded. I slipped my hand in his, tipped my head up to kiss his cheek. "I was looking for my coat, and then I was looking for you," I whispered. His hand pressed over mine. I breathed out deeply and then breathed in.

We trudged in a great line across the fields and down a road until we got to a narrow passageway that opened out onto the stupa. It was crowded there, mobs of people everywhere, Tibetans in chubas and big fur hats, white blessing scarves hung around their necks, women with striped aprons, with big turquoise rings and earrings and hair knotted upon their heads in elaborate rows of braids. "We have to get up onto the stupa," someone said, and we pushed our way through the crowd, a mob of us, and made our way through the gate up the white steps to the first level of the stupa, and then up another few steps to the next level, and then the crowds below churned like the sea. Suddenly the horns blared louder than before, or maybe it was that we were closer, and thousands of hands reached into bags and tossed *tsampa,* roasted barley meal, up into the air.

It went up, but when I think back on it, I cannot remember it landing anywhere. I think I should have returned to Pemba's home with a dusting of barley powder on my shoulders, but what I remember now is a song that someone started singing; I remember little white squares of paper covered with printed prayers fluttering off above the flags, above the rooftops, carried by the wind; I remember heads all craned in one direction, then turning suddenly toward another, following what signal I did not know; I remember the murmuring of an old woman behind me as she moved a bead down the string of her rosary. I have no memory of barley-covered shoulders, of dusting my skirt off as we walked back across the fields. "Happy New Year," Pemba called, and we followed him. We followed him to see his home once more, up to his roof where the stupa still shone across the valley and we could see it. "Happy New Year," his sister said, and wrapped one arm around my waist and one arm around Danny's. "You've washed away the old year and brought in the new."

We stayed late that night. Even after the sun set and the cold set in, we bundled into Pemba's living room, sat down cross-legged on stuffed square cushions on the floor. We drank and drank, tall, warm bottles of beer and hot cups of tea. Pemba stayed in the kitchen, washing glasses as people left and new people arrived. He smiled once through the door at me, and I thought how glad I was that he was Danny's partner. I looked away then and laughed with Danny, and whispered about how much I loved Pemba's home. It seemed that we stayed there, laughing and drinking and occasionally standing up to try to dance, until the early hours of the morning, but when we finally stumbled up and walked to the road in search of a taxi, Danny checked his watch and it was only ten o'clock. "Let's walk home," I said, and he took my hand and we did. It took us an hour in the dark night, weaving slightly and laughing through empty streets. When we were finally home and safely tucked in bed, still giddy from the beer, it really did seem that a new year had started, that the world had changed to let the light of spring begin to grow.

CHAPTER FOURTEEN

*A*nd then it really was spring. March. As if the world had started once again. The nights were cold, but already the days were hot. The early-morning mist no longer wrapped itself around buildings and between gateposts; figures no longer vanished as they walked ahead in the street. Now I gasped at the cold when I stepped out of bed, but all I had to do was open the doors to the balcony and step outside to the clear blue sky to feel a racing in my heart. The mountains shone white above the valley. The earth felt clean. Petals opened on vines, honeysuckle and sweet, sweet jasmine; rosebuds swelled on dried stems; fruit-bearing trees began to flower. The valley seemed dusted in a pale and hesitant green. The air was clear. I breathed in deeply and it seemed that movement coursed through my veins as well.

I washed my hair in the afternoons and sat out in the sun to let it dry. It was long now, almost to my waist, and hung loose for the longest time in months. I felt like a girl with a laugh constantly at the edge of her lips, with lips that it took a conscious effort to keep from curling upward. The sun on my exposed skin made it feel clean again and aired out. All of me wanted an airing after the damp, musty bundling up of winter.

Anjala was happy too, I knew she was, or happier. She sang while she worked, and sometimes she would sit with me for just a moment while I sunned myself. I tried to speak to her. "*Namaste,*" I said, and "*Kasto chha?*" She'd giggle, then very slowly she'd answer me. "*Thik chha, sanchai chha. Tapaailaai kasto chha?*"

Slowly we'd begun to speak. Her son was away in school. "*U aat barsaa bhayo.*" Eight years old. She looked as though she herself were less than twenty. Danny paid for her son's school, she told me, and it made me glow with pride for hours when I heard this until a little nagging thought made me wonder where the money came from, why there was money for that and not for other things. "*Usko naam Naresh ho.*" Naresh. What would I name a son, I wondered, what would I name a child? I asked to see a picture of Naresh, but her face clouded. She had no picture of her son, she said.

Danny changed too with the coming of spring. I could see his heart was lighter. He moved with greater grace, with greater ease, and I saw his fingers drumming constantly—not from nerves, I thought, but from anticipation. He was planning the first trek of the season. His clients would arrive soon, within a week, and then they would be off. "To the mountains," he said, "out of the valley. To the snow under the bright sun." He had so much of the sun about him that for the first time it wasn't hard to think of letting go. He'd look up occasionally from a map and shake his head. "I can't tell you what it is about heights," he said. "I wish I could. The thin air. The color of the skies. Even the texture of the wind. It's like stepping into another world."

I nodded, smiling.

"An entirely different world," he said, his eyes glowing, his fingers tapping.

I couldn't help smiling when I saw him like this.

His clients came. I went with him to meet them. They seemed as young and thrilled as we felt, all of them, even the oldest, a fifty-five-year-old man.

And then that night, home and high from beer, we sat in the living room together when the phone rang. "Let it ring. It's late," he said. I could never let a phone ring.

"Hello." The words crackled through the wires when I put the phone to my ear. "Hello, Isabel?"

"Hello?"

"Hello? I can't hear you." The crackling came in waves.

"Hello?"

"Isabel? Is that you? Isabel? It's Anna." Her voice was as soft as a flower where it carried between the static. It seemed small to me, fainter, less firm than I remembered. "Isabel? Can you hear me?" I held the phone away from my ear.

"Who is it?" Danny asked.

"Hello," I said. I looked at Danny. "I can hear you. I'm here."

And then the line went down. A great surging, a buzzing, crashing noise, as though I really were listening to the ocean, as though I could draw the phone away and my skin would be wet and salty and smell like the sea. "Hello?" I said into that great noise. "Hello?" But nothing answered. And then a click, and then we were cut off.

I came back to the couch and sat down beside my husband. "It was Anna," I said. "I couldn't hear anything. There was too much static."

"She called," he said.

"Yes." I wondered if the phone would ring again. I wondered if I would pick it up if Danny weren't here.

"Maybe she'll come," he said.

"Yes," I said. "Maybe she will."

The phone didn't ring again until well past midnight. We were both in bed. Danny had stayed up late rolling clothes into tight wads and placing them in his pack, but he had been in bed at least an hour now, and his breath was soft and even where he lay stretched out beside me. *Ring-ring,* I heard, and thought I was dreaming of riding through the city streets, *ring-ring, ring-ring,* my finger thrumming across the silver bell on the handlebars of my bicycle. But the ringing kept on and on, and finally, my mind still woolly from my dreams, I realized that the phone was ringing, that I was warm in bed, not coasting down a misty hill.

"Hello," I said, my eyes still shut, or, if not shut, open to a pitch-black room. "Hello?"

"It's Anna," I heard, and the line was clear now, clear as if she were standing next to me. I could picture her tossing her head, her dark hair falling down across her shoulders. I could picture her lighting a cigarette as she leaned against a pay phone stall.

"Anna," I said, "what time is it?"

"I'm in Thailand," she said. "I'm on my way to Kath-mandu. To you." She laughed. It must have been the rhyme she laughed at.

"When?" I said.

"Three days."

"What?"

"Three days."

"From Thailand?"

"Will you meet me at the airport? Do you have a place for me to stay? How are you? How is everything?" The questions tumbled through the line. I thought I heard her sucking in her breath. "How's Danny?"

"He's good," I said. "We're good." And then, "He's leaving the day after tomorrow. For three weeks. You'll miss him."

"I won't miss him," she said. "I'll have a whole trek with him in April."

I was suddenly glad that I was standing in a dark room, that beyond the walls of the room was the silent palace, that beyond the palace the city was sleeping, that in its sleep it was wandering through dreams I would never know. I thought Danny must be lying very still in bed. I thought of his even breathing. *What does he dream of?* I wondered suddenly, and then pulled myself back to where I stood, trembling in the dark room in my flowered nightgown. "Tell me when you'll get here." I fumbled for a light to see by and a scrap of paper on which to write as she started telling me her plans.

Danny was lying in the same stretched-out position when I crawled back beside him into bed. There was heat coming off his skin, and I pressed my body close to his, my right leg against his left. My right hand I balled up in a fist and placed in his open palm. He sighed in his sleep, shifted slightly as I pressed myself against him closer. I opened my eyes to the heavy darkness. A dog's bark broke the silence, then another and another. I waited for Danny's fingers to curl up around my hand, and when they didn't, I reached into the tangle of bedclothes, found the hem of my nightgown, pulled it up and over my head, and threw it down upon the floor. I pressed my body as close to him as I could get, my right leg almost merging with his left leg, my hand in his hand, then turned on my side, my breasts against his chest, my chin jutting in the indentation where his collarbone pulled away from his shoulder. He moved now, murmured something, his arms encircling my waist and then pushing me off his burning skin. "It's too hot," he murmured sleepily. "Too hot. Too tired." I pressed myself harder against him, circled my left leg over and around his body. Then his hands were on my hips, and he was lifting me up, pushing me off, putting me down upon the rumpled sheets. His voice, less sleepy now, said, "I'm way too tired for this. I just want to get some sleep."

When his breathing was easy again, I pressed my forehead against his shoulder and shut my eyes and breathed in deeply. I tried to match my breath with his. It was hard. His lungs were bigger than mine, I was sure, and every time we breathed in I wanted to let the air out much more quickly from my lungs than he released it from his. I tossed and turned and during the night I thought I did not sleep, but when morning came I opened my eyes surprised to see the sun. I opened my eyes and the first thing I thought was, *Anna is coming,* and then I gathered up my nightgown from the

floor and pulled it on and shut my eyes again and waited for
Danny to stir, to lean over and touch my cheek and tell me
the day was here, that it was time to wake up, time to get out
of bed.

I WENT TO Bethany and Greg's apartment once more
before Anna arrived. I went in the early morning, just after
Danny left. He kissed me on the cheek, the lips, the crown of
my head, and hugged me tightly to him before he walked out
of the door to the taxi waiting down below. I watched the
door close softly. I listened to the taxi's engine rev, and to the
gates clang shut behind the car. Then I wrapped myself in a
sweater and, key in hand, walked the dusty passageway that
separated the two apartments. *Danny's gone,* I thought.
Danny's gone. I'm all alone. He's gone.

The lock on the apartment door felt rusty. The key was
stiff, difficult to turn. Those palace keys dangled rusty from a
ring and knocked together when I moved. Their heaviness,
their size, made me imagine myself a chambermaid in a royal
castle. I tried to turn the key using just my wrist, but nothing
happened. I tried again, and this time when I bore down
with the weight of my body the key turned, the lock
moaned, and I was able to push the door ajar.

Dust gathered in that city quickly. I slipped off my sandals,
and as I walked across the floor I looked back and saw my
footprints walking on the boards behind me. When I looked,
the soles of my feet were black. There was a fine dust coating
the chairs, the tabletop; even the curtains at the window let
loose a soft, dry cloud into the air when I placed my hand

upon them and gently shook. It was quiet in that room. The air smelled old. *How long does it take to slip into the past?* I wondered. I thought I heard a stirring in the bedroom, but when I opened up the door, I saw nothing more than dust motes streaming in the sun. I walked across the room, my dark footprints following, and opened the closet door. *I've walked here before,* I thought. *I've opened this closet before.* Bethany's shoes stood in a line. I knelt down and ran a finger inside to the toe of a brown leather pump. When I drew the finger out again it was coated in a waxy black. The clothes that hung from the rod above swayed slightly at my presence. Standing up, I brushed a shoulder against a blouse and, faintly, the scent of Bethany's perfume appeared, sweet, slightly stale, then fading.

When I ran my hand across the dresses, they shimmered and rustled like a silk scarf against a throat. I held a skirt to my face, moved it slowly across my cheek. The perfume was like aging roses, sweet and musty as they crumpled and fell from their stems. As if in a dream already, I pulled the dress from the hanger, a long, loose, shapeless dress printed with blue bouquets of violets, and, scattering my own dusty clothes upon the floor, let it slip down, smoothly, across my shoulders. The feel of silk against my hips, my breasts, my belly; the whispering smell of roses all around me—I reached up and pulled my hair from its clip, let it rush down to my waist. And then I turned, and turned, and turned, dust motes rising round me, the sun streaming through a gap in the curtains, the folds of silk twining in and out between my ankles and then billowing wide into a great bell. And then I stopped, and the room was warm, and the warmth and thick silence of it all washed over me. There was the bed, and I climbed on top of the quilt tucked to the pillows and put my head down and soon was sound asleep, the silky folds of Bethany's dress washing over me like a river.

Even my dreams were tired. I dreamed of birds sleeping in their nests, a soft spring rain settling on their folded wings. I dreamed of a bouquet of flowers in a vase, their once-bright colors faded now: soft purples, browning reds, yellows faded to a deep, deep gold. I dreamed of a circle of women dancing, holding hands in a meadow, their feet weaving in and out and in and out until they tripped and fell, laughing, to the ground and, falling, fell asleep. Their long hair stretched out upon the grass, blond and brown and black. They slept forever in my dream, and had their own dreams within my dream as well. One dreamed of a child, a small, round boy. Another dreamed of mountains with snow so deep she sank down to her waist, and instead of reaching the peak she strove for, swam instead in a sea of white. The third dreamed she was an angel, flying over a field of sleeping girls. She saw into their dreams, and fanned them gently with her wings so that each, as she passed, moved her lips into a smile. The sea of white softened to a misty cloud. The boy threw his arms around his mother. Then the girls woke up and sleepily took one another's hands and, arms clasped around one another's waists, moved away from the field toward home. And I, in my dream, watching them walk away, watching them each lay a head down on another's neck, I sighed in my sleep and called to them to return. "Come back," I called, "come back for me." The birds in their nests slept on. The dried petals of the flowers crumbled in my hand. I woke and rubbed my eyes and wondered at the woman staring down at me, then shook myself and sat up with a start.

Anjala stood above me, her black hair pulled tightly back. She stood above me with a rag in her hand and I nearly jumped and I know I did scoot back. I felt my face turn red. I felt my lips begin to quiver. "It's nothing wrong," I tried to say. "They gave me the key, they asked me to keep my eye on things." But even as I started to stumble through Nepali words, even as I started to explain, I lost my train of thought—what was there really after all to say? And she said nothing. Her lips were pressed together. Her face was slightly flushed. I pulled myself up. The wooden bedstead was hard against my spine. She turned away from me and pushed the window curtains back. The room filled up with light, and then as she pushed the windows open it filled again with a cool breeze. I shivered in the thin silk dress. I shivered and pulled my knees up to my chest.

"*Bethany ra Greg bholi aaunuhos,*" she said.

Tomorrow, they were coming back tomorrow.

"*Ma wahaāharuko ghar saphaa garchu.*" She was cleaning their apartment. She spoke slowly, simply. I couldn't help but understand. "*Wahaāharu bholi Thailand batta aaunuhuncha. Wahaāharu Rana sanga telephone maa bolnubayo.*"

My eyes were still slightly blurred from sleep. A knot sank to my stomach. I felt naked there in front of her in nothing but the thin silk dress. I couldn't move. I couldn't draw my knees away from my chest. I saw her bending down, her arms gathering up my clothes quickly. My skirt. My tights. My shirt. She held them in her arms, then let them spill out upon the bed. "*Tapai kina basnuhuncha?*" Why are you here? she said.

"I don't know," I whispered, my voice as soft as a child's.

"*Tyo Bethanyko lugaa ho.*" she said. That dress belongs to Bethany.

"I know," I said again. "I know."

It was all I could do to hold back tears. I could imagine my face, dusty already, and trails in the dust where tears rolled down. I swallowed hard and shook my head. I wasn't a child. There would be no tears. I swallowed hard again.

"*Lugaa laaunuhos,*" she said. Change your clothes.

"Yes," I said, "I should change." She stared at me, and I reached forward and gathered up the clothes strewn at the foot of the bed. "Please go," I whispered. I tried to find her words to say this, but only English words came to my lips. "Please go. Please let me change alone." She didn't move. I hugged my knees. She continued to stare at me. I don't know how long we stayed there, I rocking on the bed, my knees pulled up beneath the dress, she framed by the streaming light behind her. A long time, I thought, long enough for the quality of the light to change, for a cloud to pass across the sun. Long enough for noises from the courtyard to slowly break apart and carry up to us distinctly. We stared at each other, and then she turned. Her braid swung out as she turned her head, and I watched it trailing through the air behind her, and then she was out the door, and the door was shut again and the room was silent.

I scrambled off the bed. I pulled the dress off over my head, and pulled my clothes on as quickly as I could. I hung Bethany's dress in the closet again, my fingers shaking, my chest clenched tight across my thumping heart. I darted between the hanging dresses as if through a curtain to the dusty store of carved statues behind them. I picked a small one up, a face, a face with rolling eyes and lips held back in a scowl, and clutched it to my breast.

When I finally opened the door, Anjala was on her knees in the living room, a soapy bucket close by, a rag bunched in her hand. She looked up at me quickly. Her mouth opened and then shut. I'd never noticed how red her lips were, like berries, deep, rich, round.

"*Nabolnuhos,*" I said—please don't say anything—and when she nodded her head I put a smile on my lips. "Thank you," I said. She nodded again, then turned her back to me, and I, nodding my head as if in agreement, nodding my head now to myself, slipped out the door and down the passageway and to my own apartment, where I turned on the water in the shower and stood under it, shaking, until I thought I might be clean again.

I WENT TO the airport the next afternoon carrying a string of marigolds in my hands. The flowers were plump and smelled slightly spicy and of the earth. I got there just as the plane from Thailand landed, and went upstairs to the café to watch the passengers walk along the glassed-in passageway from the plane. The fields beyond the landing strip were green, the mountains in the distance barely visible beyond the afternoon haze. There was just an intimation of the towering forms, a slight variation in the wavering sky to indicate their presence. Two men wheeled a staircase to the plane. The metal door opened. Slowly at first and then in a rush, crowds of people clambered out.

I stood at the windows among expectant crowds, children looking for their fathers, old men and women looking for their children. They pressed against the glass, pressed and waved and pointed. A little boy beside me tugged his mother's sari and cried, frustrated by the waiting, unable, I guessed, to see his father amid the stream of people. And then, slowly, as if through a lens only then coming into focus, my eyes rested on three people walking down the passageway together. The woman in the middle wore a sloping straw hat that tilted downward, covering her face. The man was tall and thin and kept reaching out to take the woman's arm. To their left, tipping her face toward them momentarily, walked a taller woman. I stared at them not thinking, not recognizing, until the middle woman pulled her hat off, her bright red hair gleaming in the sun. It was Bethany and Greg, and then, when she turned her face toward the airport, I saw who it was that they were with. Anna, tall and full of grace, Anna walked beside them. Just when I was certain I had caught her eye, she looked down and placed her arm around Bethany's shoulders, and the three of them entered the country steadfast, in a row.

Part Three

*A*nna laughed. She sat on the couch in my living room with her feet up and sipped beer from a glass and tilted her head back and laughed with such full richness that it thrilled me: Anna's face laughing in the candlelight; her shoulders shaking; her laughter like stars ringing; her hand on her belly to ease the pain of such hard, hard laughter.

"How strange to both be here," she said. "How strange traveling halfway around the world and finding you." She laughed again. I laughed too.

"How strange to be halfway around the world and to be found by you."

"I'm back to sleeping on your couch."

"Try to think of it as your couch."

"My couch. I've come to Nepal for a couch."

The world seemed just fine with Anna in it laughing. The beer was warm, but it didn't matter. Warm beer on a cool spring night—it seemed fine, it seemed almost perfect just then, in fact. I could listen to Anna talk for hours, and here she was, talking, laughing, telling me where she'd been for the past twelve months.

"New Zealand's been my favorite place," she said. "I loved the rolling hills. They were green and soft. I stayed for two months on a farm there. Every morning I could hear the sound of sheep bleating. I took a walk every day to a cliff that looked out over the sea. I helped out in the kitchen at the farm and they let me stay for nothing. They wanted me to stay the winter, but two months seemed long enough. I wanted to move. When I finally decided it was time, I hitched my way across the island. Can you imagine me thumbing it? Can you imagine me walking along the side of the road, with my backpack on and my arm stretched out? You would have laughed at me."

There was pleasure in her face as she remembered. An easy pleasure, a memory unfurled. There was nothing about her, on the couch that night, that indicated any lack of ease. *That couch seems hers,* I remember thinking, *this room seems hers.* She wore a bracelet on her wrist, a thick band inlaid with silver filigree that glimmered in the light. "It's from Bali," she said, and smiled. "I felt like I was walking in a dream when I was on that island. I don't know how to describe it. The scent of the air was like a thousand different kinds of flowers, but so faint you were never sure if you were smelling anything."

She'd been to New Zealand. To Australia. To Bali and Indonesia and Thailand. "I kept running into the same set of travelers," she said. "Every country I'd think I'd lost them, and then suddenly one morning while drinking coffee I'd look up and see a face I'd seen before. We all had the same travel books. I kept bumping into familiar faces in the lobbies of hotels."

I leaned forward while I listened. I could almost see the worlds she described. Even the sand in Bali was, in my imagination, softer and finer than sand elsewhere in the world. Even the grass in New Zealand sprung back against one's foot, and shone brighter under the noonday sun than any grass I'd ever walked on. And Anna? There was something different about her as she lay there upon the couch. Her eyes were bright, but they had always been bright. Her legs were strong, her arms thin—her body was still like mine, her long limbs still mirrored mine. But there was a freedom in her body, in her carriage, that I hadn't seen since Matthew died. Her shoulders opened when she laughed. She stretched her painted toes out long. She wrapped and unwrapped the shawl I'd lent her, pulling it along her skin without a thought: her body moved without a thought; it moved from intuition.

"And you, Isabel? Tell me about you." She sat up and drew the shawl around her shoulders. "You're married. How is it being a wife?" Her laugh was rich. I could almost taste it, it was so rich.

"It's good. It's not always what I thought, but it's very good."

"What did you think before? What did you think it would be like?"

"I'm not quite sure. It seems such a long time ago, before I was married."

"Less than a year."

"Less than a year. I think I thought that life would end there. That in a funny way life would end after we said our vows."

"Life would end?"

"That I wouldn't have to make decisions afterward. That the patterns of my life would be set. That all I'd have to do was keep on living and what I had to do would make itself immediately apparent, or if not immediately apparent, then at least gradually clear. I didn't think I'd have to make any more choices."

She stared at me. Had I just been staring at her in that same way? Her eyes glittered in the candlelight. Her lips were wet from sipping at the beer. She ran her fingers through her hair. Her hair was long like mine, but darker. She saw me looking at her hair and shook it so it hung straight down her back. "We could still be twins," she said.

"Almost. Almost twins. Same bodies. Same long hair."

"And Danny? Is he the husband you'd imagined?" She pulled the shawl from around her shoulders and draped it across her body like a blanket.

"Are you cold?"

"No. Tell me about Danny. Tell me what kind of husband he is." Her voice reminded me of the voice she'd teased me with in childhood, the rising singsong, the voice that preceded a game in which she'd end by poking me until I laughed.

"He's the only husband I've ever had. I don't know if he's

different from any other husband. I don't know if my marriage is different from any other marriage."

"Does your stomach still jump? In a good way, I mean. Does it still jump when he walks through the door and you're sitting here where I am and he's home after being away for hours, or in your case days or weeks"—she laughed—"and you see him and remember he's your husband? Do you still feel that jump?"

Didn't she think these questions strange? *It's none of your business,* I wanted to say. *It's none of your business what I feel for my husband.* "Of course I still feel it," I said.

She was silent. The doors to the balcony were open, and the faint sound of music drifted over from Bethany and Greg's apartment. I pictured them there, their living room strange in the way that it always feels strange to return anywhere—walls seem longer, corners sharper; nothing is ever as you remember it to be. I pictured them each with a drink in hand, each trying to think of a way to fill the space again with life, to make it the home they remembered having left behind. Then I felt my face coloring as I thought of their bedroom, their bed, me between its sheets, the dark corners and dust in their closet. "It's deep inside of me, that feeling," I said. "It's deep in my heart and my stomach and my toes."

The music drifting around the palace walls covered up the other noises of the city. The sweet smell of incense wafted through the open doors, rising from the Ranas' home below. It seemed that the palace was an island, that the city outside its gates couldn't enter by sound or sight or smell. "It's peaceful here," Anna said. "Peaceful in a city way, where you can guess at the movement all around you but you can't feel it.

Like you've found a cocoon. You must love the nights here."

"Nights are more peaceful here than days."

"I'm glad I got here when Danny was away." Her knees were pulled up to her chest. Her hair on her shoulders spread out like a second shawl. The candle was burning low now, the wax melted almost to the brass base of the holder. I stood to light the lantern and in the sudden brightness of the flaring match I lost sight of her. "Don't light the lantern," her voice said softly. "Let's sit in the dark awhile. Let's sit in the dark and not look at each other and see what we can say then."

The match burned out between my fingers. The candle spluttered on the table. Just before the flame died I looked up into her eyes. They were darker than the darkness that followed the dying candlelight.

We sat there, then, in that still, black room together. I tried to speak once or twice, but always the words died before they reached my lips. I could feel her across from me, could feel her and not feel her: the unsettling gap between the remembered quality of a thing and the thing itself. I could feel the Anna of my memory and another Anna altogether. I waited for her to speak, but I could hear only her breath—her breathing and the music, soft, and then vanishing—and then I stood up and said good night and we both went to sleep, she in the living room, I in the bedroom as if of old. As if of old and not of old at once.

I DREAMED THAT night of Matthew. I dreamed of us as children on that first day that he and Anna and their mother

moved next door. I dreamed of watching him from my bedroom window. He jumped out of the car and ran in circles
around the house. He ran with the limbs of a boy, but in my
dream I felt about him what I felt when he became a man.
He circled and circled until I grew dizzy watching, and I
called out to him, or tried to call, to make him stop. There
was something about the view I had, the ability to see his
patterns except in one long gap where he disappeared behind
their house, there was something in that view that sent a
quaking through my body. I pressed my face against the
screen and watched that endless circling until something
changed—I don't know what—and in my dream my mother
called me to come downstairs, and I left and let Matthew circle there alone.

MATTHEW AND I never lived together. We talked about it
often, but somehow we were always more comfortable
knowing that we each had our own space to return to. And
then there was Anna. She lived with me. How could I ever
ask her to leave? Sometimes when Matthew was over and
Anna was home and we all curled up together on the couch
it reminded me of the hours the three of us had spent
together as children, and I'm sure it must have reminded
them of that as well. Were those hours as precious to them? I
wondered. Did they remember them with the same sense of
hunger that I did?

One night Anna was at work late. Matthew and I ordered
Chinese food. We ate in the living room, our plates on the
coffee table, a video playing on the television set. We had just

reached the point where we opened fortune cookies when Anna arrived in a huff, slamming the door shut behind her. "I've had it," she said. Matthew and I looked at each other. "I've had it."

"What's wrong?" My voice was too sweet and I burrowed my fist into my knee. I hated to sound so cloying.

"Nothing. Work. Alison forgot to put my memo through. Now I'll have to work this weekend."

Alison was her secretary. It no longer startled me to think of Anna as a lawyer, but Anna with a secretary? I thought about my own job. About unpacking boxes and arranging items on dusty shelves.

"Have some food," Matthew said.

"I ate at the office."

"Sit down." I patted the couch beside me.

She shrugged. She was never worried about hiding her moods. She was never self-conscious in the way that I was. I could feel Matthew's arm around me and then I felt him pull it away and scoot to make room for Anna. She squeezed her way between us. She kicked off her shoes and put her feet up on the table.

"You don't mind, do you?" she said. Matthew reached his arm up around her to touch the back of my neck. I could feel Anna wriggle to get comfortable. The movie on the TV blared on; a soldier ran across the screen, through the jungle in Vietnam, and I stood up and took our plates into the kitchen and brought Anna back a fortune cookie to crack open. "Heed the wise counsel of others," it said. Matthew and Anna laughed. Sometimes they started giggling together and I could not tell what the joke was.

Sometimes I liked to watch them. Tonight I felt left out.

"From now on you listen to me," Matthew said.

"I haven't listened to you once in my entire life," she said.

"Then you have to listen to me," I said.

Anna turned and stared. Was it that uncharacteristic for me to say?

"Do you have something to say to me?" Anna had come home in a huff, but I hadn't realized that she was really so angry.

I shook my head.

"If you have something, you should say it."

I could feel my face color. I could see Matthew looking back and forth between the two of us. I could see him wishing—or was it my wish?—that the night had continued on with just him and me. Why didn't he say something? Why did his hand drop from the back of my neck?

"I was just kidding," I said. "I didn't mean anything. I'm sorry you had a bad day. Are you sure you don't want anything to eat?"

"No," she said. "I'm not hungry."

She shifted her weight toward Matthew. I saw him run his hand across her back. I tried to watch the television. It looked as though the soldier would stumble on a landmine. I half hoped he would. The apartment felt very crowded. How long was this night before the night on which I asked Matthew to leave? How long was it before the crowded feeling turned to one of a permanent gap, a permanent loss?

"I'm going to bed," I said at last. Anna shrugged. I turned to Matthew. "Are you coming?"

"No," he said. "I'll stay up for a little while. I'll be there soon."

I didn't shut the bedroom door all the way. I wanted to hear if she said anything about me. When Matthew finally came to bed and I hadn't heard a word, I didn't know which would have been worse—to have had her name me as the source of her irritation, or to have her anger fall on me for no reason that she could explain. "I don't know what's going on between her and me," I whispered in his ear. "Things are strange. I don't know why."

"They'll get better," he said. "It's just a phase. Sometimes I think I should leave the two of you alone."

"That's not the answer."

"Then what is?"

"There is no answer. She's like my sister. We're just going through a phase."

I felt him smile. I felt him smile in the dark. I knew what he was thinking. I knew he was thinking that we each reminded him of children, and I wondered if, having met me as a child, he would ever come to think of me as fully an adult.

"I'm not a kid," I said.

"Of course you're not."

"Anna and I are adults. We'll work through whatever's going on."

"Of course you will."

"Stop being so smug." I hit him with the pillow. I heard the water turn on in the bathroom. I shrieked when he hit me back. I heard the water turn off. I heard the click as the light switch flipped down. I giggled and rolled across him and hit him again, and thought how lonely Anna must feel, her best friend and her brother laughing together in a dark room while she curled up in bed alone.

ANNA AND ANJALA took to each other immediately. Though they didn't share a language, they seemed to understand each other all the same. I woke up late the morning after Anna arrived, and when I walked out in my robe and nightgown, rubbing sleep from the corners of my eyes, I found Anjala and Anna smiling at each other on the balcony. The tea was made. Anna held a steaming cup in her hand. "Good morning, sleepyhead," she called. This was the voice that I remembered. "It's a beautiful day. Come and look at the mountains."

It *was* a beautiful day. The snowy mountains looked so close that had I been a child I would have reached my hand to touch them. The air that morning was cold and slightly damp. It smelled of newly turned earth, and, looking over the edge of the balcony, I saw that the gardener was at work downstairs, that he was planting flowers in the courtyard.

"Do you wake to this every day?" Anna asked. Her hair was bundled up on top of her head. She wore a pair of faded jeans and a loose cotton shirt. Her skin was smooth, her face was calm, and she looked ready to belong here, ready to make this place her own.

"It *is* beautiful," I said. "The mountains look like the mountains I imagined when I was a little girl. The ones I drew when you went away in the summer. Remember the purple?—the purple jagged slopes, the peaks always covered in snow?"

She smiled. "I remember your mountains. You drew them even when I wasn't in Colorado. I remember watching you draw."

She never liked coloring as much as I did. She grew restless on rainy days, raced the animals around the house. I could sit quietly at a table for hours with my pencils, drawing flowers, drawing castles, drawing princesses with red bows in their hair. She would charge out of her house on rainy days and head right down to the sea. She'd come back with her hair in tangles, a runny nose, and watery eyes and tell me, her voice rising with excitement, about the waves she'd seen, the pools she'd hopped across, the dark green color of the ocean under slate-gray clouds.

"I don't need to draw the mountains anymore," I said. "They're here in front of me most mornings. They're here when I wake up."

"I can't wait to get up and into them. It's almost painful to see them so close and not be able to reach them right now. I've been reading everything I can about Kangchenjunga. *Five Great Treasuries of the Snows.* The third-highest mountain on the earth. I remember looking at maps with Danny when he was in New York, and how he described the route. You know what his voice is like. 'It's hot,' he said. 'It's hot and then you climb up and up and into the snow,' and I remember thinking, 'It's enough to get to base camp. I just want to get my feet to a place where I can imagine an ascent.' I don't care about conquering mountains. I just want to feel myself close to the sky. The cold, cold air. The cleanness of it. The clarity."

I put my hand upon her wrist.

"It's going to be hard," she said. "I'm not at all nervous about the trek, but it will be hard to be there with a group. I wish I could go alone. I wish I had the courage to go alone."

"You can't go alone."

"No, of course not. I believe Danny when he says the region's too remote. We need the support of the group trek. The porters. The cook. But the walking will be hard—for the others anyway. Up and down, up and down. Not everybody can handle the mountains the way I can."

Anna may have sounded like she was bragging, but it wasn't bragging really. It was the confidence that she seemed born with, the confidence I loved.

"You're right," I said. "Not everybody can. I don't think I could."

"No, you probably couldn't."

I looked at her, but her mind seemed far away.

Anjala returned to the balcony with the thermos and filled Anna's cup. "Thank you," Anna said, and Anjala smiled. She reached out and tucked a loose strand back in Anna's bun.

"Thank you, Anjala," I said, and she looked at me, then looked away, before going back inside. I blushed. "She likes *you*," I said. "She's never seemed to like me."

Anna shook her head. She took another sip of tea. "This stuff is good," she said. "It's great, but it's so filled with sugar I'm scared of what the sweetness of it all will do to me."

CHAPTER SIXTEEN

"I can't stand the dirt," Bethany said. "I can't stand the smells and the rubbish and the dust. It's the dirtiest place I've ever been, and it never used to matter but now it's all I think about. I see rats in rubbish heaps every time I take a walk. Every time. Everywhere I go."

She sat in her living room, her feet tucked up beneath her. It was a hot day—spring came suddenly, aching and hot—but even so, she piled the couch with blankets.

"Most people I know choose not to look," she continued. "But the smell of burning garbage, how can you just turn away from that smell? Or the sewage seeping along the sides of streets? You look down into the gully next to where you're walking, and it's there, the thick sludge, oozing green. And the flies. The flies on the meat at outdoor stands. The flies on the vegetables, the fruit. I'm soaking everything in iodine for longer than I ever used to. I'd rather have that taste than anything the flies might leave."

The rusty taste of iodine. Vegetables wilted and slightly oranged from the soaking. The rubbish heaps smoldering behind walls, the smell of plastic burning in the dry spring air, the haze, the heavy haze that lay upon the city during all but the early morning hours. It seemed to me we had a contract to ignore these things, that the smells we agreed to notice were those of honeysuckle on the walls and incense pouring out of temple courtyards and the tingling scent of spices that rose from pans of hissing oil.

"We stayed by the beach in Thailand," Bethany said. "A little hut along a strip of sand as white as quartz. We could see the water from our window. The waves were turquoise. The palm trees swayed in the evening. There was a porch in front of the hut. It was covered and had two wooden chairs that we sat in every night. We drank beer together, and white wine, and watched the dusk roll in. It looked like fog rolling in from the sea. I could watch the ocean forever. That ocean anyway. I'm done with mountains."

She spoke as if from sight, as if the ocean still lay before her. Anna and I sat with her for long afternoons, and often she lapsed into the telling and retelling of the last three months. *The world here didn't vanish when you left,* I sometimes wanted to say to her. *There were three months here in these empty rooms, these lonely rooms, while you watched the ocean on a white sand beach in Thailand.*

"The fruit there. Greg would go every morning to the market and come back with pineapple and bananas and melons."

In my mind I saw them: the sliced melons so bright that the faceted cleanness of their lines made them look like jewels.

"I hadn't swum in the ocean in years," she said, "but every morning as soon as I woke up I'd cross the sand to the water and walk for what seemed miles. In the morning you could walk out into that ocean, waist deep, until the shore was far away. The first time he woke to find me out there, Greg stood on the shore and called me back, and when I didn't turn, he ran as quickly as he could through the water to where I waded. He yelled at me for scaring him, but then he stopped yelling and looked around, and after that I'd sometimes wake to find him in the water ahead of me, his body in the distance a shadow against the rising sun.

"We faced east. Given a choice, I would probably have chosen west. I've never been an early riser. But sunrises are so much better than sunsets. The violet light of dawn moves into roses and yellows instead of the other way around. The darkness thinning, then clearing altogether. I imagine it a bit like smelling salts. That rising sun cleared me for three brief minutes. Sometimes, standing in the water, I'd feel an urge to duck down beneath the surface. I wanted the pause the water gave me, the pause that cut through the sun's ascent. I liked to duck down for just a moment, then rise again and discover how much farther the sun had climbed. It was quite far sometimes. Quite a lot can happen in one moment when your eyes are shut."

It wasn't always easy to listen while Bethany droned on. Any kind of closeness we'd had before she left wasn't a closeness that merited these details. Her skin, despite the months in Thailand, was pale still, a translucent, milky kind of pale. The sun was most apparent, I think, in the darkness of her freckles. Before they'd sprinkled her nose just lightly, like drops of diluted watercolor paint. Now they stood out strongly, speckles on her nose, her cheeks, her forehead. Her hands were speckled too, and the hair on her arms was so blond where the sun had bleached it that it glistened under almost any light.

I was wary there in that apartment, and watched Greg closely when he was home. Several times I tried to speak to him about the box, but always I found I didn't have the courage and also did not know quite what to say. He seemed to make a habit of leaving the apartment when Bethany began to talk. It may have been that he really did have places to go, but after the first night, when they invited Anna and me over to look at their photographs, he seemed to vanish whenever the hut in Thailand came up. "It wasn't really a hut," I once heard him whisper under his breath. "More of a cottage, and pretty plush if we're going to remember right." I looked up at him, startled to hear him whispering, but he looked away as soon as I caught his eye. He left shortly after. I wondered if he'd noticed the missing figurine, and I thought of it rolled in the scraps of the baby's quilt I'd laid aside in the far corner of my bottom drawer.

"I was in the hospital for a long time," Bethany said. "In and out, it was almost a month. Greg stayed in a hotel on Khao San Road. What a feeling to be a tourist again after years of living here. You know how it is—we keep as far away as possible from the travelers here. It wasn't that I didn't feel well enough to leave. It felt silly being in there most of the time, but you get used to it. When I lost the baby there were other complications.

"But then, after that awful month in Bangkok, we found the cottage by the sea. We'd both been to Thailand before, but we'd never stayed there any length of time. People say it's over-touristed, but look where we live—look at all the back-packers clogging the city, and it's only April. Anyway, we found the cottage, and the beach, and we stayed there and the waters were healing. I swear they were."

I DIDN'T LIKE the way that Bethany had changed. At first I felt sorry for her, a guilty, pitying feeling when I was in her presence. But that feeling changed to discomfort, and then to an overwhelming unease. When we made eye contact, she looked too long. When she stood up, she almost always stum-bled and righted herself by placing her palm upon my knee. Her boundaries were different, her sense of distance gone.

"This apartment feels strange to me," she said one after-noon. "I've lived in this palace for nearly five years, but it feels foreign now. The air feels different. We've left it empty before. Last summer it was empty for three months. But now, now it doesn't smell right. The air's not the right consistency. I don't know—it sounds crazy, but it just doesn't feel like the same place we left." Her eyes were large. Her voice was soft.

Greg stood in the corner listening. I saw him nod his head at me, and when I stood up to bring our glasses to the kitchen, he tugged lightly at my elbow and whispered in my ear, "She thinks the baby's here. She thinks the baby died here and that its spirit stayed behind when we flew to Thailand. She says she's terrified, but now that we're back she can barely bring herself to leave the apartment."

I nodded. Through the doorway I saw Anna holding Bethany's hand. How had they become so close? I saw Bethany lean back in her chair. A narrow beam of light shone in through the window and rested on her neck. Her milk-white neck. Her jutting collar bones where her loose dress gaped away from her thin shoulders. Was there something she saw in Anna that she had never seen in me?

Later I asked Anna what she thought of them. "Beth's grieving," she said. "Greg's grieving too. I feel for them. I worry about them."

"There's something very off about them, though," I said.

"There'd be something off about you too if you'd lost your baby like that."

I nodded. "You're right," I said.

GREG PULLED ME aside again one afternoon. "There's something missing," he said.

My stomach clenched. He looked hard into my eyes. I pretended nonchalance. "What?" I asked. "What's gone?"

"You don't know?"

I shook my head. "I don't know what you're talking about." I wanted to say something, I swear I did, but it was as though my tongue were locked behind my teeth.

"The closet," he said. "The statues?"

"Maybe it was Anjala."

He shook his head. "It's hard to believe. But maybe. Maybe it was her."

Later I heard him arguing with Anjala, and after that I found I couldn't meet her eyes.

THEY SPENT TIME alone together, Anna and Bethany. They spent time alone at Bethany's, Anna slipping off in the morning while I slept, or in the afternoon for tea. Sometimes she left so quietly that even if we were sitting alone together in the living room I'd look up and she'd be gone and I wouldn't know when she had left or when she would be coming back. But I'd know where she had gone. I pictured them whispering together, all alone but enjoying the sense of conspiracy that lowered voices bring. I was sure they talked about me, talked about Danny and me and how it could have been Danny waiting here for Anna instead of married to me.

Once I came upon them in the hallway. I was tired of waiting for Anna to return, and was walking through the back passageway to tell her I was leaving for a walk. I heard their voices first, whispered voices projected down the hall-way. "They seem so different," I heard Bethany say. "They're like the sun and the moon."

"They *are* different," Anna said. Her voice was softer than Bethany's, and I had to strain to hear it. "Different isn't always bad," she said. "He and I are different too."

"But the kind of different they are, it's hard for me to understand. She seems so timid."

They were walking toward me, I could hear the floor-boards creak beneath their feet. I wondered why they were walking there, where they were going—I couldn't imagine they were coming back to find me. I pressed myself against the wall, unable to keep from listening. I wiped a cobweb off my cheek. It was dusty here, dusty and so dimly lit I could hardly see in front of me.

"When Danny brought her back we couldn't believe it was real. She doesn't even look like anyone else he's been with."

"She looks like me," Anna said.

"She's tall like you, but that's all. The way you move is different. They way you smile. The texture of your hair. You're very different."

"Rose Red and Snow White," she said. Her voice was low. It made me want to cry. I pictured us as girls together, wrapping ourselves in blankets, hers red, mine blue. They were cloaks, the blankets, and we played at being sisters from the fairy tale. She was Rose Red with her dark hair and dark red lips. I was Snow White only because I was paler. In this story, unlike the one where Snow White finds the Seven Dwarfs, in this one Snow White and Rose Red are sisters in the world together. We'd make skits, and sometimes Matthew, lanky, almost teenage, would flop down on the floor to watch us. Did Anna carry those same scenes inside her heart? "We're very different," she said. "But different can be good."

"It can be." Bethany sighed.

"It can."

"You know, when he left Nepal last winter, things weren't going well for him. He'd had an affair with a Dutch woman, and I'd never seen him so in love. She came and lived here in the palace for a little while. And then something happened. He said they got tired of each other. She ended up leaving the country. She's traveling now. Through China, the last I heard. When Danny told me he was getting married, I couldn't help but think he was trying to prove something. That he could commit to somebody. That he could love someone without causing her pain."

"He caused me pain."

"He did."

And then they stopped. They were just around the corner from where I stood, my back against the wall. There were rows of shutters in that section of the passageway. I heard a muffled thud, the creak of a rusty hinge, and then the passage flooded with gray light.

It hurt my eyes at first. Sometimes in the dark when you concentrate on listening, you forget that your body exists. The light spilled down the hall, and suddenly my hands were in front of me, white on top, black with dust on the palms, and they seemed foreign, the fingers too long to belong to me. The hall was even dirtier than I'd imagined, the ceiling hung with thick soft strings of dust, the plastered walls on either side spidered with cracks and bare where large sections of the plaster had fallen to the floor and turned to chalky rubble. It seemed wrong to me, that light. I worried that they'd see my shadow around the corner. I couldn't move; I felt so bare that I could hardly breathe.

"This is where they say it happened," Bethany said. "This is where she jumped."

And then I realized what it was they were doing in the hallway. They were chasing ghosts. Our ghost. The Ranas' maid.

"She was pregnant, they say. There was nothing else that

she could do. Look down at the courtyard. You'd never know, would you? You'd never know."

I wondered what Bethany looked like there in the dusty, crumbling hall. Anna always looked alive no matter where she was, but Bethany, Bethany looked like a ghost herself these days. She must be leaning toward the window, her eyes cleared by now from the bursting light. Her hair might be the only color in the hall. I pictured it gleaming like copper where the light struck it, gleaming like fire against the snow of her skin.

"I used to hear her walking at night when we first moved in. It would be a steady creaking back and forth down the passageway. I could hear it from our bedroom, the footsteps nearing the apartment door, then growing distant, then drawing near again. I never really liked to walk down here alone, but when Danny moved in we started using it with greater frequency. Or I did." She giggled, a high-pitched, nervous giggle.

"You can't see either of the balconies from here." Now Anna must be leaning forward. Did the sunlight make her squint her eyes? Did she lift her hand to shade them? Did she have dust on her hands as I did, gray, on mine? "Think of what she must have felt. Think of what it means to fall. Her dress raying up around her. Her bare legs showing as she hurtled through the air. The courtyard waiting down below. Just try to think of it." There was something about Anna's voice, a slight rising in timbre as she worked her way through the sentences, that I recognized. I heard her take a deep breath. *Don't breathe deeply here,* I thought. *You'll fill your lungs with dust.* "No wonder she still haunts this place. I'd haunt it too if I died like that."

And suddenly her voice seemed closer, just beyond the corner, and I could feel the floor move as her weight shifted toward me. There was just the corner separating us. I couldn't move now. What would I say if they found me? What would I say if I had to look into Anna's eyes?

"The hall turns here," Bethany said, and her voice seemed almost next to mine. "It leads right to Danny and Isabel's apartment. There aren't any windows along that part—only along this straight strip here. I'll show it to you."

I sucked my breath in hard. A long creak sounded in the hall behind me. Had I shifted my weight? The creak sounded again and I was certain someone stood behind me.

"Hello?" Bethany called.

I bit my lip. I bit my lip and trembled and tried to still my trembling.

"There's someone there," Bethany said. "Hello?" Her voice echoed from wall to wall.

"Let's go back." Anna's voice was low and quiet now.

"I'm going to find out what it is."

"I'd rather not." And that was when I thought that Anna knew it was me. Never in our lives had Anna shied away from investigation of any sort. Never had she shied away from mystery. Did she protect me still? Did she love me still? "I'd rather just go back and clean myself up," she said. "The dust is so thick here I can hardly breathe."

They turned around. Their voices grew faint. I let my breath out. The hallway shimmered, pale in the half light that seeped in through the opened shutters. Dust motes rose from floor to crumbling ceiling. Cobwebs swayed gently, draped the fold from wall to ceiling like soft, thick-spun lace. I walked back down the passageway, away from the flecks of light, away from the open window. The darkness closed around me. I slipped into the shadows, toward my own door, my own door that led to open windows of my own, and just before I reached it, I passed through a sudden icy cold and then what seemed a cloud of roses, soft and sweet, soft and then gone completely, an invisible garden present only through its scent.

When I looked into the mirror on my bedroom wall, I saw that my face was streaked with dirt. I wiped away a lock of hair, and where I wiped, the streaks grew wider. I stripped then, and was standing under steaming water in the shower when I heard the door to the apartment open, heard Anna's voice calling to say that she was home.

CHAPTER SEVENTEEN

We didn't talk about my presence in the hall. We didn't talk about what I'd heard her say to Bethany. We did talk, though, about the maid. We made up stories for her. I said she wasn't a maid at all, but a prince's concubine who secretly loved another. Anna said her name was Dev Kumari, and that she had a beautiful singing voice, and that when she moved her fingers quickly, her hands, covered in rings, looked like butterflies. She wore bracelets to her elbows. She painted a deep red point between her brows and lined her eyes with kohl. Her perfume smelled like jasmine.

"No, like roses," I said.

Her perfume smelled like roses, like white roses with a touch of amber. She slept in the room with the other concubines, women, girls really, piled in beds one next to the other, the beds raised high above the ground, the quilts of batted cotton, thick and soft. Sometimes at night she'd slip down from her bed, run through the darkened halls to her lover, sing sweet songs to him in a low-pitched voice until the sun rose in the east. But then one night her lover vanished. Her petticoats rustled beneath her nightgown as she ran back through the palace. The noise they made sounded like the wind whispering. It whispered something that she still could not make out. Her hands that moved as quick as butterflies trembled as she stood outside the door to the bedroom she had left. When she took a breath, finally, and opened the door, she found the room ablaze in candlelight, the rows of blanketed concubines sitting up and rubbing their eyes, one of them staring at her with a half-open mouth and a tongue showing slightly in a hiss between sharp teeth.

They would have killed her. The Rana prince would have had her killed. And she would have gone silently to her death. But first they killed her lover, hanged him from a rope in the center of the courtyard. She had ropes around her hands now, ropes that couldn't still her fingers' quivering. The Rana prince sat in a mahogany chair raised on a dais that was covered with a tiger skin while Dev Kumari's lover was led to the noose. She stood below the chair, her hands bound behind her back, wearing white already, white to die in, white to mourn in, white in which she would become a ghost. Her lover met her eyes once. They draped the noose around his neck. He raised his eyes toward her once more, and then they pulled the floor from beneath his feet, his body dropped, the rope pulled tight, his body jerked and then was still, and the air seemed still to her as well, and the voices that rose up seemed only to add texture to the silence. She was led back to the palace and her hands untied. She was led to the hallway where the doors were locked on either end but the shuttered windows were open to the courtyard down below. She was kept there to watch the body of her lover sway gently from the rope, to watch the body hang as a warning: *This is what happens to a thief. This is what happens to a man caught stealing from the prince.* She stared at her lover and at the white peaks of the high mountains in the distance. She'd come from the mountains once, she thought. She remembered the rugged slopes, her bare feet, child's feet, treading hard on stones as she ran down a slope toward a stream.

It was twilight while she watched. Between two worlds, neither light nor dark, the dusk in the valley before her pooled silvery and purple. She could see herself already as a ghost. Her hands in the silver gauze of twilight seemed to shimmer at their edges, skin blending with the coming dark, the coming dark merging with her skin. Already a ghost, she sighed, and moving quickly, she climbed to the sill of the window, and with a prayer on her lips, threw her body to the air, to the mountains, to the dusk, to her lover.

My story. My ghost dying for a lover.

In Anna's story, the girl—we called her Dev Kumari again; once we found the name it was difficult to believe another— was a maid, a maid from the hills, whose parents could not afford a dowry. She worked in the kitchen. She hardly ever left the kitchen, except sometimes to carry a tray up to the room where the concubines were kept, or to the room where the wives jealously brushed each other's scented hair.

She climbed dark steps up to these rooms. She carried silvered trays. There were other maids who waited at the chamber doors, who scolded her for her dirty face, her dirty feet. They walked in slippers, and slipped the slippers off when they entered the ladies' rooms. Dev Kumari smelled smoke sometimes when those doors cracked open. She smelled incense, myrrh and sandalwood and sage. She smelled deeper scents as well, carried in thick clouds of smoke and the whispering of water hissing through a pipe. Sometimes she heard laughter. Sometimes languorous singing. She would wait there by the door until the ladies' maids returned the trays to her, the food gone, the silver slopped with thickening lentils, tiny bits of meat or bone swimming in grease at the bottom of the bowls.

She didn't like walking through those palace halls. The darkness closed around her. There were always noises above her and below her, behind her and in front, but she was never certain of their source. Once she tripped and fell. A blessing: the dishes on the tray had already been emptied. But the plates and cups and bowls fell clattering to the ground, and in the stale, dark passageway she couldn't find the pieces of every scattered dish. Her knees were scraped. Her hands were caked with dust. She got back to the kitchen late and got a beating from the cook. Scattered dishes in the passageway. Bits of food for the palace rats to eat. She didn't sleep that night, groping along the passageway on her hands and knees, a candle stub and the tray beside her. It was nearly dawn when she thought she'd gotten everything. She was almost at the end of the corridor when she heard a voice, a man's voice singing, a drunken slurring singing, and before she could blow out the candle, there was the Rana prince, looking down at her where she huddled on the floor.

He raped her, standing, against the wall. She was a tiny thing, but even her muffled sobs were loud. He left her in the hall where another maid found her and sent her to the kitchen with a scolding. "That's what you get when you get in a prince's way," the cook said, seeing a red mark on her neck where the prince had locked his hand.

Three months later her stomach was swollen and her legs felt weak and she found she couldn't climb up steps quite as quickly as before. The cook looked long at her one afternoon. "If you're pregnant," she said, "you can expect to leave. I won't have a pregnant girl with no husband working in my kitchen."

This was the first she'd thought of being pregnant, but placing her hand on her belly she knew. Something was growing inside her. A child was growing. She beat on her stomach in anger and horror. A child was growing. She threw herself down on the floor and cried.

Her belly swelled and two months later the cook took another look at her and told her to pack her things. "I won't have you in here," she said. "I won't have a girl like you working for me."

"Let me stay," she begged. She couldn't return like this to her parents. "Let me stay." The cook told her she could sleep there one more night but that in the morning she'd be on her way.

"A girl like you," the cook said. "Be thankful for what I'm giving you."

Dev Kumari went that night back to the passageway. It was winter and the nights were cold and she shook in her cotton skirt and pushed a shuttered window open wide. She could see the stars from where she stood, the stars but not the mountains. She took one deep gulp of air and shut her eyes and threw herself down to the courtyard below. They found her in the morning, her body cold, her stomach frozen in its swell.

"That's the ghost that haunts us," Anna whispered.

I looked away from her. "Maybe so," I said. "But I'd rather it was love that killed her."

"I'd rather it was love as well."

"Then let's believe it was. Believe it for me."

She nodded. "Believe it for yourself," she said. "Love that kills rings true. Who it kills is something else entirely."

TWO DAYS LATER, almost three weeks after Anna had arrived, Danny was home again. She saw him first. The taxi pulled into the compound late on a Friday afternoon. I was napping in the bedroom. The spring had changed again. The evening breezes gave way to near-constant sweltering heat. The fan turned above my head. My eyes were shut, and my mind moved softly between sleep and waking, circling with the circling fan, a gentle, dreamy state.

The car's wheels moved slowly through my half dreams. *A carriage,* I thought; then, *no, a rusting taxi;* then, *maybe a carriage after all, a rusting carriage, a creaking carriage.* I lay on top of the covers, my cotton dress loose across my skin. Danny's footsteps on the stairs, bounding footsteps I think they must have been, became the crack of an ax through timber, of wood splitting, of tree trunks listing between strokes—one more tap of the ax and the tree would fall. I think I tossed. The listing tree trunk became a listing mast; the dress across my body, a sail that fluttered in the wind; the fan's wind, the sea's wind. And then his voice sounded through the door, his rich voice, his voice that draped my body like cloth of gold. I remember stretching, my arms reaching out wide as if to reach him, his voice so rich it still seemed a part of my dreams. *Rich as sunlight,* I remember thinking, *rich as clotted cream.* And then Anna's laugh, her joyful yelp of greeting. *There's a puppy out there,* I thought as I heard her scramble up.

There are moments between waking and sleep when a choice is made about which way to turn. How often, upon the first sign of waking, have I willed myself back to sleep? How often have I turned toward the downy gauze of afternoon dreams, rolled over on my belly, pressed my face into the pillow, and whispered, "Sleep," silently in my mind? I did this then. I heard Anna's voice, and I snuggled down on the bed, kept my eyes shut, concentrated on the fan that pushed the air around in warm and gentle circles, the laziness of it all steering me back toward my dreams. *A carriage now, draped in velvet. A small black dog, its tail wagging, running anxiously back and forth. Circles of air moving like circles of water.* I dreamed and sighed and continued dreaming, and Anna was with Danny first.

I'M NOT SURE how much longer I slept. I know I slept too long, because later that night, after Danny and I made love, I

lay next to him with my eyes wide open; even the act of
shutting my lids was a movement toward sleep greater than I
could manage. I tossed and turned that night, and once
Danny put out his hand and laid it, heavy, on my back. "Stop
kicking," he whispered thickly, "stop turning. Just try to
relax." He whispered that, and then he dropped off back to
sleep with his hand still on me like a weight. But there are
other reasons I know I slept too long, and one is that my
dreams got deeper, and as the afternoon heat grew denser in
the room, as Danny and Anna caught up alone outside the
bedroom door, my dreams moved from the light dreams of
drifting sleep to the nightmares of deep slumber.

I dreamed of Matthew falling. In my dream I saw him not
as the gangly boy I'd first met but as the man he was when I
saw him last. As the man he was when we loved. As the man
he was when we parted. In this dream I hovered above him
as before, but not from my bedroom window. Now I
watched him from the sky, from far away, so that when he ran
in circles around his house, a tall man running circles, I could
watch the circles all the way through. He raced as if he could
not stop. He raced as if he were not allowed to stop. And
then the borders of the lawn that hemmed the house in
changed—or I became aware of them, not having noticed
them before. They wavered and then dropped off. The house
stood alone on a hill, a hill like a mesa, a swath of emerald
grass that cut down in a sharp edge, cut down and down and
down, and even from my new perspective, hovering above at
untold heights, I could not see the bottom of those edges.

I could see him getting tired as he ran. His legs pumped
fast, but his chest seemed to heave, and his breath grew hard

and sharp and loud. I had no body in this dream, just the sight, just a vision. I could not reach out to him. I tried to raise my voice. I tried to scream, "Matthew, Matthew, Matthew," but I found I had no voice within this dream. What good would it have done if he could hear me? "Matthew, Matthew, Matthew. Come back to me," circled in my head and heart while I watched him run and run and run. "Come back to me. I'm sorry." And then he stopped.

He stopped and slid, his legs laid long before him, but what at first seemed a throwing of his body forward changed quickly to a clutching back, and his fingers, I saw his fingers grab at the earth, at the grass, and the lawn, the lawn was suddenly smooth as ice. "Matthew," I called silently, "come back," and then he was gone. And the house was still, as if he'd never been there, and I could no longer see the edges of the lawn, and if I hadn't been so sure in my heart of the terror I had felt and the terror I had watched him feel, I might have thought the house had always stood alone, in the middle of a grassy yard, the green a shade too bright, a yard that stretched to the ends of the earth.

I woke up then. A blackout must have started, because what woke me was a lack of breeze from the fan shutting off. The afternoon had turned to early night. I woke with a blanket of heat upon me, the weight of heat pressing down on my chest as if it were an iron. The room was full of shadows. It was that twilit moment, neither night nor day but moving always away from day, and I thought, on the bed, to control my panic, *If I just lie here until night comes, the heat will lift, it will lift away from me.* But still, I could not keep from moaning. And then I heard their voices, laughing, in the living room, and I was not sure yet who was laughing, just that there was a man and woman there and they were laughing and I could not move. I moaned. I swear I moaned. I moaned and thrashed but could not move off the bed. "Anna," I called, and "Matthew," but the words came out as no more than a moan. Then "Anna," I called again, and "Danny," and the heat pressed me there and I tried to call and tried to call until my eyes filled with water and tears streamed down my cheeks and washed down the hot skin on my throat.

And then I woke once more. And this time when I woke I saw that the fan was off from the blackout and the evening was hot and there were tears running down my neck, but I sat straight up and looked around and there was no mistaking the sleeping from the waking now. I woke with a throbbing of grief in my heart, with disbelief that the day had vanished while I slept. I woke with the terror of losing Matthew and the terror of losing myself, but I woke, I woke, and the room was the same room I'd lain down in. And the voices I heard, I knew these voices now—my husband's, my friend's! I wobbled to standing, my limbs weak from sleep, and stumbled in a sleepy zigzag across the floor. My arms were rough, and I noted in my sleepy mind that the pattern of the quilt had indented itself on my skin. Even as I noted this I thought, *Why am I noticing this? What does it matter?* But somehow it did matter and somehow it added to my stumbling, to the weakness in my wrist as I twisted the knob upon the door.

Then there they were. Sitting together on the couch. Anna had her knees bent, she always hugged her knees, and Danny leaned back against the cushions, his face still scruffy from the trek, his hair a dusty halo of curls. *They're beautiful,*

I thought briefly, *beautiful,* and they were, seated there, laughing in the dying light. He reached his hand out toward her ankle. It was large and easily wrapped itself around her narrow bone. And then they both turned and looked at me and the smiles changed slightly on their faces and I tried to smile, I tried to do something with my trembling lips, and I watched Danny's hand slide quickly away from Anna's skin.

THEY SAY THAT time changes according to one's state of mind. I cannot disagree. Time slowed down. It slowed to an excruciating, slow-paced, jerky limp. I counted days in my head. I counted hours. I counted minutes, and to count minutes it's difficult to keep from counting seconds. *Six days until they leave,* I counted. *Five days. Four.* They planned their trek well, poring over elevation maps, Anna counting the meters to passes and doing the conversions, Danny sitting by her side, his neck craned too, telling her where they would sleep, how many hours of walking they would do each day. Three weeks they would be gone. Three weeks through villages, through rough wilderness on foot, three weeks they would be walking. They went to trekking stores in Thamel, buying last-minute supplies. *Three hours they've been gone,* I'd count. *One hundred eighty minutes, one hundred eighty-one.*

Three days before they left I told them I was going too.

"You're what?" Danny said when I told him.

"I want to go too."

"You're crazy. You've never been in mountains like this in your life. That trek we did together was hard for you, and that was just the hills. You can't go."

"I want to come with you."

"Your boots are barely broken in. It's a three-week trek. You can't turn back. You can't come back early."

"My boots are fine. I'll be fine. I want to come."

"You can't. I don't have supplies for you, I don't have an extra porter for you, I don't have a permit for you, or a plane ticket, or even a good sleeping bag for you. You can't come."

"I want to."

"You can't."

Anna said nothing while Danny and I argued. She sat silent at the table, looking down. The map was open in front of her. Their route was highlighted with a yellow marker, their campsites marked with circles in blue pen. Her hand rested on the map, her finger frozen where she'd been counting ridges, imagining the elevations rise. I knew her—she was trying to visualize the whole thing. She was trying to see it all spreading out before her.

"I want to."

"You can't."

Anna sat with lowered eyes and finally, almost shaking, I ran crying from the room.

I WOULDN'T LET Danny fall asleep that night until he agreed that I could go. I went to bed first, and when he came in and lay down beside me I knew that he knew I was still awake. "What?" he finally said.

"I'm going."

"We've talked about this, Isabel. You can't."

"I have to."

"No, you don't. You can't."

I'm not sure what I finally said that changed his mind. I remember his lying beside me in the dark, his breathing heavy. He tossed while we argued, propping himself on his side, lying flat on his back, reaching out his hands to turn me toward him. I wouldn't look at him until he said yes. Maybe that is why he changed. Because I wouldn't look at him. Because I wouldn't turn. Eventually he asked me why I wanted to go.

"I want to be with you. I'm tired of being left behind."

He sighed. "This is my work. I'm doing my job."

"You're leaving me behind."

"Why haven't you wanted to come before?"

"I don't know. I didn't feel this way before."

He touched my arm. "Would you look at me?"

"No," I said. "No, I won't."

It was late. I hoped Anna was asleep in the living room. I wondered what they'd stayed up so late discussing—was it me? Did they ever talk about me? Did they ever talk about each other? Their parting was because of circumstances, not the end of their desire for each other, and I wondered if they talked about the parting, if they voiced the questions they must still have. I wondered if they'd lain together in New York, side by side in Anna's bed, and felt my presence alone behind the door. I wondered if Danny could feel her presence now even as he tossed in the bed beside me. What did he think of all of this? What did he think, and why was I so afraid to ask?

"Is it Anna?" he whispered. His voice was like a feather, like a shiver.

"I don't know."

"If it's Anna, that's a stupid reason. It's a three-week trek. We're climbing to over sixteen thousand feet. Anna's not a reason to come."

"Why do I have to have a reason?"

"Why do you want to come?"

I could picture myself walking. I could picture myself walking on a narrow trail with steep mountains rising up beside me. I could picture green valleys and terraced slopes and smoky teahouses that served milk tea in cracked glass cups. I pictured Danny walking ahead of me that first time we left the valley, the muscles moving in his legs, his arms swinging, the moment when he stopped and looked back at me, smiling, opening his arms wide as if in welcome; I thought of him walking ahead of me and how I thought I could follow him forever and be happy as I followed. And then I thought of Anna.

"I want to go to be with you," I whispered. "I just want to be with you."

I felt his lips upon me then, on my shoulder, on my throat. His lips were warm and only when he kissed my lips did I feel a dampness on my cheek and realize that he must be crying. We made love then, quietly, and still I can feel the sweep of his hand across my breasts, across my hips, can feel him taking my measure from head to toe. His tears were sticky on my skin but his hands were warm and I moaned and hushed my moans—Anna was just a door away. I half hoped that she could hear me.

"Okay," he whispered just before he fell asleep. "Okay. You'll come with us."

I pressed his hand against my cheek and then against my heart. It was only after he'd fallen asleep, after his breath had evened out, had turned into a gentle, constant murmur, that I reminded myself about his tears. What was it that I'd said that made him cry? *I want to go to be with you. I want to be with you.* Who had he been crying for? For himself? For Anna? For me? I held his hand against my face and listened to his breathing.

Part Four

CHAPTER EIGHTEEN

*T*hree days later we climbed down from the plane in Tumlingtar, a tiny village in eastern Nepal above the Arun River. We flew from Kathmandu in the early afternoon, and the day was still hot when the plane touched down. Eight of us climbed out, shaking, from the rickety plane: Melissa and Saul, a married couple in early middle age; two men, Gordon, in his early fifties, and Bob, in his late thirties; Danny, Anna, and I; and Pemba, as the guide. Ten porters met us there, one of whom doubled as head cook. We were to trek to Pang-pema, to the frozen north side of Kangchenjunga, and from there down to Taplejung and the flight home. Three weeks in the mountains. Three weeks, camping most of the way. The porters would carry food and tents and fuel and our packs. We would each have a water bottle and a day pack.

A scattering of houses lay at the side of a grass-covered landing strip in Tumlingtar. The heat of that deep valley settled over us like fog as we climbed unsteadily from the small airplane. There was *daal bhat* for dinner, lentils in a thin sauce and rice, and large bottles of warm beer and small bottles of Coca-Cola. We had dinner at a teahouse, the doors open to the airstrip. The light cast from the free-hanging light bulbs that dangled from the ceiling was thinner, somehow, than electric light should be. A slight breeze blew, stirring the heat where it settled but doing nothing to get rid of it. We toasted the days ahead, and I wondered where the porters were, who they ate with, and Pemba said they'd sleep and eat that night at the inn next door.

Danny and I had a room on the second floor of the teahouse, at the top of a steep staircase. Our beds were wooden platforms with lumpy cushions laid on them as mattresses. A candle flickered on the table between the beds. The walls were thin and we could hear the only other couple, Saul and Melissa, rustling in the room next to ours. "I feel like I'm inside a fairy-tale cottage," I whispered to Danny. Was that excitement ringing in my voice, in the quick rush of words? "I feel like I'm inside a dream."

He smiled. He lay on top of his sleeping bag and shifted in the heat. A dog barked in the distance. There were dogs everywhere in this country, it seemed. Another dog echoed the first bark, this one closer. I heard the sound of doors closing downstairs, of a lock turning, of the innkeeper's soft voice below. The scent of fire smoke drifted up and I leaned over and blew our candle out. Danny whispered, "Good night."

I hugged myself in the dark, hugged myself with pleasure

at the thought of falling asleep in this small room in this tiny airport town, tucked away to sleep to the sound of my husband's breathing. "Good night," I whispered back. I could see the moon through the open window, a thin crescent at the edge of the field. Danny tossed in the heat on top of his sleeping bag. I fell asleep wishing that we could stay there for days, sleep there for nights and nights and nights without moving. I'm sure I smiled as I slept. I'm sure that even in my dreams I avoided the thought of the mountains that lay ahead.

That first night was short. When I woke in the morning I could hardly believe I had fallen asleep at all.

Our trek began at dawn. We each drank a glass of tea in the thin breaking light. The town was misty and the air already hot. The porters had gone ahead, bundling our packs inside their baskets as soon as we brought them down. "It's going to be a hot one," Danny said. I sipped the steaming, milky tea. I could see beads of sweat where they formed above his eyebrows. "We walk to Chainpur today. We climb three thousand feet. It will be a rough day, but by tomorrow afternoon we should be getting into cooler territory." I placed a hand upon my own forehead and when I pulled it away the skin was damp and sticky and I realized I too had begun to sweat.

We walked south out of town in a line. The river lay to our right. The dirt path we followed moved through the grass as if across an open field. Then suddenly the grass closed in, tangled weeds and rushes all around, and though we passed by a house here and there, when the airstrip vanished behind us it was difficult to believe it had ever been there. In twenty minutes the path forked. We moved downward, first, down to a valley where the Sabhaaya Khola and Hewa Khola rivers meet, and then across the waters and up, up into the east. We had not been walking an hour when my calves began to burn and my shirt was wet against my back and the still air became so heavy that I felt it like an extra weight on my shoulders.

We climbed up through a forest. Pemba walked first. Anna and Melissa walked behind him, Anna turning her head to Melissa from time to time and laughing. Her laugh was like water through the silvery forest light. Saul walked behind Melissa, and behind him was Danny and then Gordon and then Bob. I walked last. I walked slowest. I kept time to my breathing. My legs moved. My lungs filled. My ribs ached where a cramp was forming. The sun was higher in the sky now, and the world we walked through at times was a tropical world and at times was a world that whispered momentarily of cooler mountain air. Now the mountains peeked from behind corners, Makalu and Chamlang, snow-covered, to the north and west. It made me gasp to see their frozen, jagged slopes here amid this verdant green, amid thatched houses and farms and air that was almost too hot to breathe.

We reached Luwakot by mid-morning. By the time I struggled over the ridge, panting and near tears, the rest of the group was seated at tables at the teashop. Pemba had passed out packets of sweet arrowroot biscuits, and there were cups of tea on the table. It took me time to catch my breath, there on that ridge, and the sweat on my back cooled, and when I sat down I thought I would not be able to stand again. Two thousand feet above where we'd started, and the rest of the day would be spent ascending as well.

"Are you okay?" Danny asked me.

I looked around. I coughed. I wiped my hand across my brow and vowed to become a faster walker.

"I'm fine," I said. "Just getting used to it."

"You'll tell me if you're not okay?"

"I'm fine." I cleared my throat. "I'm fine."

After half an hour the group was off again. Another climb. Kharaang waited in an hour, Kharaang and lunch. My stomach growled. My breath came out in gasps. I felt a hand on my back and turned. Anna stood beside me.

"You'll be fine, Isabel. You'll be fine in a day or two. Don't worry."

She was lovely there with the sun behind her, her black hair spilling out of a high ponytail in silken strands around her face. I nodded. She touched her hand to my cheek.

"Look around," she said. "This is why we're here."

And it was true. As we climbed higher, as we followed the ridge, then crossed back and forth and back and forth to continue the ascent, the world opened up at times. The views of the distant mountains broadened and closed, broadened and closed, and the country seemed a dizzying and glorious place.

But the climb. It was only in moments few and far between that I could lift my eyes from the path and look out. Once I'd breathed in, it was all I could do to tell myself to breathe out again. My lungs hurt so much that at times I was certain I was drowning in the hot, watery air. I followed Gordon's ankles. I watched the muscles in his calves stretch and flex and stretch and flex, and I breathed with each footstep and could not stop thinking, *This is the first day, it's only the first day,* and then I thought that I could barely keep myself from sitting down and sinking to the earth.

In another hour we reached Kharaang, where three of the porters were waiting for us with lunch. They squatted on the ground, cigarettes in their hands. They barely looked at us and when they did they shook their heads from side to side. We ate *daal bhat.* "*Daal bhat* at every meal," Danny said. I wondered if he was serious. The rice was heaped up high on plates, the lentils thin and salty. We ate with our fingers, the way the porters ate, lifting up large, sticky chunks of rice and popping them in our mouths. I shivered in the air. It was cool now. We were as high as we would go that day. Chainpur, where we'd sleep, was just an hour and a half away, perched upon a ridge crest at the same height as where we'd stopped. The green hills below to the south and west looked like the folds of a rumpled skirt. I could not believe that we had climbed out of them.

The food was good. The rice, wet with lentils, soft on my lips and tongue, filled my belly, and I thought I could sit there for hours eating rice. *Three weeks of this,* I thought, *three weeks.* This was nothing like the trek that Danny and I had done what seemed so long ago. Already it seemed we'd climbed into the sky. The air smelled faintly of smoke, of firewood burning. Three boys ran toward us and called out, "Hello, hello, *namaste.*" They circled around us, giggling, and then ran away, disappearing behind a turn in the path. I lifted my water bottle to my lips and drank the medicinal, orange-tinted water. "*Namaste,*" I heard again, and the boys were back. They followed us like darting flies after that, followed us as we gathered up our things. They trailed behind us, laughing and calling, for almost an hour.

It was late afternoon when we reached Chainpur. I was not the only one who was tired. We walked in as if we were just off a caravan through the desert, dusty, sure of the fact that we had conquered something, and tired—radiantly tired. I could see that Melissa walked slowly, and Gordon, ahead of me, stumbled once and almost fell upon the cobbled streets of that high town. He swayed to the left. His day pack slipped fast toward the ground, and I reached forward to catch his elbow, but then he caught himself, pushed his left foot out and righted his balance. "Whoa," he said, then glanced quickly over his shoulder to see if anyone had noticed. I shifted my gaze down to the path and didn't look up until I was certain he had turned around.

We came to a rest in what seemed the center of the town. Pemba spoke in quick Nepali with the owner of the largest inn, then nodded his head at the porters. They waited, crouching in the shade, their baskets propped against a wall. When he nodded they sighed and hoisted the baskets to their backs. But they were done for the day as well. They carried the baskets into the inn and emptied them so that our packs were scattered across the floor. Then they sighed again and vanished quickly. I wondered where they'd sleep, but I didn't ask this time.

The inn had blue shutters on the windows. The ceilings were low when we climbed up to the second floor, but the rooms were lit with the warm glow of the setting sun. I sat down on a bed and fumbled at my boot strings. "Tired?" Danny asked. His smile was kind.

"Yes," I said. "I could sit down for days." My feet were damp with perspiration, dented and grooved where the toes had pressed against the boots. Danny sat down beside me and took my feet in his hands. He rubbed them and pulled at them until they were soft once more.

"Stay there," he said. "Lie down. I'll come and get you when it's time for dinner."

I nodded. He slipped back downstairs. I fell asleep with the low sun shining in on me and when I woke again it was almost dark.

I woke disoriented. I woke with aching limbs. The shutters were open, but dusk had settled and I could not see down to the street below. I thought for a moment that I'd slept an entire day and into the next night, or that it was almost dawn. By the time I pulled my reeling mind back in, I found that I was shaking. I tried to bend a leg. I could barely lift it. I could barely curl my toes.

When my eyes grew used to the light, I stood up shakily and hobbled to the stairs. Voices rose from down below. I heard Anna ask a muted question. I heard Melissa's laughing answer. "Two years ago," she said. "Two years last December. The second time for both of us."

"How old were you with the first?" I pictured Anna leaning forward, a smile playing on her lips, her dark hair pulled back from her face. I always thought her smiles encouraged intimacy.

"Young," Melissa said. "Too young."

"Much, much too young," Saul called out. He must have been sitting across the room. His voice was softer than the others and seemed to come across a distance. I tried to picture the room below, and couldn't quite grasp the dimensions. What kind of tables did they sit at? What was the light like there? A glow rose from below the stairs, a reddish glow, and I thought there must be candles lit, that the room must have very dark corners and rich pools of light. "I was twenty-two when I got married first. Melissa was twenty-five. We both were divorced by the time we were thirty. We met each other just after that. Thank God we both came to our senses."

I gritted my teeth. My legs ached—they ached so much it surprised me they would bend at all. I stumbled down the steps. Someone called out, "Here she is." I thought it was Bob, though the timbre of each voice was still not completely recognizable. I could feel my face color. It took a moment to get used to the change in light. The doors of the inn were open to the street, so that one whole side appeared to have no wall. I could see that traces of the sun were still visible in the sky, but I could see too that darkness was closing in fast. A woman with strong cheekbones and almond eyes passed out cups of tea. A large gold disk pierced her left nostril and glittered in the candlelight. Anna sat with her back against a wall, her knees bent to her chin, her feet propped up on the bench she was sitting on. Melissa sat beside her.

"Hey, sleepyhead," Anna called. I rubbed my eyes. "Did you get a good rest?"

I nodded. My mouth was dry. *My legs,* I thought. *Oh, my legs.* "What time is it?" I said.

"Seven o'clock. You're just in time for supper."

It took me a moment to locate Danny. He stood at the doorway, stretched his arms out, and stepped down into the street. He turned black and flat against the light behind him. His back was to us. I wondered if he'd been this quiet since I fell asleep, if he sat so quietly always on a trek. He walked out into the street, and for a moment disappeared. A man passed, stopped, stared in at us, then moved by.

Dinner was *daal bhat* again. The plates we ate off of were metal. I sat on a bench, squeezed in between Gordon and Bob. Anna sat with Melissa and Saul. Danny and Pemba sat alone together, a map spread out between them. I kept glancing over my shoulder all through dinner, wondering what it was they talked of. The *daal* was salty. The fried greens that accompanied the meal were bitter and swam in grease. Gordon bought a bottle of beer and poured some for me and Bob. "To the first night," he said. I raised my glass and took a sip. It was warm and as thin as water. "Yes, to the first night," Bob said.

"Hear, hear," Melissa and Saul called out, and opened their own bottle.

My legs feel like wood, I thought. I forced a smile. "Hear, hear," I said. "Hear, hear," I took another sip. *Here, here,* I thought, and now my smile was real. *I'm really here.*

After dinner Danny asked us to gather round. "There are some things we need to talk about," he said. His voice was low, and watching him stand up, I was proud that he was our leader, that we were in his charge. "We're going high into the mountains. They're higher than mountains back home. You all know that. I want to make sure we all know what to be careful of.

"It's easy to get sick out here. You can't drink any water, ever, without treating it, just like in Kathmandu. There's always someone up above you—the water is never clean, no matter what it looks like. We have medicine with us, but we don't want you to get sick. There are no roads anywhere we're going, no roads to take you home if you do get sick. The only way out is by helicopter or to be carried out. You break a leg, we carry you. You break an arm, you walk.

"But more than that, more than the water or anything else, I want to make sure you understand about the altitudes we'll be gaining. Pangpema lies at over sixteen thousand feet. We'll be ascending slowly, but altitude sickness can still hit any one of you. Most times, when someone gets sick, they get too confused to notice it themselves. You have to watch out for each other. People die out here from altitude sickness. Watch for shortness of breath. Watch for headaches. Watch for vomiting and loss of coordination. If I notice these signs at altitude in any one of you, you'll descend with me immediately. I'm not kidding." His voice was gruff. "If any of you has these signs at any point on the trek, at any time of day or night, we'll go down at once."

We nodded. We shook our heads and vowed to watch out for one another. I wondered if Danny gave this speech on every trek. When he was finished, the lightness of the night was gone. *Who has he marked for sickness? Who has he pictured ill?* I wondered. I looked across the room at the faces of these fellow travelers. I wondered what it would mean to watch out for one another.

I couldn't sleep that night. The nap had done me in. I lay on top of my sleeping bag and the nylon fabric stuck to me. The night still warm despite the climb, the bag catching on my legs each time I moved. I tossed and tossed and Danny once raised his head and whispered, "Shh." I opened my eyes and stared at the shadowed ceiling, at the beams that ran across it, cracked and dark. My legs ached, my back ached, and I could not find a position in which to stop the throbbing pain. My heart thrummed. My mind spun. I tried to imagine the days ahead. *Three weeks,* I thought, *three weeks,* and felt a sudden stab of loneliness, my heart aching along with my legs. I heard a scampering close by, and when I shut my eyes I was certain that mice ran back and forth across the floor. Danny's breathing in the bed beside me was even. He breathed out and then paused; breathed in and paused. His breath was like the rocking of a ship, back and forth across the waves. I longed for sleep. I longed to dream. I longed for the aching in my heart to ease.

CHAPTER NINETEEN

*W*e spent the next three days climbing higher into the mountains. My calves were on fire the second day; they were as hard as wood by the third. There was so much to look at—each time we entered a new village it seemed we had entered a new world as well. Children ran after us for long stretches along the winding trails. Women and men passed by with large loads on their backs fastened with rope pulled tight across their foreheads. It looked, sometimes, as though they were carrying whole houses on their backs. I walked with only a day pack and a water bottle, and watched with open mouth as men and women, taking tiny steps, moved quickly up the slopes ahead of me.

This was not wilderness that we walked through, despite the fact that there were no roads for cars. These paths *were* roads, roads that formed a net from village to village, and crested at the top of ridges where square stone walls sat around pipal trees to prop a heavy pack upon and rest for a moment in the shade. There was planning in these roads, I thought as I panted and moaned up hills. Someone thought about this. Someone placed stone upon stone to form a shaded seat; someone cut steps from the bottom of the valley to the top of the ridge before any paths were formed.

We walked through forests of rhododendron. They grew like trees, not like the bushes that edged my parents' house back home. The light in those rhododendron forests glowed like gems: gold filtered through brilliant red trumpeting blossoms, dazzling red and pink and white. I could feel that light as it dappled my skin. I opened my mouth in the glow, breathed in deeply, as if I could drink in the brilliant colors and the buzzing of bees. In the shade of the forest the warmth of that colored light was welcome. Each time we passed into a grove of trees I forgot the weight of the heavy air, forgot the sweat that lay thick on my neck. I gathered blossoms to my face and ran my fingers in the grooves of long, thick, waxy leaves.

A woman walked past me once on the trail, a baby tied across her chest, a basket hanging down her back from a strap that ran across her forehead. Her head was tilted down. The basket was filled with jugs of water. She moved slowly, but her steady motion carried her up the path faster than my lighter steps took me. We had just passed through a flowering forest and were back out now under the heat of the direct sun. I thought my head would explode from the heat and I stopped often to take in breath in short, quick gasps.

She moved slowly straight upward and when we came to the top of the hill I could see her far away, moving up the twisting path of the next inevitable ascent.

We reached Gupha Pokhari on the afternoon of the fourth day, a lake nestled on the far side of a ridge. The lake lay still as ice, not a ripple moving across its flat surface. We'd walked for days through the dips and crests of those hills, the intricate, tight windings up and down and around, and now, after days of twisting, turning, rising slopes, the flat mirrored expanse of that water seemed a miracle. I stumbled over the rock wall that hid the lake, and gasped at the sight of water. Silent. Cold. A cluster of hotels lay at the far side of the lake. Smoke glazed the sky where chimneys peeked from hotel roofs. The mountains rose white in the distance. From where I stood it looked as though they rose directly from the water, and I thought we'd found a paradise. *This is it,* I thought. *This is where we should stay.* The mountains above the water, the mountains reflected in the water—*It's too much for this earth,* I thought.

We camped that night on the flat ground beside the lake. Our tents were arranged in a circle. The sky was clear, and after the sun set on the distant slopes of the Kumbu range to the west—the white snow turning orange, then pink and then purple—the blackness of the clear sky looked thick as shadowed moss, the stars as bright as glinting ice. I remember laying out our sleeping bags and thinking how small the tent looked, remember imagining sleeping beside my husband in that shelter. Of the eight of us, only Anna and Pemba slept in tents alone. Melissa and Saul, Bob and Gordon, Danny and I—we all fitted neatly into pairs. Had I not been there,

Pemba and Danny would have been tentmates, I thought. And then I caught myself as I wondered—had I not been there, would Anna really have slept alone? I caught myself and looked at the clean, calm water and told my mind to remember the water and calm itself as well.

That night was cold. We camped by the lake where the foothills crested and the air was thin. The stars reflected on the lake. We clustered round the kerosene stove and waited for water for our tea. I had pulled mittens from my bag, and now, sitting on a rock, an itchy wool hat pulled down over my ears, my hands swathed, I felt like a sexless child.

"Up here in these mountains it's hard to believe that a city like Kathmandu exists," Saul said. He and Melissa sat together to my right, and I looked at them and nodded my head. The stove cast only a small circle of light, and their faces, even so close, were hidden deep in shadow.

"I don't think I believed it, that there weren't any roads." Bob's voice was low, and it was sometimes difficult to know if he was joking. "Or maybe I believed it, but didn't have a sense of what it meant. No roads, no cars, only feet to get you where you need to go. I'm still not sure if I believe it."

I laughed because I felt I should. Most of me was watching my husband where he sat beside Anna across the fire.

They'd walked all day together, I was sure of it. More than anything, this was why I cursed my lack of speed and strength. Pemba walked at the back of the group and Danny walked in front. He led the rest of us—Anna kept pace beside him. What were their private conversations, as they moved across hills and valleys, up slopes and down, up and down, up and down? Did they speak? Did they point out sights? Did they laugh together and then forget to show the rest of us what they'd laughed at when we, panting, worn, arrived? Did he hold her arm to steady her when they walked on unstable ground? Did she fling her hand up when she stumbled—if she stumbled; did she ever stumble?—and laugh and end up with it curled around his neck? *They must create an entire world together as they walk,* I thought, *an entire world without me.* Anna's face was lit by the end of the days, and her skin glowed.

Pemba handed me a glass of tea. His cheekbones jutted high. His eyes were warm. "We walk almost all day downhill tomorrow," he said. "We'll sleep quite low tomorrow night in Gorja. Even more beautiful views in Gorja. And also a view of the road at Taplejung." He paused, then said, "If you're too tired there, you can leave, you know." His voice was kind.

Danny had told me before we set out about this break in the route. "You can come," he'd said, "but you have to decide at Gorja if you can keep going. If not, we'll send you from there to Taplejung, and a bus back to Kathmandu. The route we'll take from Gupha Pokhari is one day down and then straight up for days, and then we'll be at high altitudes for the bulk of the trek after that. I can't have you slowing us down. These people paid a lot of money to come here. I can't have you changing the trip for them."

I'd nodded then. I'd said I understood.

I would be lying if I did not admit I was relieved at this possibility of early return. For the past four days, climbing up those endless slopes, those endless slopes cut like steps, I eased myself by dreaming of a bus ride home. *Home,* I whispered like an incantation, *home,* and for the first time realized that when I thought of home, I thought of our net-covered bed in the palace. I thought of shutters opening to the balcony, and Mr. Rana downstairs with tea. I pictured myself alone on the bus, deep gullies beneath its tires as we curved along mountain roads. I thought of my face pressed against the window, watching the world move by, and the thought comforted me. Now, on this clear night, I looked back at Pemba, his brown eyes kind, his dark hair creeping out from beneath his hat, and nodded.

Danny came to bed late that night. He settled down inside his sleeping bag. The tent grew warm with the heat of another person. His breathing evened out, fell heavier, and when I was certain that he slept I rolled over and looked at him. He slept on his back. Just his face was visible above the quilted padding of the bag. His beard was coming in in patches. Beneath the stubble his cheeks were thin. I wanted to touch him then, to draw my hand out from the warmth of my own sleeping bag and run it over the hills and valleys of his face. "I trust you," I whispered. "I trust you." He sighed. He shook his head slightly in his sleep. I listened for sounds outside, but the world beyond the tent seemed frozen. I reached my hand and touched his face. His skin was warm. He shook his head again in his sleep and smiled. Then he shifted so that his head was turned away.

IN THE MORNING, a dusting of snow covered the ground. Tea was waiting when we woke and stumbled as a group from out of our tents. The porters sat by the stove, their hands wrapped in tattered gloves. I had eyes only for the tea and the circle round the kerosene stove when I made my way from the tent, but I heard Melissa's voice say, "Look," and when I raised my eyes there was Kangchenjunga to the east in the clear morning light before any dust was raised, white like a bride with her veil drawn down, white like a blizzard frozen in its motion. We climbed to our feet and stood and stared. This was where we were going. This mountain was our goal. The whiteness made me want to sob. I felt an arm slip through mine, and there was Anna beside me, sleep still in the corners of her eyes, a cup of tea in her free hand.

"She's beautiful," Anna said. "Can you believe we're here?"

I shook my head. I couldn't believe, not with that mountain so bright in front of me—I couldn't believe that this was me, that I was here, beside a lake at the far side of a ridge, giddy in the lightness of the air. The mountain glittered with the frenzy of a mirage, already growing hazy with the first heat of the day.

"I can't stop thinking about Matthew," Anna said. "Sometimes I think that walking these trails is like a prayer for him."

I looked at her. Her eyes were fastened on the mountain. Her lips quivered slightly, then raised to form a smile. My heart melted suddenly toward her then, and I pulled my arm tight where hers ran through its crook.

"I know he can hear you thinking that," I said. "I know he can hear himself in your thoughts."

"Do you think about him too?"

"Yes," I said. "Yes, I think about him. I dream about him. I dream about him often."

She leaned her head on my shoulder. I reached a mittened hand up and touched her face.

"Girls!" we heard Danny's voice call out. "Enough of the mountain. Time to take your tents down. Time to get a move on."

Was it my imagination, or did her face harden as she whirled round? When I saw her next, her day pack was on her back, and her hair was tied neatly in a braid. The flecks of sleep had vanished from her eyes, and her face was scrubbed clean. I looked back at the lake as we moved over the ridge to begin the descent to Gorja, and it lay unrippled behind us in the early morning light. *The lake's the same whether we're here or not,* I thought. The ridge crest beyond the lake was topped with small stone cairns. From there the trail dropped down and down and down. I took a breath and followed the path and whispered good-bye to the silent lake, the perfect view of the mountain looming like a vision, the cold, clean morning air. I took a breath and began to climb back down into the tropics, back into the hot, wet air, back to the earth below.

I DIDN'T LEAVE in Gorja. That day was a whole day of climbing down. Now my lungs stopped hurting and my thighs began to burn. Danny dropped back to walk with me. "Lace your boots as tight as you can," he said. "Try to keep your toes from slipping to the bottom of the boot. Tense your thighs. Bend your knees." It was a relief, after days of walking up, to head down again, but the thought of losing all that height only to make it up again in the days to follow almost made me sit down and refuse to move.

I meant to leave in Gorja. I dreamed of walking down across the Tamur Khola valley, parting ways from the group where the paths diverged, and climbing up again, alone, to Taplejung. I dreamed of the sound of buses pulling away from that town, the rumble of diesel engines, the furious honking of horns. I dreamed of the mountains at my back. Walking down through rhododendron forests that day, where bees buzzed and clustered flowers looked like bundled ribbons in a young girl's hair, I dreamed of sitting on a bus, of the cramped and narrow seats, of tattered vinyl sticking to my skin. *Back to the city,* I thought. *Back to the city, back to my bed.* I was bursting with the news when I reached the camp, but when I got there and found the circle of erected tents, I couldn't find Anna, and then when I looked for Danny, I discovered that he was missing too.

He belonged to Anna first, I thought, but I could not sit still knowing that they were alone somewhere together. I could not keep my fingers from shaking long enough to take my boots off. I could not mop the sweat from off my brow. I could not look up at Kangchenjunga, mysteriously at our backs now—it followed us, I swear; it tracked us even while we thought it was our daily effort that drew us nearer to its icy slopes. I could not eat, I could not think, I could not leave. Most of all I could not leave.

They came back eventually—of course they did. They came back laughing about a villager they'd met, an old woman who had taken Anna's hand and pulled her inside her house. They'd sat by the fire and drunk salted butter tea. "It was horrible," Anna said, laughing, "like drinking fatty brine." They'd sat on carpeted beds in that smoky one-room house, and after the tea they drank *chang,* home-brewed beer, and I pictured the woman asking if they were married, and Anna looking at Danny and blushing and the two of them pretending for the moment that they were. Of course I could not leave.

"He's my husband, you know," I said softly to Anna that night after the sun had set on the slopes of Kangchenjunga and we sat bundled side by side. I thought at first she had not heard me. She was staring out across the river valley far below, across what we could still see of the valley as the night closed in. We sat in silence for what seemed a very long time.

"I can't forget that for a moment," she said, finally. "I try very hard to forget it, but I can't seem to keep it from my mind."

It was a relief of sorts, then, to hear her speak of it.

"He was mine first," she said. I could smell the sour home-brewed beer on her breath. "I try to understand. I try to think you two were meant for each other, that I was just your way of meeting, but I cannot work it out. I cannot think that he was meant for you." She laughed. There were many timbres to her laugh. I'd always loved to hear it. Now I turned away.

"He won't leave me," I said. "He won't leave me here, in this strange land, among these mountains. I do not doubt him. He won't leave."

"We'll see," she said. Her voice was low. I had to lean to hear it.

I could not leave then. Of course I could not leave.

CHAPTER TWENTY

It was one more day down after that, across the Tamur Khola, and then five days up again to Ghunsa. I grew stronger as we went along. I walked behind Gordon, then Gordon fell back and I walked behind Melissa, and then Melissa fell back and I walked behind Saul. My strength came from anger. Always just far enough away so that I could not see them clearly and could not reach them, Danny and Anna walked together. After Pemba they were the fastest of the group, the most agile, the two most suited to these mountains. But Pemba, who could have joined them in the race ahead, took his time, moving forward, dropping back, making idle conversation along the trail. And it was Pemba's hand upon my shoulder that brought me at times back inside myself.

Why didn't I speak to Danny then about my fears? I cannot say. Perhaps I did not want him to see that weakness. Perhaps I did not want to admit to him why it really was that I was there.

We rose steadily with the Tamur Khola rushing farther and farther below us to our right. We rose through oak and rhododendron forests and thatched-roof towns to higher villages where the houses were made of stone and the roofs were flat, where worn and tattered prayer flags hung on great poles at the village entrances and a language closer to Tibetan than Nepali was spoken. We passed waterfalls. We crossed and recrossed the river on rope bridges. The Tamur Khola dropped down more than a thousand feet below. The sun shone hot upon us, heavy and unyielding. We kept our eyes on our feet as we walked, and I, at least, prayed for balance.

In Phole, on the morning of the tenth day, Pemba arranged a visit for us to the *gomba,* the Buddhist monastery at the outskirts of the town. The walls were dark with smoke from butter lamps. The tapestries were torn. The air was thick with incense. The lama, an ancient, shrunken man whose long gray beard reached almost to his waist, sat and nodded as we stepped inside. He cradled a tiny dog in his lap, the dog's fur tangled in the maroon robes. Pemba knelt in front of him, a white scarf held forward in his hands. The lama lifted the scarf from Pemba's outstretched arms, placed it over Pemba's neck, and struck him lightly on the head with a rosary made of bone. We bowed too, awkwardly, and then we left. We had no white scarves of our own to offer. We ate our lunch, and gathered up our things for the trek. A short day lay ahead. In two hours we'd reach Ghunsa.

We passed through more forests then, larch and juniper and rhododendron, the high air dry, the fierce sun filtered through the leaves. The air was thin. We did not dip below ten thousand feet now, and even the Ghunsa Khola beside us to our left, a river wide and icy blue, seemed to move at a slow pace. It wasn't true that it was slow—that river was as wild as any. "Keep your eyes on the trail," Pemba called back, and when I rested my eyes for a moment on the river it was as if I were carried with the water's wild rush in a torrent down the mountain. When we came to a rope bridge that crossed the river, the icy water swirled far below. Melissa went ahead of me. I saw her fingers clutch at the rope rails, her hands turning white from the squeezing pressure. She stopped halfway across. The bridge was empty in front of her where Saul had moved quickly on. Gordon pressed close behind me. Melissa couldn't move. The churning water screamed. I raised my hand, put it on her shoulder. She seemed to wake. "Just take one step," I said. I'm not sure if she heard—the river was that loud. But she took a step, and then another, and following slowly behind her, focusing on her movement forward, I didn't have time to notice if I myself was frightened. I just watched her neck, her straight blond hair where it escaped from beneath a baseball cap, just watched her neck and the banks of the river drawing closer in behind it.

Ghunsa lay ten minutes beyond the river, a spread-out village of flat-roofed wooden houses. Potato fields lay outside the village, and beyond the fields the forest stood thick. The high mountain air was cool. Smoke rose above the houses. Another *gomba* lay just at the edge of town. I heard a jangling of bells, and there beyond the town were yaks, giant, rugged, long-haired cattle, their herder small beside them.

The porters had set up the tents at the foot of the hill on which the *gomba* stood. The tents arranged in a ring looked like a kind of home by now, a ring of covered wagons. I looked forward to the day of rest that awaited us. Ghunsa marked the halfway point of the trek. From here we'd continue toward Pangpema, the base camp for northern ascents of Kangchenjunga. The world around us opened up and stretched out like a desert. Even the forests seemed dry.

The villagers stayed away from us for the most part. Many of the men, Pemba told us, were at higher altitudes with the yaks. The lama of the *gomba* lived a solitary life, refusing to receive visitors. The air lay still. The wind, bitter in winter, had eased off now in spring. The town seemed a silent place. I drank tea quickly, then retreated to my tent. For the first time since we'd started there seemed time to rest. I loosened my sleeping bag from the roll and spread it out. I lay down and shut my eyes. Danny's voice was loud outside, and when he unzipped the tent and crawled inside as well I stretched my arms out wide to him. "Lie down with me," I said, my eyes still closed.

I felt his breath upon my face. I felt the warmth of his skin as he drew near. I felt him leaning his face in close to mine. "Lazybones," he said. His voice licked at my ear. "Lazybones, it's not everyone who can lie down in the middle of the day. I'm working here. I can't just collapse inside my tent." I felt his breath on my face, and then he disappeared.

They say it's hard to sleep at altitude, but they say less about the dreaming queasiness it means to stay awake. I don't know how long I lay there, but I could feel the earth beneath me spin. When I finally roused myself, the edges of my hands were cold and the late morning had passed into early afternoon. I stumbled out through the tent flap. The camp was empty. The air was clear. The valley rising up beyond the village appeared to rise up endlessly: dry, enormous, wild, strewn with rocks. Smoke drifted from the village. A slight breeze blew. I tied my hair back in a braid and pulled my mittens on.

I walked beyond our camp. I walked out into that wild valley. I saw a yak far off, and then another, each with its horns tied with red ribbon. It was like the moon at the bottom of that valley, the barren moon, but forests covered the slopes that rose up at its sides. A sluggish stream, a river tributary, ran through the valley, the water an icier shade of blue than the sky. The earth seemed flat to me, somehow, flat despite the steep inclines to the sides, the white-peaked mountains up ahead. I turned around when I'd walked for ten minutes or so, and the camp had vanished. The wind picked up and unraveled my braid. Cool air blew up through my sleeves where they gaped open at the wrists. I sat down on a large rock and watched the world. Alone. I liked the cold air. I liked the wide valley. I liked the silence and the vastness.

I don't know how long I sat there. There was nothing to rush back for. It was a day to rest, *to rest*. I leaned against the back of the rock. My stomach felt giddy in a way that has always meant expectation. When I shut my eyes for a moment and opened them again, there was Anna, staring at me from beside the water, and I lifted my arm and waved to her and she lifted her arm and waved back.

Her hair was tangled beneath her hat, pulling out in strands. The light pressed against her from the back, and she looked like a cut-out angel, an angel with a halo of dark hair. "It's beautiful here," she called. "Isn't it beautiful? Isn't it more beautiful than you could ever have imagined?"

I nodded. I patted the rock beside me, motioned to her to come over. She came. She sat down beside me, nestled close to me for warmth. I thought we felt like two birds in a nest. Like two cats without a fire to curl up by, each warm against the other's body. "It is," I said. "It's like the moon."

She leaned her head on my shoulder. Her hair smelled of smoke and I wondered if mine smelled the same. "I miss Matthew here," she said. "I miss him more here than any-where, I think."

I was silent. Of course she missed him. Of course she car-ried him with her. I put my arm around her shoulders. I pulled her to me tight.

"It's been almost two years," she said. "Almost two years, and I'm not used to being an only child yet. I'm not used to life without my brother."

"I know." The world seemed outside of time up there. I thought the sun would hover in the sky forever. I thought the air would lick at our skin always with the same degree of icy gentleness. I thought there was nothing more to life than Anna's shoulders beneath my arm, than Anna's head as it rested on my shoulder. I thought I could lean over now and whisper that, since we were both alone, she could be my sister.

"Do you still miss him, Isabel?"

Matthew. I thought of my hand in his. I thought of the

length of his fingers, the callused roughness of his skin. I thought of him racing down the stairs as a boy, and pressing his hand against the small of my back as a man. I thought of the last time I had seen him, his long face gaunt, his dark eyes, rimmed with red, staring back at me. "I miss him," I said. "I miss him, but I try to push it from me as much as I can."

"I know," she said. "I do that too."

We sat in silence for a moment. The moment stretched out, endless, timeless. She stirred beside me on the rock. She stirred, and I shifted my weight, and just before we both shook our heads and pulled ourselves awake, I said, "I miss you too, Anna. I miss you too." She didn't answer. She turned, instead, and stared at me. Her eyes were dark, her lashes thick. Her cheeks were pink in the cold. She stared and then she smiled slightly and took my hand. She pressed my hand to her heart, and I thought it meant she missed me too. I thought it meant a fissure between us was healed.

WE HAD *tongba* that night, warm millet beer to celebrate our coming day of rest. Danny bought it from one of the women in the village. We huddled in a circle, the milky, sour liquid hot upon our tongues. The millet grains floated on top of the beer like tiny seeds and we picked the nut-brown grains from our lips after every sip. My hat was pulled down low over my ears. Bob had a harmonica and he played blues riffs. The moon in the sky was close to full.

"Let's tell each other why we're really here," Melissa said. The harmonica moved like a train behind her voice. "Saul and I wanted to come to Nepal for our honeymoon, but we couldn't afford it then. We've been waiting two years to get here."

"Was it worth it?" That was Anna. Her voice sounded deeper than usual. Maybe it was from the beer.

"Definitely worth it," Saul said. His arm lay across Melissa's shoulders. She laid her head down against it. She looked like a little girl under the light of the moon, her face small, her straight blond hair spiking out around her face. "Definitely," she said.

"I came for the food," Gordon said. We laughed, but politely. "No, seriously, my kid just started college. It's lonely at home without him. My wife thought this would make me feel better. You know, a beginning for me at the same time as my kid is beginning the rest of his life. I'm not sure what I'm supposed to be beginning, but I think it's a good place to make a change."

"Very good," Pemba said. "Many people come here to change. Or at times when their lives at home are changing around them. Many people."

The porters were drinking tongba as well where they sat in a circle close to their one large tent. Their laughter rose high, and then one broke into a song that rose above the sound of Bob's harmonica, rose high and dipped and rose again. One voice rose louder than the others, arguing, then quieted again. "They're here to get paid," Gordon said. "They're here to make some money."

"Can you imagine carrying someone's bags up mountains for a living?" Anna's voice was louder than I thought she'd intended. I looked for her face and saw that she sat across the fire next to Danny. Did they sit together every night? In that thin air I could not remember.

"It's not work that I could survive," Bob said now, his harmonica on the ground beside him. "It's hard enough climbing these mountains without a pack, but carrying someone else's things? I think I'd go crazy. I think I'd end up throwing whatever I was carrying off a cliff and into the river."

"I might too," Saul said. "I couldn't do it."

Pemba poured more hot water into the mash in everybody's cups. Millet seeds rose to the top once more. The steam and the fire light through it softened all our faces. When he came to me, he pressed his hand down on my shoulder, squeezed it, then rested his weight briefly on my back. "Are you doing okay?" he whispered. I nodded. I could not say why I was there, that I was there because I feared betrayal.

"I came because of my brother," Anna said. I wondered how much of the tongba she'd been drinking. "Matthew died two years ago. In the mountains. He was hiking alone. He was caught in a snowstorm. He died of hypothermia."

There was silence then. What could anyone say after that? I felt a stab of pain inside me. What was there to say?

"We grew up in the mountains together. In the summers. We lived with my mother on the East Coast for most of the year, but we lived with my father in Colorado every summer. If anyone should have known how to stay alive it was Matthew. To tell you the truth, I don't really understand it. He wasn't *that* far away from home. He wasn't *that* deep into the wilderness. But it took a long time to find him. It certainly felt long, anyway. A week. He was missing for a week and then he was found dead."

Danny had moved closer to her. I could see by the light of the moon. I could see through the high flames of the fire. We all sat still. We all looked into the smoke, only our eyes moving to watch it billow to the sky. *What about me? I wanted to cry out. What about what I went through? I lost him too. I lost him too.*

Anna shivered, and then a shiver seemed to shake through each of us. "Anyway," she said, "anyway, I wanted to come to these mountains for him. He always wanted to visit the Himalayas. He talked about it all the time when we were growing up. That's why I'm here." Her voice was almost a whisper. "That's why I'm here. For my brother. For Matthew."

We slipped away to bed, then. Or almost all of us slipped away. I walked unsteadily around the fire, leaned down and buried my face in Anna's shoulder. She reached her arms up and circled my neck. Her mind seemed far away, though, and her arms that circled did not close tight around me. "Go to bed, Isabel," she said. Her voice was low.

"Okay," I said. "Okay. I love you."

"Go to bed. Get some sleep."

"I miss him too," I said. "I miss him more than I can say." She nodded.

I could feel Danny's eyes on both of us. The beer was in my head suddenly, and I stumbled, unsteady, the world spinning. "Go to bed, Isabel," Danny said. "I'll come in soon. Go lie down."

I nodded too. I kissed them both good night. Unsteady kisses. Tipsy, wobbly kisses. And then I was in the tent, my clothes off, my long johns on, ready for bed, ready for sleep.

It's hard to sleep at altitude even if you're drunk, as I was. I faded in and out of sleep. My dreams were thin. I saw visions, and those visions became memories of the day before, and those memories of the day before slipped and distorted and became stories, took on a life of their own. I wasn't really sleeping, but I wasn't really awake either. At times I could hear Melissa and Saul murmuring in the tent beside mine. At times I thought I could still hear the fire crackling outside. A dog barked over and over, a village dog. It sounded like a giant, I thought, a giant dog with fierce, sharp teeth.

And where was Danny? I lay in that tent half dreaming, alone. *Go to bed,* he'd said. *I'll come in soon.* But I lay there by myself. I had a headache almost immediately, and then I felt hungry, but with no appetite, and then I thought I should just get up and pee. I don't know how much later it was when, my head throbbing, I climbed from the tent in my long johns. An hour? Two? It's hard to keep track of time when you're trying to fall asleep.

The stars were bright when I stumbled forth. They were enormous stars. The moon had set and the stars looked like jewels in the sky. And the earth—the dry earth under those bright lights seemed to glow. The tents spread out in a circle were as still as sleeping cattle, as still as stones. The flat-roofed houses in the valley beyond the tents were silent. The dog's howl ripped through the night, one loud, ferocious bark, then silence again. And the cold. It was hard for me to move through it, the windless, penetrating cold. It was like moving through the faceted surface of a diamond.

And then a sound. A low, low voice. There was no way to

hide beneath these stars, even with the moon gone from the sky. I walked toward the voice, and heard another. Two voices, low, by the burnt-out fire. Two voices moaning by the frozen ashes. I took another step. The cold, it slowed things down. There was a world, I thought, between me and those voices. There was a world in which to decide to turn back. I took a step and then another and then another, as if being drawn toward a magnet, as if caught on an ice floe.

I know I saw them before they saw me. With Danny's arms reaching down and Anna's arms reaching up to his face, they looked like a many-armed sculpture of a Hindu god. Her face was tilted up toward his, and his lips were pressed against hers, and his right hand reached down inside her coat. *To her breast,* I thought, *his hand is on her heart.* She shifted her weight and she sighed and moaned and I thought, *I've heard that moan before, I've slept outside her door enough times to know that moan.* I stared. I could not help but stare. Their moving hands. Their tilted heads. Their legs, swathed in thick, warm pile, twined together. I stared and then, as if on its own, a cry moved from my lips.

Anna looked up first. She looked up, and her eyes narrowed as she refocused. She looked into my eyes. Then Danny turned his head as well, his eyes wide, his mouth dropping open, and then he looked down again. "Isabel," he said. "Isabel."

"Isabel," Anna said, but she froze too; whatever words she'd planned halted on her lips.

"How could you?" I whispered. "How could either of you do this?"

They stared at me. They didn't say a word.

"You're not alone here. Did you think you were alone? Did you think no one would find you? Did you think I wouldn't know?" My voice had risen now. I could feel it from the effort it took to speak into the dark. "How could you do this, Anna? He's my husband. How could you do this to me?"

He stared at me. He stared at me and didn't say a word.

Anna stared too, but now her mouth was open.

"He was mine first," she said. "He was mine and you did it to me first. He was my consolation and you took him from me. You took him. You were my friend and you took him away."

I was next to her then. I was close enough to touch them. Her voice rose loud. Her breath was warmer than the air.

"He came," I screamed. "I didn't take him. He came to me. He came by himself. He wasn't yours."

"He came because I wasn't there. If I had stayed he never would have thought to touch you. You took my life. This should have been my life. You stole it away from me. You took my brother first, and then you stole my life."

And there he was with us. Half a world away. Back from the dead, almost. Back before us in this mountain valley, so high we could almost touch the stars, and here was Matthew, haunting me, haunting his sister, here was Matthew between us.

"It wasn't my fault," I shouted. "It wasn't my fault."

But it was, and of course neither of us could forget it. Neither of us could forget how Matthew left, his heart in my hand, how Matthew left and how I didn't call him back.

"It wasn't my fault," I said again, and this time my hand moved as if on its own. It lifted, it swung back, and then it cracked across her face. Cracked like a branch breaking. Cracked like a whip on a horse's flank. Her eyes were inside my eyes. Her face turned red, a red I could see even under the starlit sky. And then she turned. She whirled around and ran. Away from the tents. Away from the cold ashes. Away from me. And then Danny turned and followed her.

CHAPTER TWENTY-ONE

*I*t snowed that night. More than a dusting. Clouds closed in over those icy stars. It snowed a good six inches, and the first I knew of it was when, waking up alone inside the tent, I realized that the texture of the silence had changed. The air in the tent was warm, or warmer than it had been, and the rustling I made as I pulled myself from my sleeping bag seemed muffled. My head throbbed. The air outside the tent was crystalline.

Pemba and the porters were already awake. The red hood of Pemba's jacket was pulled up over his head, and even though he wore sunglasses I could tell he'd seen me. Shortly after I emerged he walked over.

"It's a lot of snow," he said. "A lot of snow to go up higher."

I nodded. I thought it was beautiful, and I had a headache and I thought I might like to crawl back into bed.

"Wake Danny up," he said. "We need to talk about what we're going to do."

I looked at him. He looked back at me. "I can't wake him up," I said. His glasses were dark across his eyes, but I could tell he stared. "I can't wake him up," I said again. "He didn't sleep in our tent last night. He never came to bed."

There was silence then. Pemba looked down. "Any idea where he is?" he asked finally.

"Anna's tent." My voice was flat.

"Anna's tent," he said, and nodded. "I'll find him. Thank you."

AFTER MATTHEW AND I finally said good-bye, I threw a party. I rounded up friends to help me celebrate my freedom. It was October when he left and the leaves had already begun to fall. I remember walking to the liquor store with leaves gusting across the sidewalk. I remember buying a bottle of vodka. I remember the weight of the plastic bag that dangled from my arm. Anna came home, and some other friends of ours, and we drank vodka martinis and had the music turned up loud, and it seemed perfect then, perfect and terrifying and right to have said good-bye.

And then the phone rang. I went into the bedroom to pick it up. Something told me not to answer it, and I sat on the bed and let it ring for what seemed quite a while. But then I looked up and Anna stood in the doorway and she smiled at me and nodded her head and I thought, *This is someone who I trust.* I picked up the phone. Matthew's voice spoke through it to me.

"This is the last time we'll ever speak," he said.

"Matthew," I said.

"This is the last time you can say it," he whispered. "This is the last time you can tell me not to go."

"Matthew," I said again. I heard his breathing. I heard him gasp quickly, what sounded like a sob, and then I put the phone down.

"It's okay," Anna whispered, "it's okay. It was time for both of you to move on. It was time."

It was October. In New York the leaves were thick and dry on the ground. In Colorado, in the mountains, a storm was building. In Colorado, Matthew was preparing to walk into the wilderness alone.

ANNA'S TENT WAS empty. Her sleeping bag was laid out neatly. Her clothes were folded in her bag. "Nobody has seen them," Pemba said. "Nobody knows where they might have gone."

The group was silent during breakfast. We huddled round the kerosene stove and sipped lemon tea from tin cups in mittened hands. "We planned to take an extra day here any-way," I heard Pemba telling Saul. "We can't go on in this snow. We can't continue up to Pangpema in weather like this. We'd have to wait it out here another day."

"What do we do?" Saul's voice was shaky, and I wondered

what he thought of being out here, in the snow, in this high valley, the mountains looming all around, the road a ten-day walk away.

"We stay here. We'll look for Danny and Anna, and then we'll figure out what to do."

I felt a hand on my shoulder and looked up. Melissa smiled at me. I tried to smile back. She kept her hand on my shoulder for a moment, then walked over to Saul and Pemba. This all seemed far away, the snow beyond my boots, the climbs that lay ahead, my husband gone. Anna gone. I took a sip of tea. The hot liquid on my tongue was real, but all the rest—all the rest seemed too far away to believe. I thought of my hand on her face. I thought of their backs as they disappeared into the night. It all seemed to be at a great distance from me, and I would not believe it.

We started looking for them then. Melissa and I went to the village and knocked on doors. Pemba and Gordon and Bob and Saul and all the porters moved down together to the valley. Turning to look over my shoulder, I could see that group far away, the bright colors of their jackets, and then they disappeared into the snow. I could still hear their voices then. And then their voices, calling, vanished as well. We knocked and knocked, but we couldn't make ourselves understood. My stuttering Nepali didn't have much weight here high up in the mountains. They speak a Tibetan dialect, I remembered Danny saying; of course they couldn't understand me.

Melissa and I went back to camp and stayed there alone. We sat in the mess tent, the porters' tent, with the zipper pulled shut, and Melissa tried to find out what had happened.

I wouldn't tell her. "I don't know," I said. "I went to bed, and then I woke up and they both were missing."

"You didn't see them leave?" she said. "You don't know what direction they might have gone in?"

"No," I said. I shook my head. "I don't know. I don't know anything about it."

"Are you okay, Isabel?" She looked into my eyes. Her eyes were gray. I thought they were nice eyes.

"Yes," I said. "Yes. I'm fine. I know they're fine."

AND THEN, HOURS later, they returned.

The whole search party returned, their voices just a shift in the wind at first, then separating and becoming a vague calling in the distance, and then emerging as loud voices, loud like the ringing bells on a sleigh. They came back and when Melissa and I unzipped the tent and looked outside, we saw them walking, and in amid the group of men were Anna and Danny, their arms around each other's waists. "We found them," Saul called out. He waved his arms. "We found them. They're back. They're safe."

They're back. They're safe.

They didn't let their arms fall from around each other for even a second.

THEY HAD SPENT the night in a cave. By the time Danny caught up with Anna she had wandered far away from the camp. It was late. The moon had set. The sky had clouded over. They sat for a little while talking, and when they turned to go back the snow had begun to fall and they couldn't tell in what direction the camp lay. They both knew the mountains. They both knew not to keep walking once you realize that you're lost. But they tried anyway. They tried to find the camp, and they wandered farther away, and finally when the snow started falling thick, they found a cave and clambered in. A dark cave. A cold stone cave. They spent the night clinging to each other.

This I gathered. I couldn't speak to either one of them. I tried. When they came stumbling back to camp, Pemba brought them first into the mess tent. He gave them hot tea and pulled their wet clothes off and sent us back to our tents to find them dry things to cover themselves with. He gave them food. He held their hands in his until they warmed. Anna could not stop shaking, and Pemba wrapped his arms around her and pulled her to his chest. He looked toward me to do the same with Danny, but when I approached, Danny shrugged away. Gordon reached to put his arms around him. The porters sat down at the far end of the camp and lit cigarettes and talked amongst themselves. They shook their heads. The thick smoke drifted toward us and Anna started coughing. Pemba said something loud and sharp and they put the cigarettes out but continued to shake their heads and click their tongues. *A pity,* their tongues seemed to say, *such a pity.*

Such a pity, echoed in my heart. *It's all such a terrible pity.*

IT WASN'T ONLY my fault when Matthew left. There were, of course, many factors involved. He wanted more from me than I wanted to give. He wanted a home away from the city, a home and a wife for his home and children, and we'd been together since I was sixteen, since I was *sixteen*—we'd been together for what seemed forever and he wanted it to just keep going. When I asked him to leave, he didn't believe me at first. When I asked him to leave, I wasn't sure I believed myself. But then I found myself waking in someone else's arms and realized, more easily than I'd thought I could, that it was time for things to end.

Before he left for Colorado, he came to pick up the last of the things he'd kept at the apartment. Anna was out. I stood by the door with my arms crossed while he gathered his clothes up in a bundle. His back was turned to me. I watched his shoulder blades move beneath his shirt. Later, when he left, I did not want to meet his eyes and instead I concentrated on his neck. Something was different, and it was only when the door closed behind him and I went to lie down on my bed and cry that I realized what it was. His necklace, the marble that he'd worn on a leather string since the day we met, was curled up on my pillow. I cupped it in my hand. The glass was cold. The surface was smooth. I dropped it in the drawer of the table beside my bed, and then I turned over on my side and wept.

This is the last time you can tell me not to go, he said on the phone with Anna standing next to me. And it was. It was the last time we ever spoke.

"WE CAN'T KEEP climbing toward Pangpema," Pemba said that night at dinner. "We can't keep climbing into deeper snow. It's three days from here. Three days up and three days back. We can't do it. It's just not worth the risk."

No one spoke. It was dark outside, and I think if we could we would all have gladly climbed into a plane, left immediately from that place and not looked back.

"Either we can turn around and go back the way we came, or we can make the loop we originally planned—over the Sinion La and back down toward Taplejung—but without heading up toward base camp. It takes us along a mountain ridge. The passes bring us up to fifteen thousand feet, but the climb is steady and relatively easy. The views are beautiful."

I saw the group begin to nod.

"Won't there be snow that way too?" Gordon asked.

"Yes," Danny said. His voice was low. "Yes, there will be snow."

"Will there be more snow than here?"

"We don't know," Pemba said. "There's no way to know."

Turn around, I wanted to say, *let's turn around. Let's go back down to those warm valleys we climbed up through. Let's go down from this high country, let's go down.* But I couldn't get a word out. I looked across the darkening tent at Anna, and she shifted her eyes away from me. I looked across at Danny, and he kept his eyes straight on Pemba's.

We had a vote. We decided to keep going. Everyone laughed and appeared relieved, and when I asked Melissa why, she said, "We flew halfway around the world for this trek. We can't turn around. It's a terrible thing to have to turn. I'd rather keep moving forward than turn back around even if it means walking into danger. Wouldn't you? Wouldn't you rather keep moving on? No matter what lies ahead, wouldn't you rather just keep going?"

ANNA NEVER SAID a word in blame to me when Matthew disappeared. How could she? I was frozen by the phone. I didn't sleep for days. I blamed myself and she held me in her arms and told me that his vanishing had nothing to do with me, that he had no one but himself to blame. I never told her about the necklace lying cold inside the drawer.

We took care of each other, and we said at least we had each other, and then Anna planned her trip. A year after her brother's death, a year after he lost himself in the wilderness, she decided that she needed to be alone. She needed to be alone in a world that she didn't know, and she started planning and she took me with her to meet the man who would be her guide in Nepal, and that is where my story started. My story started when Anna was to leave me, too.

AND SO THAT night we decided. Come morning we would walk along the ridge to Mani Bhuk. The following day we would head across the Sinion La, across the Mirgin La, and begin our descent toward Taplejung. If there was snow, we would walk through snow. We would stop often and walk tightly as a group. Danny would lead and Pemba would walk in the back. We would walk south with Kangchenjunga to our left and Jannu at our backs.

Early the next morning we set off.

CHAPTER TWENTY-TWO

*T*here was less snow than we'd expected at Mani Bhuk. It lay like dust across the earth. A stream ran by, thin and with a rippling song. We arrived in the early afternoon. The porters set our tents up and boiled water for our tea. We spent the day quietly, the quietness of that place working its way inside of us, a thorough stillness, a thorough quiet. The air was thin but the sun shone hot and by late afternoon the snow had melted and the earth was brown.

I asked Danny to come back to our tent that night. I found him at the edge of the campsite, staring out at the rising face of Jannu to the east. The mountain was fading already as the sun set in the west, the glittering slopes turning to coal as night descended. He turned to me when I approached and for a moment I thought he would reach out to me. "I'm sorry, Isabel," he whispered.

I put my hand on his arm then, and breathed my words into his ear. "Come back," I said. "Come back tonight."

He didn't move my hand away, but he turned as if I weren't there, and I felt my face go hot. How could everyone not have been watching? What else was there to watch in that small world? I left and spent the night alone.

WE SET OUT early the next day to cross the Sinion La. The climb was steep, the path bordered by stone cairns erected as prayers to the gods. I walked as though walking through water, the thin air weighing heavy, my breathing taking effort, taking memory. Kangchenjunga, white and silent to the east, seemed to ride beside us, measuring our pace.

We all walked slowly. I could hear Gordon's shallow breath behind me, and when I looked over my shoulder I saw that Melissa lagged far below. She stumbled once. I saw her feet drag across the bumpy path and then an ankle gave. When she stood up again she seemed to veer to the left and right as she followed on the path. *She's moving like she's in a trance,* I thought, and then I shrugged. It all seemed the product of a trance—the barren slopes, the snow beneath our feet, the cold sighing of the wind, Danny turning away from me, me in my tent alone at night.

By noon we reached the pass. Tattered prayer flags snapped in the wind. The Simbua Khola valley lay before us, down below. We stopped at the pass and the porters set the stove up and boiled water for tea and we ate ramen noodles dry, straight from the packets, and crumpled up the plastic and stuffed it in our pockets. *This is the highest I will ever go,* I thought, and then I said it aloud, "This is the highest I'll probably ever go."

"Me too," Melissa said. Her voice was slow. "This is high enough for me."

The path below split in two as it descended toward the valley, and we could see the split from where we stood. "That way goes to Kangchenjunga," Pemba said, "to the south base camp. The other leads to Taplejung and home."

"Let's go to Kangchenjunga," I heard Anna say behind me. I turned around. She stood next to Danny and was staring toward the distant mountain.

He looked at her. He opened his mouth to speak, and I was certain he would say yes, that she would take him and they would leave. I was certain of it, but the words never left his lips because with a startled cry Melissa stumbled and fell.

Later we weren't sure what had happened. It was too high to move quickly there. I would have thought it was too high to move in any way that could cause real damage, but there she was, on the ground. In the thin air it seemed her cries were very far away, but when Saul rushed forward and took her hand, her cries grew louder. When we tried to help her up it became clear that her wrist was broken. She had fallen on it with all her weight and now it swelled. But it wasn't her wrist that she was crying about. It was her head. "I can't think," she whispered, and her whispering grew loud. "I can't think. My head hurts so badly, I can't hear anything."

She sat on the ground with her legs crossed and her head

bowed down. Saul wrapped his arms around her and she shook slightly. Danny knelt down and held her chin in his hands. "Look at me," Danny said. "Look at me. I want to see your eyes."

Behind, I heard the stamp of feet. I turned around. Gordon had his hands tucked inside his pockets and was moving his legs up and down. It was cold, I realized, and then I too began to shiver. I looked back at Melissa. Danny had pulled her up. He asked her to walk toward him, but as she walked, she veered off to the left and then she stumbled. Saul rushed forward and caught her before she fell again. "My head," she gasped. She'd shut her eyes. "My head." She breathed in deeply, then coughed. Her cough sounded like a rattle shaking.

"I'm taking her down," Danny said. "I'm taking her down now."

"Aren't we all going down?" I said.

He looked at me. He shook his head slightly. "It's from the altitude—look at her eyes. Listen to her chest. It's the altitude that made her fall. I'm going to take her down fast. Faster than we could travel as a group. I don't even want to take the time to wait for a helicopter." We stared at him. Whether it was because of the thinness of the air or something else, it was hard to follow what he said. *Take her down? In what?* "We'll carry her out," he said. We nodded. It was cold there on the pass. An hour had gone by while they tended to Melissa. I think we would have agreed to anything. The sun was lower in the sky. *Take her,* I thought. *Take her and leave.*

One of the porters was clearing out his basket. Melissa hung her good arm around Saul's neck and cried and cried.

Anna and I looked at each other quickly. Then we looked away.

"I'm coming too," Saul said.

Danny looked at him. "You can't move fast enough." His voice was flat. Saul's mouth opened, and then he shut it again.

They piled her in a basket, her legs bent toward her chest and dangling out the top. A porter carried her on his back and Danny carried another pack that they'd hurriedly filled with supplies. A tent in case they needed to stop for sleep. Water. A cooking stove. Packets of noodles. Clothes to keep them warm. They set off quickly, and though we followed fast behind them, they soon vanished from our sight.

"I should be with them," I heard Saul say, his voice rising high from the front of the line. "I could keep up. I should have gone."

Nobody said a word. We were all concentrating on the steep path down, the path that led us toward the valley, the path that led us back toward home.

WE CAMPED THAT night outside a teahouse in Whata Phedi. We heard rumors there of Danny and the porter and their basket heavy with the weight of a sick woman. We heard rumors of their having stopped for food and, having eaten, setting off still farther down though night would be drawing on soon. We seemed like trackers then, eager for news, restless to keep moving ourselves. It was warmer here, though still quite high, and we stayed up later than we had the past few nights.

Whata Phedi lay just above a tributary of the Simbua Khola, a small, noisy stream that rushed past the town. The air was almost wet here, dense trees crowding in, small, bright flowers peeking from beside the path. It was like coming down from the wilderness and finding ourselves in a dream, in a village where smoke curled from a chimney and a laughing brook promised to lull us to sleep at night, and where the inn in which we ate our dinner smelled of sweet fresh hay. But we didn't sleep. Or I didn't. I lay in my tent alone and wondered where Danny was and whether Anna was sleeping, and when I did finally sleep it was a restless, shallow sleep and I screamed at Anna all night long in my dreams. When I was finished screaming at her, I screamed at Danny, and when finished with Danny, I screamed and screamed at Matthew.

We rose at dawn the next day. The walk ahead would not be easy. We were climbing up again, over a pass at Lassi Than and on to the high pastureland of Lassi. It would take us all day, Pemba said. All day, and at Lassi the porters would have to walk still farther to find us water. Fourteen days in the mountains by now. The city seemed a world away.

When I first started on the trek, days ago, weeks ago, my muscles burned and I could barely straighten my legs at night. Now my muscles seemed used to the steepness of the slopes, to the work of moving up and down whole mountains, but now a different kind of tiredness had set in. Walking that day, each step seemed the sum of fifty others, and all I could think was, *Tired.* Just to lift my foot and place it on the path seemed an enormous act of will. *Keep moving,* I told myself, and wondered what there was to move toward. *Keep moving,* but all there seemed to be was an endless sea of ups and downs, dips and crests and dips and crests. I knew that I was walking slowly. Without Danny there, Pemba walked at the front of the line. All at once I realized that I had dropped very far back, that even Gordon had passed me now. For all intents I was alone there climbing up toward Lassi. I was alone on the rocky path with the high Himalayas towering at my back.

I didn't mind walking alone. I stopped when I wanted now. I stopped and rested my feet and took long sips of rust–colored water from my bottle. The path seemed clear. It passed up through thick fir forests. I came to a stream, and the path crossed it, and then the trees opened up and I sat on a rock in the sun.

I don't know how long I sat there. The sun was warm on my neck as it streamed down and I took off my day pack and stretched my arms wide and let the light soak into my skin and pretended that the world was all in order. *I'll just stay here,* I thought, *I'll just stay here forever. I'll stay forever and feel the sun on my neck and on my face and sleep cozy against this rock.* I'd filled my water bottle at the stream. I could see the iodine pill dissolving. My back was warm. I shut my eyes. I moved my feet against the earth and breathed in deeply—the rushing pine scent, the sun above, the breeze through the trees at the edge of the clearing. *I'll stay. I'll stay. I'll stay.* And then I heard my name.

"Isabel . . . Isabel . . . ," came softly through the trees, as if from far away. I opened my eyes. "Isabel," I heard, "Isabel," but the voice through the trees, through the distance, was so soft that I couldn't recognize its owner.

It grew louder. I stumbled to my feet and then there, suddenly, in the clearing was Pemba, and running behind him, breathing hard, was Anna. She bent double to catch her breath. Her braid flopped over her shoulder and for a moment all I could hear was a deep wheezing in and out, and then she straightened and they both stared at me.

"We thought you were lost," Pemba said. "We got to the pass and realized you weren't with us. We waited and waited and you never came. We thought you'd fallen. Or had taken a wrong turn."

"We didn't know what to do," Anna said. "You scared us half to death."

Both of them were staring at me now. Both of them looked me up and down. I looked back at them, but I couldn't match their gaze, and finally I bent my head and stared down at the ground.

"What were you doing?" Anna said.

"I don't know," I whispered. "I was tired. I sat down to rest and then I lost track of the time. I didn't realize I was so far behind. I didn't realize you'd be worried."

"I didn't realize I would be either," she said sharply. She turned. "I'll see you back at the pass." She looked at Pemba. "You'll walk with her?"

He shook his head. "I have to go back quickly. I can't leave the group up at the pass just waiting for Isabel and me to catch up. You stay with her. You walk the way with her. I'll get them to the campsite, and then I'll come back and find you. I'm sorry. This is the way we have to do it."

Anna nodded. I felt my mouth gape open.

And then he was gone.

"Let's go," Anna said. She turned. I walked behind her.

ঙ৩

WE HAD BEEN walking for an hour before either of us said
a word. I walked slowly and rested often, but even at our
slow pace Anna began to lag behind. At first I said nothing
and then when I forced myself to ask if she was all right she
just nodded hard and turned her head away. Finally, though, I
stopped and turned and put my hands on my hips and she sat
down and told me. There was something with her muscles,
she said, they felt loose somehow, as if the hardness that they'd
built to over days had turned to something else—something
rubbery, something not quite tight enough. "They don't feel
right," she said. "It started this morning." Then she pressed
her lips together again in silence.

The path that we followed brought us back to rhododendron forests. It rose through great flowering groves, dark
where the leaves blocked out the sun. The air in the forests
had a certain density, but as we climbed up through them it
thinned again, clean and cool.

I concentrated on my breathing as we walked. On my
breathing and on Anna's breathing, which I could hear
behind me. I watched each step, and at the back of the step
was Anna, slowly lifting up her leg, slowly putting it down,
lifting it up again, and down. I turned my head. Her leather
boots were worn. Her pants were the bright blue color of
the sky. Where there had been a rhythm to her walk, a steady
pace, now her walking matched the rush and falter of her
breath.

We reached the pass at Lassi Than by mid-afternoon. The

white peaks of Kangchenjunga and Jannu towered in the distance. The mountains moved around us as if chasing in a game of tag. They never seemed to grow smaller. They never seemed fixed in place.

"The camp is supposed to be an hour from here," Anna said as we sat panting at the top. "A flat hour, I think. Pemba said it's an easy walk from here."

I nodded. I looked at her and wondered if she'd be able to stand up. I took a sip of water and handed the bottle to her. There was a jumping in my stomach, a sudden giddiness. The mountains winked in the sun. "Come on," I said, "Let's go."

"Let's wait here just a minute more."

She sat on a rock. Her head was in her lap. Her black braid dangled over her shoulder. Her shoulders moved up and down as she breathed.

"I can't move quite yet," she said.

"You can," I said.

"I can't." Her breath came out in one long gust. "I really can't."

And then I put my hand upon her forehead. Her smooth skin. Her skin turned brown by days in the mountain sun. My fingers are long and they stretched across her brow and she leaned into them as if my hand were her mother's. Her skin—it burned. "No wonder you can't," I said. I tried to keep my voice from shaking. "You have a fever. No wonder you're going so slow."

Her teeth began to chatter. The wind blew across the pass. The earth spun and spun and she could not raise her head.

"Up," I said. "Stand up. We're going."

She had a fever. She could not stand up. I imagined that

the earth was shifting beneath her feet, that the mountains reeled and quivered in the distance.

"Get up."

I stood behind her and my hands were underneath her arms. I bent and straightened and tried to hoist her up. I cannot say she helped me. I grunted with the effort. She seemed to try to sink her weight. But suddenly, despite her fevered efforts otherwise, I found that we were both standing, that she leaned her weight against my body.

"Just keep moving your feet," I said. "I'll get us there. Just keep walking with me."

We moved together then, stumbling along, half her weight resting on my body.

"I'll get us there," I said again and with her head upon my shoulder I was certain that she believed me.

Later, when I thought back on it, I saw that we'd walked an easy trail, but at the time the path seemed as thin as a rope, and Anna cried that it heaved like the ocean, up and down. I whispered to Anna as we walked. "You'll get there," I said. "We'll get medicine for you and you'll feel better soon." Once she broke away from me and turned and crumpled and fell down upon the path. I reached my hand out to help her up, but she curled away and retched, and I stroked her hair while she sat on the dusty path and vomited.

"Drink water," I said when she was done. "Drink it in sips. Small sips. Get some fluids inside you." But the water made her gag.

It was like walking through a whirlwind, that walk, the world spinning around us, the slightest breeze sending Anna into shakes.

When we finally reached the camp it was close to night. Dusk had settled over the mountains, and the ring of tents looked like a ring of yellow jewels. Anna kept her arm around me and I moved with her weight upon me. The feel of her shoulders, the feel of her waist—just the feel of them, I thought, gave me strength to move her forward.

They put her to bed in her tent right away. They unrolled her sleeping bag and I helped her peel her clothes off and get inside the bag, and Pemba brought her water and I sat next to her and rubbed her forehead and told her to try to fall asleep. Later, when she slept, I listened to the worried talk of the others as they sat beside the fire. "It's not the altitude," I heard Pemba say. "It's some kind of infection. Isabel said she was sick already by the river. She was sick before we ever started climbing up again."

"Still"—I thought the voice was Bob's—"still, shouldn't we take her down, just in case?"

"I think we'll watch her," Pemba said. His voice was soft. I thought how different it was from Danny's. It was hard to catch his words across the distance, through the thin canvas wall. "If her fever comes back, if it gets worse through the night, we'll have to move her. We're three days from the airport now. Three long days, but three days going down. We'll be down to six thousand feet tomorrow. If it's the altitude that's making her sick, she'll be better tomorrow."

I climbed out through the narrow door. They stood side by side with their arms crossed. Their faces looked worried. "I'll sleep in her tent," I said.

I shut my eyes. *I'll sleep beside her,* I thought. *I'll sleep beside her and I'll take care of her and everything will be all right.*

IT WAS LATE when I slipped back inside her tent. She woke with a start at the sound of the zipper pulling. The tent was small. It seemed that she was as close to me as I was to myself. "Isabel," she whispered. "Isabel, is that you?" Could she doubt that it was me? Could she doubt that I would not forsake her?

"It's me," I answered, and laid a hand upon her head.

"I'm sick," she said. "I'm sick. My stomach."

"You'll feel better soon," I said. "The fever's gone." Her long hair was loose now, and I could feel it on my cheek as I bent over her. It smelled slightly of the campfire, of wood and smoke and the cool night air. It brushed against my lips and I thought it felt like spiders' webs, or lace.

"I feel so weak," she said.

"It's three more days. Three more days and then you can sleep in a bed again."

"Your couch?"

"My bed. Your bed."

Her hand on my forehead. Her long hair against my lips. The thin walls of the tent now seemed as thick and solid as those of any house I'd ever slept in.

"I won't sleep in my own bed again," I said. "I won't go back there."

She coughed. "It doesn't matter."

"You can go back, but I won't go back. I want to go home. I want to go back to New York. I want to start my life again."

There was silence. Then she drew away. She drew away

like the ebb tide of the sea, the imprint of my hand on her forehead like the shells left behind when the water's gone. Finally she whispered, "You don't have to leave for me."

I sighed. "I do," I said. "I do."

IT TOOK THREE days to get out of the mountains. The path dropped steadily, and by the time we reached the airstrip at Taplejung, it was as if we'd been walking through lush jungle forever. The air was wet as we got lower, the foliage along the paths bright green, so green that all I could think about was envy.

I took care of Anna along that walk, though we hardly spoke. When she slipped I was there behind her, a hand on her shoulder to steady her. When she stopped to sip water, I stood over her so that the shadow of my body shielded her from the sun. We left her fever in the mountains, but as we descended farther a cough shook in her chest and by the time we reached the airstrip she doubled over when she coughed.

And then, one day, we found ourselves in a tiny airplane circling out above the hills, above the rhododendron forests, away from the towering mountains. The city lay ahead. The windows of the plane were streaked with dust. The noise of the engine closed in like a great wind. I shut my eyes, then opened them to watch the land unfold below us. Hill upon hill upon hill swept by, as many as the waves in a small ocean. I looked to my left and there was Anna, staring past me through the window. I tucked my arm through her arm and leaned my head upon her shoulder and then I put my lips to her ear.

"Good-bye," I whispered. "In case I don't say it later. Good-bye."

She looked at me. Her eyes were large. "Good-bye," she whispered back. She placed her hand upon my hand where it rested on her arm. "Good-bye," and the plane swooped through the hills, and the city, ringed by mountains, awaited our return.

CHAPTER TWENTY-THREE

*W*e reached Kathmandu just after nightfall. A van waited at the airport to meet us, and, bone weary, I dropped to sleep when I put my head against the vinyl cushions. I was sleeping when we entered the city, was sleeping when the van pulled to a halt in front of the Yak and Yeti Hotel. I woke with a start, and instead of waking with a normal logy sleepiness, I woke fully alert, my heart beating quickly, unable to see out of the misted window into the night. I jumped up and hit my head on the ceiling of the van. I was the last to file out.

Danny stood outside the van. His face was shaven. I thought his skin would smell clean. I thought his skin would smell, just faintly, of nutmeg. Our eyes met briefly. He reached his hand out to me. I turned away from him.

A taxi came. Pemba flagged it down for me. He touched my shoulder as I climbed in. "Thank you," I whispered.

"Be careful," he said. "Care for yourself."

I didn't look back at Danny or Anna. I leaned forward and told the driver to take me to Thamel. As if I were a tourist. I wanted to be a tourist. I didn't argue when he named his price and we drove off without the meter ticking. Five minutes later I stood outside of a budget hotel, neon lights blinking down on me, another traveler in this foreign city.

The room they led me to was plain, but the bathroom had hot water and I turned the water on as soon as I locked the door. I peeled my clothes off piece by piece. The room was hot, but even in the heat I shook. My skin was white, I saw. It felt soft and damp beneath the woolen layers. It felt in need of breath. When I stepped beneath the steaming water my hair smelled first of smoke, and as the smoke washed away and I worked in shampoo, it began to smell of lavender.

I covered myself with soap. I covered myself, my aching legs and shoulders, my callused feet, my scraped knees and tender breasts, with frothy suds, rubbing the bar across my skin in circles until I could see no more skin, just foam, then standing under the running water, my lips pressed shut, my eyes closed, until the water had washed the soap away. *I'll just stay in here forever,* I thought, but the hot water turned to warm and then to cold and I opened my eyes again and reached my hand out, turning off the tap.

I slept naked in that room that night. The windows were open against the heat, and music carried up from the street below, the Rolling Stones and Jimi Hendrix blaring from a bar next door. Even with the music, I slept deeply. The sheets were clean against my skin. A slight breeze reached me with the music. I think I didn't dream a thing. I woke late the next morning, the folds of the sheets creased into my skin, my lavender-scented hair in a tangle around my head. I woke and thought, *If I were waking beside Danny he would say my hair looked like a halo,* and then I shook my head and shut my eyes again. The mountains seemed a world away. The last night I slept with Danny in the tent, the last time he touched my hair, touched my face—another world, another life. I woke and turned on the water and washed my skin again and dressed. When I was done, I locked the door and left.

I was at the travel agent's office on Durbar Marg by eleven. Her red nails tapped away at her computer when I told her what I needed. The nails matched the red roses on her sari. Her black hair was cut to her shoulders and blown out wide. "I can get you on a flight next Monday," she said.

A week. A week to say good-bye.

"I can get you on a plane to Thailand then."

"A week is fine," I said.

I left the office, and then I walked. I walked the back streets, the winding alleys, and when I looked up I was in the knot of streets that make up the old city, inward-sloping buildings caving toward me from above. The sun was bright and sweat trickled down my neck. Sometimes when you walk and your mind is circling inward, it takes some time to notice the world around you. That is what happened then. Sounds moved toward me on their own, as if a river rushing forward, as if they were carried on the neap tide of the sea. As they grew closer, as I grew closer to the world, the noises pulled apart: honking horns; women laughing; women calling out their wares; the whirring spokes of bicycles as they passed close by; the caw of birds in cages; the low growl of a dog; the smacking lips of leering men. The cacophony of emergence; the fevered voice of the city waking; the fevered voice of my own self, waking.

WHEN I ENTERED the airport a week later, I walked through the glass doors behind an American man. He dragged three enormous suitcases behind him. He moved slowly. The lines through the baggage check were long. I stood behind him as we waited. Once he looked over his shoulder and I met his eyes and smiled. He smiled back. The creases at his eyes were deep. His shoulders were thin. He wore long brown canvas shorts. His legs were thin as well, and his knees were knobby. His elbows jutted out at his sides.

"Too heavy," I heard the ticket agent say. I sighed. I thought I could feel the plane outside waiting. I thought I could feel already the freedom of the air.

"They're not too heavy," the man ahead of me said.

"You're allowed only seventy pounds."

"I'm moving my brother's possessions home. I have an extra allowance."

"It doesn't say so on your ticket."

"I have an extra allowance. My brother and his family were on the flight last summer."

I didn't want to look now. I didn't want to hear him argue. The suitcases were large, locked like trunks, and I could picture them opened, lined with shelves that were stocked with everything a home could need: pots and pans, pressed and folded cotton sheets, small, pliable teaspoons, candle stubs, lanterns; I pictured them packed with the material stuff of his brother's life.

"I'm here to clean his house. I'm here to take his things home. I shouldn't have to fight about this."

His voice was even. I wondered if this was his first time here, whether he'd been to visit his brother when his brother was still alive. Was he an older brother? A younger brother? Had they been friends? I wanted to know everything. I wanted to know the inside and the outside of this man.

"I'm sorry, sir. There are rules," the ticket agent said. "I'm sorry. We can't let this on."

MY OWN BAG was small. When I went back to the apartment I'd taken only a duffel bag with me, had stuffed it only with what my eyes first rested on. Anna stood with her arms folded across her chest. Danny wasn't home. I'd grabbed my money from the drawer and lifted armfuls of folded clothing out and pushed it deep inside the bag. It was only half full when I felt dizzy and that I had to leave. I couldn't go back. *This is all I have of my life,* I thought. *All I have. All I have to take with me.* I prayed the cash was enough for the ticket and when I counted it outside in the hall I saw there was just enough left to get me home.

"FUCK THE RULES," the man said. "Fuck the rules. My brother died on your plane."

The ticket handler's face was coloring. A deep rising red. He turned his head from left to right. Was he looking for a supervisor? Was he looking to see who was watching? He pressed his lips together tightly.

"Excuse me," I said. My voice was louder than I'd intended. The man looked around. "Excuse me. I only have this bag. I could take one of your bags for you." Even as I spoke I felt ashamed to admit I'd been eavesdropping.

"That's not necessary," the man said. "They owe me this. That plane's not leaving until they put these bags on it." He turned away again. His shoulders looked as though they were shaking inside and he was doing everything he could to keep the shake from getting to the outside, to where his muscles would actually move.

Another man joined the ticket handler. They shook their heads from side to side. I looked to see if other lines had formed, and the airport, then, was full. Long lines snaking to the doors. People breaking off from lines to form a mat of human bodies, a moving fabric, threads twisting in and out amongst one another. It made me dizzy, watching. It made me dizzy, and hot, and tired of standing, and tired of being dizzy.

WHEN I WENT back to the apartment to gather my things from the dresser drawer, only Anna was there. When I left, I wondered as I walked across the woven mat, as I concentrated on feeling the rough texture beneath my feet, whether Anna was right behind me. Was she watching me as carefully as I was avoiding watching her? Did she miss me already with the strength that I missed her? I stopped at the door and turned around. She stood within a foot of me. She stood and for the first time I felt myself as tall as her, and her eyes were locked on mine.

"You were my sister," she said.

"And you were mine," I said.

We stood there and looked, and her eyes were so dark that I realized suddenly I'd forgotten where I was looking. I tried, then, to see the bottom of her eyes. To see the bottom of my closest friend's heart. I reached my hand out and touched her arm. She let it rest there for a moment, then shook her head slightly and stepped backward.

"Good-bye," I said.

"Good-bye," she said.

I lifted the strap of the bag to my shoulder and left.

THEY FINALLY PULLED the man ahead of me aside and waved me through. There wasn't much to search in my bag, and even when the metal detector shuddered to a halt and the screen that showed the insides of the bags crackled and ran with crooked lines, they let me pass. The afternoon was bright. I drank a cup of tea in the restaurant upstairs and waited for my flight to board and stared out at the landing strip and the rice fields beyond.

WHEN I TURNED away from Anna in my bedroom, her bedroom, the bag hanging from my shoulder was heavy. I'd gathered the unfinished baby's quilt, the wrapping for the figurine, and pushed it to the bottom of my bag. "Good-bye,"

I'd said, and my shoulder sagged down. When I counted the money I thought of the bills peeled off month after month and of how secretive I'd been, how scared to let Danny know how much I'd spent. I shook my head and heard a strange sound rise from my throat.

I took the figurine to Ram and Anthony. I walked past the dusty carpets, past the woman drinking tea. She stood up to stop me, but I was already beyond the door, already held the goddess out, already saw Ram's eyes light up as he felt its weight in his hand. "Where is it from?" he said.

"It doesn't matter," I said. "What matters is how much you'll pay me for it."

"How do I know it isn't stolen?"

"You don't know."

"How do I know I won't get in trouble for it?"

"You don't."

When I arrived at the store in Patan that afternoon, a new roll of hundred-dollar bills was in my pocket. "I'm leaving," I told Radika.

"We need you," she said.

"You don't," I said. "You don't need me. You have Gina. She wants another box. I needed you, but you don't need me anymore." When I left, I left the roll of hundred-dollar bills with Radika.

I SPENT MY last night in Kathmandu sitting on the floor of that hotel room. It was a cement floor, and was cool even in the sticky late-spring heat. My feet were bare. Even when a bristling millipede skimmed across the floor, I stayed sitting there. My back was propped against the bed. My knees were at my chin. I think my mind was blank, because I watch myself sitting there and cannot imagine what it was that I thought about. *Time is elastic,* perhaps I thought. *Time is elastic and I have lived three lifetimes in the space of less than a year, or one day stretched out into eight months.* Or perhaps I thought, *I will never see my husband again. I will never see my dearest friend again. This is ruin that I have wreaked, this is ruin for me alone.* Or perhaps I went over the days I had lived with Danny, counted each one, relived each night we had spent together. Perhaps I traced his hands on my body. Perhaps I gulped in air as if it were his kisses I was swallowing. I cannot remember what I thought. I can only remember the cold floor on my bare feet, the bed against my back.

AND THEN, SOMEHOW, I was on the plane. Tucked in a box. Safe and sound. And then the plane was moving down the runway, and the dry fields were swerving past. The plane lifted with a jolt. The mountains rose up around us. The fields sank far below. I leaned my head against the back of my seat and stared and stared, amazed at the world dropping away, amazed to rise above it.

When I turned my head from the window, I saw the man from the airport, sitting alone across the aisle, the seat beside him empty. He leaned down, his face on his knees, his hands cupping his head, and his shoulders shook. I wondered if his shoulders hurt from the weight of dragging the suitcases. I wondered if he'd noticed the lurch at liftoff. He sobbed and I watched him and I wondered if he noticed anything.

I WAS WAITING for Danny, that last night. I was waiting for his knock on the door. He came. He came eventually. It was late at night. He knocked and I rose to my feet. My legs were cramped from all that sitting on the cold floor. I hobbled to the door and opened it. He stood there, and he looked a different man from the man I had first seen, the man behind the table at the café in Greenwich Village whose boots stuck out from under the table. "Stay with me," I tried to whisper, "stay," and I thought the ghost of the words found their way to my lips.

I remember his hand on my cheek then. I remember his hand on my hips. He pushed me back through the doorway, back into the room, and sat me down roughly on the bed. The door was still open, and during our conversation half of me was thinking that from the outside I could hear him as clearly as I was hearing him there, on the inside.

"Why doesn't anyone talk about the plane that crashed?"

"The plane?"

"The plane that crashed last summer. We saw it. The first time you took me to the hills. I didn't know what it was then. You didn't tell me. They'd dragged the wreckage from the mountain, but the magazines were there still. Why didn't you tell me?"

"I don't know," he said. "We try to live in the present here. We try to forget the things that trail behind us. We try to see each moment as new."

I nodded.

A horn blared. A woman's laugh rose from outside on the

street. My husband's face was lit by the neon lights shining in through the window.

"This is my good-bye," he said.

"Good-bye."

"I loved you," he said.

"Good-bye."

"I loved you from the moment you stumbled into that café. I saw you and I thought I'd love you, and then I saw you let yourself fade behind your friend—I saw you let Anna step in front of you and I saw you give up the world to her. Forgive me, Isabel."

"Enough," I said. "Good-bye."

He left then. I could feel his hands on my hips when he went. He shut the door behind him. He shut the door, and I thought with half of myself that now no one outside could hear what I could hear inside, and the other half of me thought, *I hear nothing. I hear nothing but my own heart beating.*

WE CIRCLED OUT of the valley. We winged above the mountains. I watched the man across the aisle. I waited for his crying to cease, but just when I thought it had ended, I saw his shoulders shake again. His shoulders shook and I could see the mountains beyond him through the window and then we lifted higher up and behind him I could only see the sky: blue in the sunlight, blue and clear in the distance.

ABOUT THE AUTHOR

Johanna Stoberock is a graduate of Wesleyan University and received her MFA from the University
of Washington. She lives in Brooklyn, New York,
with her husband, Christopher Petit.